FIRST BLOOD

Dr. Harold Smith knew now he never should have stopped his car for the beautiful blonde girl, no matter how much of her black brassiere was showing between her straining blouse buttons. He knew it as soon as he saw the man with her, and saw the man's hand—not a hand, really, but a three-fingered metal claw.

The claw opened with the muted sound of a dentist's high-speed drill. It took him by the throat and the dentist drill sound filled his ears, louder and louder, reminding him of past pain, even as he felt the choking sensation that told him his windpipe was being crushed.

Was this the end for Harold Smith, the revered head of CURE and the boss of Remo and Chiun? The unspeakable answer was not at all. For Harold Smith, and for his two star employees, the horror was just beginning. . . .

The #71

Destroyer

RETURN ENGAGEMENT

Created by

WARREN MURPHY & RICHARD SAPIR

A SIGNET BOOK

NEW AMERICAN LIBRARY

PUBLISHER'S NOTE

This book is a work of fiction. Names, characters, places, and incidents either are the product of the author's imagination or are used fictitiously, and any resemblance to actual persons, living or dead, events, or locales is entirely coincidental.

SIGNET TRADEMARK REG. U.S. PAT. OFF. AND FOREIGN COUNTRIES
REGISTERED TRADEMARK—MARCA REGISTRADA
HECHO EN CHICAGO, U.S.A.

SIGNET, SIGNET CLASSIC, MENTOR, ONYX, PLUME, MERIDIAN and NAL BOOKS are published by NAL PENGUIN INC., 1633 Broadway, New York, New York 10019

First Printing, January, 1988

1 2 3 4 5 6 7 8 9

PRINTED IN THE UNITED STATES OF AMERICA

For Will Murray, who figured out a way to bring them back.

1

He had waited almost forty years for this moment.

Forty years. And now the waiting would end here, on this winter day, with dirty snow clotting the road and the sun high and remote and cheerless in the bleak New Hampshire sky.

He touched the lever, and the wheelchair shifted closer to the darkened window. The smell of old oil filled the interior of the van. Down the road, a car neared, weaving slightly from wheels that were out of alignment.

"Is it him?" he called, his voice cracking. Was it just his age that made it crack? Once, it had been a strong voice, a powerful voice. He had been a powerful man with a strong physique that caused the young women to throw themselves at him. But now that magnificent physique was no more, and there was only one woman left.

"Hold on," Ilsa called. She ran out into the road, her body bouncing attractively. Ilsa tossed her long blond hair back from her soft oval face and trained Zeiss binoculars on the approaching car.

"The color is right," she called breathlessly. "Light blue. No, wait. The plates are wrong. Out-of-state plates. No good."

He slammed his left fist down, metal striking metal. "Damn!"

"Don't worry," Ilsa said through the tinted glass as she waved the passing car through. "He'll be along. He always comes to work by this road."

"Never mind that. I banged my hand. It stings!"

"Oh, poor baby. You really should get a grip on yourself."

Ilsa talked at the window. She couldn't see his face behind its smoky opacity. It didn't matter.

"Forty years," he said bitterly.

"Actually thirty-eight years, seven months, and five days," Ilsa offered brightly.

He grunted. She hadn't been born then. Then, he had been as young as she was now. Had he known her then, he would have taken her. By force, if necessary. He would take her now—if he had anything left to take her with. Perhaps when this was over, he would find a way to take this foolish girl who had adopted the lost cause of a past generation as her own.

"Another car coming," she said, dashing out into the road again. He watched her. Her black pants were snug, hugging her shapely girlish figure. Her white blouse was uniform crisp. She wore her armband inside out, so that only the red cloth showed. Even so, it reminded him of the old days.

"Is it him? Is it Smith?"

"Yes," Ilsa said excitedly. "It's him. It's Harold Smith."

"At last."

Harold D. Smith saw the girl first. She stood in the middle of the road, waving her arms.

She was attractive. Perhaps twenty-five or twenty-six, with a beautiful face that needed no makeup. A glimpse of a black lace brassiere showed between two straining blouse buttons. Smith noted these things absently. He had stopped looking at young women as sexual creatures about the time his white hair had started to recede, more than ten years before.

Smith braked his car. Then he noticed the van. It was one of those custom jobs, painted bronze and decorated with airbrushed designs. It had pulled onto the slushy shoulder of the road. The plastic cover was off the rear-mounted spare tire.

The blond bounced to his side of the car and Smith let the window down. She gave him a sunny smile. He did not smile back.

"Can you help me, sir?"

"What seems to be the trouble?" Harold Smith asked.

The trouble was obvious—a flat tire—but Smith asked anyway.

"I can't get the spare tire down."

"Just a moment," Harold Smith said. He pulled off the road, slightly annoyed that he would be late for work. He did not feel up to the exertion of changing a tire, not with what felt like three pounds of his wife's infamous five-alarm oatmeal congealing in his stomach.

He stepped out of his car as the blond came bouncing up like a happy puppy.

"I'm Ilsa Gans," she said, putting out her hand. Uncertainly, he took it. Her grip was strong—stronger than he expected—and with her other hand she reached behind her back and removed a cocked pistol. She pointed it at him.

"Be nice," she warned.

Harold Smith tried to let go, but she squeezed his hand harder and spun him around. Her knee slammed into the small of his back and he fell against the car hood.

"I must warn you, young lady. If this is robbery—"

But then the muzzle of the gun was at his back. He wondered if she was going to shoot him then and there.

"Hold still," she said. Her voice was a bar of metal. She undid her red armband, and, carefully turning it right-side-out, blindfolded Harold Smith. She marched him to the disabled van.

Had Smith been able to see himself just then, he would have recognized the black symbol in a white circle that burned the front of the red blindfold that had been securely knotted around his head. He might have understood then. But then again, he might not have.

"Harold Smith?" His mouth was dry. He took a drink. Why should he be nervous? It was Smith who should be nervous.

"Yes?" Harold Smith said uncertainly. He could not see, but Smith knew he was inside the bronze-hued van. The floor was carpeted, and his bald head had brushed the plush roof as he was forced in through the sliding side door. Cool hands pushed him down into a seat. It swiveled.

"Harold D. Smith?"

"Yes?" Smith's voice was calm.

The man had poise, if not courage. He wondered if that would make it easier.

"The first ten years were the worst."

"I don't understand," Smith said.

"The walls were green. Light green above, and dark green below. I could do nothing but stare at them. I thought of you often in those days, Harold Smith."

"Do I know you?"

"I'm getting to that, Smith." He spat the name out. His nervousness was leaving him. Good. Ilsa smiled at him. She was kneeling on the rug, looking like a dutiful daughter, except for the pistol she kept trained on the hated Harold D. Smith.

"We didn't have television then," he continued in a calmer voice. "Television was new. In America, people had television. But not where I had been consigned. No one had television there. So I stared at the green walls. They burned my retinas, they were so green. To this day, I cannot bear to look at grass. Or American paper money."

Harold Smith tried to see past his blindfold. He kept his hands carefully placed one on each knee. He dared not make a move. He knew the blond girl had the pistol—it had looked like a Luger—pointed at him.

"Eventually," the dry voice continued, "we had television. I think that was what saved my sanity. Television fed my mind. It was my window, for the green room had no windows, you see. I think without television I would have let myself die. Even hate can sustain a person just so long."

"Hate? I don't know you."

"You can't see me, Harold Smith."

"Your voice is not familiar."

"My voice? You last heard it in 1949. Do you remember?"

"No," Harold Smith said slowly.

"No! Not even a stirring memory, Smith? Not even that?"

"I'm sorry, what is this about?"

"Death, Smith. It is about death. My death . . . and yours."

Smith gripped his knees tighter.

"Do you remember where you were on June 7, 1949?"

"Of course not. No one could."

"I remember. I remember it well. It was the day I died."

Smith said nothing. This man was obviously deranged. His mind raced. Would another car come along? Would it stop? But this was not a well-traveled road.

"It was the day I died," the voice continued. "It was the day you killed me. Now tell me, Harold Smith, that you do not remember that day."

"I don't," Smith answered slowly. "I think you have the wrong man."

"Liar!"

"I said I don't remember," Harold Smith said evenly. He knew that when you dealt with unbalanced minds, it was better to speak in a calm voice. He also knew that you shouldn't contradict them, but Smith was stubborn. He wasn't about to go along with a madman's ravings just to humor him.

Smith heard the whirring sounds of a small motor and the dry voice came closer. Smith suddenly understood that the man was in a wheelchair. He remembered the handicapped decal on the back of the van.

"You don't remember." The voice was bitter, almost sad.

"That's correct," Smith said stiffly.

Smith heard a new sound then. It was a softer whirring, more like the muted sound of a dentist's high-speed drill. The sound made him shiver. He hated visiting the dentist. Always had.

The blindfold was swept from his eyes. Smith blinked stupidly.

The man in the wheelchair had a face as dry as his voice. It resembled a bleached walnut shell, corrugated with lines and wrinkles. The eyes were black and sharp, the lips a thin desiccated line. The rest of the face was dead, long dead. The teeth were stained almost brown, with the roots exposed by receding gums.

"I don't recognize your face," Smith said in a voice

calmer than his thoughts. He could feel his heart racing and his throat tightening with fear. The man's features grew furious.

"My own mother wouldn't recognize me!" the man in the wheelchair thundered. He pounded a dead dry fist on the wheelchair's arm. Then Smith saw the blindfold hanging in the man's other hand.

But it was not a hand. Not a human hand. It was a three-fingered claw of stainless steel. It clamped the blindfold that the girl had worn as an armband. Smith saw a black-and-white insignia distorted in the red folds. The steel claw opened with that tiny dentist's-drill whirring. The blindfold dropped on Smith's lap and he recognized the Nazi swastika symbol. He swallowed uncomfortably. He had been in the war. It was a long time ago.

"You have changed too, Harold Smith," the old man said in a quieter voice. "I can scarcely recognize you, either."

The steel claw closed noisily. Its three jointed fingers made a deformed fist.

"Modern science," the old man said. "I got this in 1983. Electrodes implanted in my upper arm control it. It is almost like having a natural hand. Before this, I had a hook, and before the hook, my wrist ended in a black plastic cap."

Smith's face was so close to the man he could smell the other's breath. It smelled like raw clams, as if the man's insides were dead.

"Fire did this to me. Fire took my mobility. It took my speech for many years. It nearly took my sight. It took other things too. But I will not speak of my bitterness any longer. I have searched for you, Harold Smith, and now I have found you."

"I think you have the wrong man," Harold Smith said softly.

"You were in the war? World War Two?"

"Yes," he said.

"He was in the war, Ilsa."

"He admits it then?" Ilsa said. She rose, clutching the Luger tightly.

"Not quite. He is stubborn."

"'But he is the one?" Ilsa demanded.

"Yes, this is the day. I told you I felt it in my bones."

"We could tie him up and throw him in a ditch," Ilsa offered. "Then cover him with gasoline. Whoosh!"

"Fire would be appropriate," the man in the wheelchair said. "But I do not think I could bear watching the flames consume him. Memories, Ilsa. No, not fire. I must witness his death."

Harold Smith knew then that he would have to fight. He would risk a bullet, but he would not let himself be executed. Not without a struggle.

Smith came to his feet abruptly. He pushed the wheelchair back and narrowly ducked a vicious swipe of the old man's claw.

"Should I shoot him? Should I?" Ilsa screamed, waving her pistol.

"No. Brain him."

Ilsa swung at Smith's balding head with the heavy barrel of the Luger. But there wasn't enough force behind the blow and the gun sight merely scraped skin off Smith's head.

Smith grabbed for the gun. Ilsa kicked one leg out from under him and leaned into him. Smith fell against the swivel chair with Ilsa on top of him.

"Hold him there," the man in the wheelchair said. Smith, his head hanging back, saw the upside-down image of the old man advancing on him with the chilly whirring of machinery.

The steel claw took him by the throat and the dentist's-drill sound filled his ears, louder and louder, reminding him of past pain, even as he felt the choking sensation that told him his windpipe was being crushed. His face swelled as his blood was forced up through the arteries in his neck. His ears popped, shutting out the drumming sound of his feet against the floor.

And all the time he could see the hideous old man's face staring at him, the black eyes tiny and bright in the middle of the red mist that seemed to be filling the van's interior.

When the red mist completely filled Harold Smith's vision, he lost all conscious thought.

"Damn!"

"What is it, Ilsa?"

"I think he wet himself."

"They do that sometimes."

"But not all over me!" She stood back from Smith's contorted corpse, looking like a woman who had been splashed by a passing car. Her hands fluttered uselessly in the air.

"You can change later. We must leave."

"Okay. Let me lock you down."

"First get rid of the body."

"You don't want it?"

"No!"

"Not even for a souvenir? I thought we were going to skin him or something."

"Not him. He is not the one."

"He said his name was Harold Smith. I heard him."

"He is not the right Harold Smith."

"Oh no, not again. Are you sure?"

"His eyes are blue. Smith's eyes were gray."

"Damn," said Ilsa, kicking Smith until his body rolled out the side door. She shoved the door closed on screeching rollers. "I thought you were sure."

"It doesn't matter. What is one less Smith? I am sure this one was a nonentity whom no one will miss. Drive, Ilsa."

2

His name was Remo and he was building a house.

Remo drove the last support into the hard earth. The post sank a quarter-inch at a time, driven down by the impact of his bare fist. He used no tools. He did not need tools. He worked alone, a lean young man in chinos and a black T-shirt with strangely thick wrists and an expression of utter peace on his high-cheekboned face.

Standing up, Remo examined the four supports. A surveyor, using precision equipment, could have determined that the four posts formed a geometrically true rectangle, each post perfectly level with the others. Remo knew that without looking.

Next would come the flooring. It was important that the floor of the house sit well above ground level, at least eight inches. Like all houses in Korea, Remo's home would sit on stilts to protect it against rainwater and snakes.

Remo had always wanted a home of his own. He had dreamed of one back in the days when he lived in a walk-up flat in Newark, New Jersey, and pulled down $257.60 a week as a rookie cop. Before his police days, Remo had been a ward of the state and bunked with the other boys at St. Theresa's Orphanage. After he was suspended from the force—after they killed him—there had been a succession of apartments and hotel rooms and temporary quarters.

He had never dreamed that one day he would build his house with his strong bare hands here on the rocky soil of Sinanju.

Two decades ago Remo had been sent to the electric chair on a false murder charge, but he did not die. Remo had been offered a choice: work for CURE, the supersecret American anticrime organization, or replace the anonymous corpse that lay in his own grave.

It wasn't much of a choice and so Remo had agreed to become an agent of CURE. They turned him over to an elderly Korean named Chiun, the head of a fabled house of assassins, and Chiun had transformed Remo Williams into a Master of Sinanju, the sun source of the martial arts.

Somewhere along the way, Remo had become more Sinanju than American. He did not know when it had happened. Looking back, he could not even pinpoint the year. He just knew that one day long, long ago he had stepped over that line.

And now Remo had finally come home—to Sinanju on the West Korea Bay.

An aged Oriental in a subdued blue kimono strolled up the shore path and watched at a slight distance Remo's attempt to lay hardwood planks on top of the floor frame. He was tiny, and the fresh sea breeze played with the tufts of hair over each ear and teased his wispy beard.

At length, the Master of Sinanju approached.

"What are you doing, my son?"

Remo glanced back over his shoulder, then returned to his task.

"I'm building a house, Little Father."

"I can see that, Remo. Why are you building a house?"

"It's for Mah-Li," Remo said.

"Ah," said Chiun, current Master of Sinanju—the town as well as the discipline. "A wedding present, then?"

"You got it. Hand me that plank, will you?"

"Will I what?"

"Will you hand me that plank?"

"Will I hand you that plank what?"

"Huh?"

"It is customary to say 'please' when one requests a boon from the Master of Sinanju," Chiun said blandly.

"Never mind," Remo said impatiently. "I'll get it myself."

Remo hefted the plank into place. The floor was forming, and next would come the walls, but the hard part would be the roof. As a kid, Remo had never been good in woodworking class, but he had picked up the basics. But as far as he knew, no American high school had ever taught classes in thatching. Perhaps Chiun could help him with the roof.

"Mah-Li already has a house," remarked Chiun after a short silence.

"It's too far from the village," Remo said. "She's not an outcast from the village anymore. She's the future wife of the next Master of Sinanju."

"Do not get ahead of yourself. I am the current Master. While I am Master, there is no other. Why not build Mah-Li's new house closer to mine?"

"Privacy," said Remo, looking down the hollowed tube of a bamboo shoot. He set several of these on end, in a row, and chopped off the tops with quick motions of his hands until they stood uniform in length.

"Will that not be hard on her, Remo?"

"How so?" Remo said. He split the first shoot down the middle with a vicious crack. The halves fell into his hands, perfectly split.

"She will have far to walk to wake you in the morning."

Remo's hand poised in mid-chop.

"What are you talking about?"

"You are not even married yet and you are already treating your future bride disgracefully."

"How is building her a house disgraceful?"

"It is not the house. It is where the house is not."

"Where should it be?"

"Next to the house of my ancestors."

"Oh," said Remo, suddenly understanding. "Let us sit, Little Father."

"A good thought," said Chiun, settling on a rock. Remo sat at his feet, the feet of the only father he had ever known. He folded his hands over his bent knees.

"You are unhappy that I'm not building closer to you, is that it?" Remo asked.

"There is plenty of space on the eastern side."

"If you call twelve square feet spacious."

"In Sinanju, we do not dwell in our homes for hours on end, as you did in your former life in America."

Remo looked out past the rock formation known as

the Horns of Welcome, past the cold gray waters of the West Korea Bay. Somewhere beyond the horizon was America and the life he used to live. It was still all so fresh in his mind, but he shut away the memories. Sinanju was home now.

"A home on the eastern side would cut off your sunlight," Remo pointed out. "I know you like the sun coming through your window in the morning. I would not deprive you of that for my own pleasure."

Chiun nodded, the white wisps of beard floating about his chin. His hazel eyes shone with pleasant approval of his pupil's consideration.

"This is gracious of you, Remo."

"Thank you."

"But you must think of your future bride. On cold mornings, she would have to walk all the way from this place to your bedside."

"Little Father?" Remo said slowly, trying to pick the best words to phrase what he had to say.

"Yes?"

"Her bedside will be my bedside. We will be married, remember?"

"True," said Chiun, raising a long-nailed finger. "And this is my point exactly. She should be at your side."

"Right," said Remo, relieved.

"Right," said Chiun, thinking that Remo was getting the point at last. Sometimes he could be so slow. Residual whiteness. It would never go away entirely, but in a few decades Remo would be more like a Korean than he was now. Especially if he got more sun.

"So what's the problem?" Remo asked.

"This house. You do not need it."

Remo frowned.

Chiun frowned back. Perhaps Remo had not gotten the point after all.

"Let me explain it to you," the Master of Sinanju said. "Mah-Li's place is at your side, correct?"

"That's right."

"Good. You had said so yourself. And your place is at my side, correct?"

"You are the Master of Sinanju. I am your pupil."

Chiun rose to his feet and clapped his hands happily.

"Excellent! Then it is settled."

"What is settled?" Remo asked, getting up.

"Mah-Li will move in with us after the marriage. Come, I will help you take this unnecessary structure apart."

"Wait a minute, Little Father. I never agreed to that."

Chiun looked at Remo with astonishment wrinkling his parchment visage.

"What? You do not want Mah-Li? Beautiful Mah-Li, kind Mah-Li, who has graciously consented to overlook your unfortunate whiteness, your mongrel birth, and accept you as her husband, and you do not want her to live with you upon your marriage? Is this some American custom you have never shared with me, Remo?"

"That isn't it, Little Father."

"No?"

"I wasn't planning on Mah-Li moving in with us."

"Then?"

"I was planning on moving in with her."

"Moving in?" Chiun squeaked. "As in moving out? Out of the house of my ancestors?" Chiun's many wrinkles smoothed in shock.

"I never thought of doing it any other way," Remo confessed.

"And I never thought you would dream of doing it any other way than the way of Sinanju," Chiun snapped.

"I thought you'd want your privacy. I thought you'd understand."

"In Korea, families stick together," Chiun scolded. "In Korea, families do not break apart with marriage as they do in America. In America, families marry off their young and live many miles apart. In their apartness, they grow cool and lose their family bonds. It is no wonder that in America families fight over inheritances and murder other family members out of spite. American whites are bred to be strangers to one another. It is a disgrace. It is shameful."

"I'm sorry, Little Father. Mah-Li and I talked it over. This is the way it is with us."

"No, this is the way it is in the unfriendly land of your misbegotten birth. I have watched your television.

I have seen *Edge of Darkness, As the Planet Revolves.*" I know how it is. It will start with separate homes and escalate into contesting my will. I will have none of it!"

And saying no more, the Master of Sinanju turned on his heel with a flourish of skirts and sulked up the shore road back to the center of the village of Sinanju, nursing a deep hurt in his magnificent heart.

Remo said "Damn" to himself in a small voice and went back to building. He sliced dozens of long bamboo shoots with fingernails that had been made hard by diet and exercise, until he had enough to make the siding for his new home.

Remo had never dreamed that he would feel so miserable when he finally had a home to call his own.

It was near dusk when Remo finished the sides. The scent of smoking wood wafting from the village told him the cooking fires were going. The clean scent of boiling rice came to his nostrils, so sensitized by years of training that to him the aroma was as pungent as curry on the tongue. His mouth watered.

Remo decided the roof could wait.

When Remo stepped out from among the sheltering rocks that protected the village of Sinanju from the sea winds, he spotted Mah-Li, his wife-to-be, below. He slid onto a boulder and watched unnoticed.

In the village square, the other women had gathered around her. Mah-Li was a young girl, several years younger than Remo, but the older women of the village paid court to her as if she were the village grandmother.

Remo felt a swelling joy in his heart. Only weeks before, Mah-Li had been an outcast, living in a neat hovel beyond the rocks, far from the mainstream of the tiny village.

Weeks earlier, during the terrible days when it appeared that Chiun was on his deathbed, Remo was surrounded by the villagers of Sinanju, who despised him because he was not Korean. He had felt a greater loneliness than he could ever remember knowing.

It was then that he had met Mah-Li, herself an orphan, shunned by the other villagers and called by them Mah-Li the Beast. Remo had first found her living in her small hut, wearing a veil. He had thought she was deformed and felt pity for her. But her gentle ways had soothed the confusion in his soul, and he grew to love her.

When, in an impulsive moment, Remo lifted the veil from her face, he had expected to find horror. Instead, he had found beauty. Mah-Li was a doll. Mah-Li was called a beast because, by the standards of the flat-faced Sinanju women, she was ugly. By Western standards, she made the obligatory female newscaster on most TV stations look like hags.

Remo had not thought twice about proposing. And Mah-Li had accepted. Remo, whose life had lurched from one out-of-his-control situation to another, now felt complete.

Mah-Li's laugh tinkled up from the square. Remo smiled.

As the bride of the next Master, she was respected. There was a certain hypocrisy about it. Until he had agreed to shoulder the burdens of the village, they had spat whenever Remo had walked by too. But that was the way of Sinanju villagers. For thousands of years they were the moths that circled the flame of the sun source. They were not encouraged to work, nor to think. Only to be led and fed by the Master of Sinanju, who plied the art of the assassin for the rulers of the world.

The first Masters of Sinanju had taken to their work to support the villagers, who, in times of need, were forced to drown the youngest children in the bay waters. Perhaps it had been that way once, Remo thought, but instead of the motivation for Sinanju, the villagers had became more of a convenient excuse.

Either way, they were not to blame.

Mah-Li happened to look up then, and Remo felt a shock in the pit of his stomach. Her liquid eyes never failed to do that to him. She was so gorgeous, with a face that was perfection.

Remo started down off the rocks. But Mah-Li was already on her feet, her delicate hands lifting her long traditional skirts, and met him halfway.

They kissed once, lightly, because they were in public. Over Mah-Li's shoulder Remo saw the faces of the village women looking up at them with a rapt softness in their dark eyes that took the curse off the harsh planes of their square jaws and flat cheekbones.

"Where have you been, Remo?" Mah-Li asked lightly.

"It's a secret," Remo teased.

"You cannot tell me now?" She pouted.

"After we're married."

"Oh, but that is so long a time."

"I'm planning to talk to Chiun about that. I don't know why we can't get married right now," Remo complained. "Today."

"The Master of Sinanju has set an engagement period. We must obey him."

"Yeah, but nine months?"

"The Master of Sinanju knows best. It is his wish that you learn our ways before we are wed. It is not so difficult."

"It is for me. I love you, Mah-Li."

"And I love you, Remo."

"Nine months! Sometimes I think he was put on earth to bust my chops."

"What are chops?" asked Mah-Li, who had learned enough English to talk to Remo in his own lanaguage, but was confused by slang.

"Never mind. Have you seen Chiun lately?"

"Earlier. He looked unhappy."

"I think he's upset with me. Again."

Mah-Li's face tightened. The Master of Sinanju was like a god to her.

"You had words?"

"I think he's going to have trouble adjusting to our being married."

"The people of this village never argue with the Master. It is not done."

"Chiun and I have been arguing for as long as we've known each other. We've argued all over America, across Europe, from Peoria to Peking. When I think of the places I've visited, I don't remember the people or the sights. I remember the arguments. If we're fighting about my refusal to grow my fingernails long, this must be Baltimore."

"It is strange. In America, you show your love by arguing. After we are wed, do you expect me to argue with you as a token of my love?"

Remo laughed. Mah-Li's face was puzzled and serious, like a child confronting some great, complex truth.

"No, I don't expect ever to argue with you at all." Remo kissed her again.

He took her hand and they walked down to the village square. The villagers made way for them, all smiles and crinkling eyes. The village was full of contentment and life. As it should be, thought Remo.

Except for the House of the Masters, in the center of the village. It was a great carven box of teak and lacquers set on a low hillock. Built for the Master Wi by the pharaoh Tutankhamen, it was the largest edifice in the village. Back in America, it wouldn't have impressed a newlywed couple as a suitable starter home. In fact, it was more of a warehouse than it was a dwelling. The earnings of centuries of past Masters of Sinanju lay piled in elegant profusion inside its walls. It was there that Chiun lived. Now the great door was closed and the windows curtained.

Remo wondered if he should go to Chiun and try to explain things to him again. But then he remembered that every time he had explained himself in the past, Chiun had always gotten his way. Even when Chiun was wrong. Especially when Chiun was wrong.

"He'll keep," said Remo half-aloud, thinking how hungry the smell of boiling rice was making him.

"Who will keep what?" asked Mah-Li.

Remo just smiled at her. With Mah-Li around, there was no one else in the universe.

3

Dr. Harold W. Smith was never happier.

Strolling into his Spartan office in the morning was a pleasure. The sun beamed in through the one-way picture window, filling the room with light. Smith deposited his worn briefcase on the desk and, ignoring the waiting paperwork, sauntered to the window.

Smith was a spare, pinch-faced man in his mid-sixties, but today a thin smile tugged at his compressed lips. He noticed the faint reflection of the smile in the big picture window and forced his lips to part slightly. Good, he thought. The flash of white teeth made the smile warmer. He would have to practice smiling with his mouth open until he got used to it. Smith adjusted the red carnation in the buttonhole of his impeccable three-piece suit. He liked the way the flower lent color to his otherwise drab apparel. Perhaps one day he would buy a suit that wasn't gray. But not just yet. Too much change too rapidly could be overwhelming. Smith believed in moderation.

Dr. Harold Smith had worked in this very office since the early 1960's, ostensibly as the director of Folcroft Sanitarium, on the shoreline of Rye, New York. In reality Smith, an ex-CIA agent and before that with the OSS during the war, was the head of the counter-crime agency called CURE. Set up by a President who was later assassinated, CURE was an ultrasecret enforcement organization that operated outside of constitutional restrictions, protecting America from a rising tide of lawlessness.

CURE's one agent, Remo Williams, and his equally difficult mentor, Chiun, were safely back in Sinanju. Smith expected he would never see them again. He hoped so. The present President had been led to believe Remo was dead—killed during the crisis with the Soviets—and that Chiun had gone into mourning.

It had nearly been the end of CURE, but the President had sanctioned CURE to continue operations. But with no enforcement arm. Just Smith and his secret computers—just like in the beginning, the good old days. Only now, America was getting back on track. True, there were still problems. But the Mafia's back was being broken in major cities all over America. Public opinion was tipping the scales against drug use. White-collar crime was on the decline, thanks to the heavy exposure of corporate crime on Wall Street—exposure that Smith had helped to bring to light.

But best of all, no Remo and no Chiun. Smith had grown to respect both men, even to like them in his uncommunicative fashion. But they were difficult, unmanageable. Life was so much simpler without them.

A tentative knocking at his office door shook Smith out of his dreamy thoughts. He adjusted his Dartmouth tie before turning from the window.

"Come in," he sang.

"Dr. Smith?" Mrs. Mikulka, Smith's personal secretary, thrust her matronly head inside. Her face was troubled.

"Is something wrong, Mrs. Mikulka?"

"That was what I was going to ask you, Dr. Smith. I heard strange sounds in here."

"Sounds?"

"Yes, whistling sounds."

Smith tried his new smile on his secretary.

"I believe that was me," he said pleasantly.

"You?"

"I believe I was whistling 'Zip a Dee Doo Dah.' "

"It sounded, if you'll excuse me for saying so, like the steam radiator had popped a valve."

Smith cleared his throat. "I was just thinking how good life is now. I always whistle when I'm happy."

"I've worked for you for over five years, and I can't recall you ever whistling before."

"I was never happy at work before."

"I'm glad, Dr. Smith. It's nice to see you come in at a

more reasonable hour, too. And spending more time with your family."

"That reminds me," said Dr. Smith. "My wife will be here at twelve-thirty. We'll be having lunch."

"Really?" said Mrs. Mikulka. "How wonderful. I've never met your wife."

"I thought she'd like to see Folcroft. She's never been here. Perhaps you'd like to join us."

"I'd be delighted," said Mrs. Mikulka, who was astonished at the change in her tightfisted boss. "I hope I'm dressed properly."

"I'm sure the cafeteria workers will find you presentable," assured Smith.

"Oh," said Mrs. Mikulka, realizing that her employer hadn't changed quite that much.

"Will that be all?" asked Smith, returning to his desk.

"Oh. I left you a newspaper clipping I thought you'd want to see. It's another odd one."

"Thank you, Mrs. Mikulka."

The door closed after the bosomy woman, and Smith leafed through the papers on his desk. He found the clipping. It was a brief item, a UPI dispatch:

> Authorities are puzzled by the mysterious deaths of two New Hampshire men, only days apart, in Hillsborough County. Harold Donald Smith, 66, of Squantum, was found beside his parked car on a section of Route 136. His neck was crushed. Harold Walter Smith, 61, of Manchester—only twenty miles from the site of the earlier death—was discovered in his apartment. His skull had been shattered by a blunt instrument. Robbery was ruled out as the motive in both cases.

Smith tripped the intercom lever.

"Mrs. Mikulka?"

"Yes, Dr. Smith?"

"You're slipping," Smith said in a light voice.

"Sir?"

"I've seen this one," he said cheerily. "You clipped it for me two weeks ago."

"No, sir."

"I remember it distinctly," said Dr. Smith, still in that light tone.

"That was a different clipping," said Mrs. Mikulka. "Those were two other Harold Smiths."

Smith's voice sank. "Are you certain?"

"Check your files."

"One moment."

Smith carried the clipping to his file cabinet. In it, news cuttings were filed by the week. Smith had told his secretary that he collected unusual human-interest stories, the more bizarre the better. It was his hobby, he had said. In reality, Mrs. Mikulka was just another unwitting information source for CURE.

Smith riffled through the files and pulled out a clipping headlined: "SEARCH FINDS RIGHT NAME, WRONG VICTIM."

The clipping told of the bizarre murders of two men, both about the same age, living in different states. The two deaths were believed to be unrelated. The coincidence came to light when the wife of the first victim reported him missing, and a nationwide search turned up the body of a man with the same name. The first man's body was also later discovered.

The name the two dead men had shared was Harold Smith.

Smith returned to his desk with a stunned look on his lemony features. He sat down at the desk heavily, laying the two clippings side by side on the desktop as if they were alien bug specimens.

Smith touched a button and a concealed computer terminal rose from the desktop and locked into place. Smith booted up the system and initiated a search of all data links.

He keyed in the search code: SMITH, HAROLD.

Moments passed as the most powerful computer system in the world scanned its files, which were the combined files of every data link in America. Smith's computer plugged into every systems net accessible.

"Dr. Smith?"

It was Mrs. Mikulka. She was still on the intercom.

"One moment," Smith said hoarsely.

"Are you all right?"

"I said one moment," Smith barked.

The computer screen began scrolling names.

SMITH, HAROLD A.

SMITH, HAROLD G.

SMITH, HAROLD T.

Swiftly Smith scanned the reports. A Harold A. Smith, used-car salesman, had reported a car stolen from his lot. Smith keyed to the next file. A Harold T. Smith was murdered in Kentucky three weeks ago.

Smith input commands to select only death reports.

There were thirteen of them. Thirteen Harold Smiths had died in the last seven weeks.

"Not unusual. There are a lot of Smiths," Harold W. Smith muttered, thinking of his relatives.

And to prove his own point, Smith saved the data as a separate file and requested reports of the deaths of all Harold Joneses in the same time period. Jones was as common a name as Smith.

There were two.

Smith asked for Harold Brown.

The computer informed him that three Harold Browns had died since November.

Puzzled, Smith returned to the Harold Smith file. The newspaper clippings had given the ages of the deceased Harold Smiths. All four victims were in their sixties. Smith requested age readouts from the file.

The first number was sixty-nine and it made Smith's heart leap in fear. But the next digit was only thirteen, and he relaxed.

But the rest of the numbers caused a fine sheen of perspiration to break out on his ordinarily dry forehead.

Every Harold Smith on the list but one had been over sixty. The oldest was seventy-two. The one exception—the thirteen-year-old—had died of leukemia, and Smith dismissed it from the file as a coincidental anomaly. All of the others were in Smith's own age group. All of them had Smith's name. All had been murdered.

Smith reached for his intercom, and in his agitation,

forgot it was already on. He turned it off and spoke into the mike. "Mrs. Mikulka. Mrs. Mikulka." He was shouting it the third time when Mrs. Mikulka burst into the room.

"Dr. Smith! What is it? What's wrong?"

"This intercom. It doesn't work!"

Mrs. Mikulka examined it critically.

"It's off."

"Oh. Never mind. Call my wife. Tell her I'm too busy to see her today. And forget lunch. Have the cafeteria send up a cheese sandwich with no mayonnaise or salad dressing and a tall glass of prune juice. I don't wish to be disturbed for the rest of the day."

Smith returned to his computer, his gray eyes fevered.

Someone was killing Harold Smiths. Even if it was a random thing, it deserved investigation. If it wasn't, it could have serious implications for CURE. Either way, Harold W. Smith knew one thing was certain.

He might be the next victim.

4

When Chiun did not emerge from his house to join in the big communal dinner in the village square, Remo decided to pretend not to notice.

Chiun was probably still angry with him, and pouting among his treasures was the surest tactic to get Remo to come to him, begging forgiveness. It wasn't going to work this time, Remo told himself. Let Chiun pout. Let him pout all night. Remo went on eating.

No one else seemed to notice that Chiun wasn't there. Or if they did, they didn't remark on it.

The villagers sat in the smoothed dirt of the square all around Remo and Mah-Li. Closest to them squatted old Pullyang, the village caretaker. During the period of Chiun's work—his exile, he had bitterly called it—in America, Pullyang ran the village. He was Chiun's closest adviser. But even he didn't seem concerned about Chiun's absence.

Pullyang leaned over to Remo, a little cackle dribbling off his lips. Remo knew that cackle meant a joke was coming. Pullyang loved to tell jokes. Pullyang's jokes would shame a preschooler.

"Why did the pig cross the road?" Pullyang whispered, giggling.

Remo, not thinking, asked, "Why?"

"To get to the other side," Pullyang howled. He repeated the joke to the crowd. The crowd howled. Even Mah-Li giggled.

Remo smiled weakly. Humor was not a Korean national trait. He would have to get used to it.

Remo decided that it might be better to introduce a more sophisticated brand of humor to the good people of Sinanju. He searched his mind for an appropriate joke. He remembered one Chiun had told him.

"How many Pyongyangers does it take to change a light bulb?" Remo knew Sinanjuers considered the people of the North Korean capital particularly backward.

"What is a light bulb?" asked Pullyang, deadpan.

Remo, taken aback, tried to explain.

"It is a glass bulb. You screw it into the ceiling of your house."

"Won't the roof leak?" asked Pullyang.

"No. The light bulb fills the hole."

"Why make the light bulb hole then?"

"The hole doesn't matter," Remo said. "The light bulb is used to make light. When you have light bulbs in your house, it is like having a little sun at your command."

"Wouldn't it be easier to open a window?"

"You don't use light bulbs in the daytime," Remo said patiently. "But at night. Imagine having light all night long."

The crowd all wore puzzled faces. This was strange to them. Ever since Remo had agreed to live in Sinanju, he had promised them improvements. He had told them the treasures of Sinanju had gathered dust for centuries and were going to waste. Remo promised to use some of the gold to improve the village. Remo had been saying that for weeks, but so far nothing had changed. Some wisely suspected that old Chiun was holding up these improvements.

"Light all night long?" repeated Pullyang.

"That's right," said Remo, grinning.

But no one grinned back. Instead there was a long uncomfortable silence.

At length Mah-Li whispered in Remo's ear.

"But how will we sleep at night?"

"You can shut the light bulbs off anytime you want."

"Then why would we need them?"

Remo thought hard. Why were these people so dense? Here he was doing his best to bring them civilization and a higher standard of living, and they made him sound so stupid.

"Suppose you had to relieve yourself in the middle of the night," Remo suggested.

The crowd shrugged in unison.

"You do it," a little boy said.

"But with a light bulb, you can see what you're doing," Remo pointed out.

The little boy giggled. All the children of the village laughed with him, but the adults looked mortified.

No one was going to say the obvious to Remo. Who would want to watch himself performing a bodily function? They all thought that, but to voice it to a Master of Sinanju, even if he was a white American with a big nose and unnaturally round eyes, would be disrespectful.

Out of the corner of his eye Remo saw the door to the treasure house of Sinanju open a crack. Remo's head swiveled, and Chiun's eyes locked with his. Satisfied that Remo's senses were focused on the dwelling of the Master of Sinanju, who was ignoring him, Chiun slammed the door.

Remo muttered under his breath. He had looked. And Chiun saw him look. Had he not looked, everything would have been fine. But not now. Now Remo could no longer pretend that there wasn't a problem.

Remo excused himself from dinner, squeezed Mah-Li's hand, and made for the treasure house.

"Might as well get this over with," he said to himself.

The door was locked, forcing Remo to knock.

"Who knocks?" demanded Chiun in a querulous voice.

"You know damn well who knocks," Remo snapped back. "You didn't hear me come up the path?"

"I heard an elephant. Is there an elephant with you?"

"No, there's no goddamn elephant with me."

The door shot open.

Chiun's beaming face stared back at Remo's.

"I thought not. An elephant makes less noise than you."

"Can I come in?" Remo asked, controlling himself with an effort.

"Why not? It is your house too." And Chiun moved back into the taper-lit interior.

Remo looked around. The heaps of treasure which occupied every room had been moved about. There were Grecian busts, Chinese statues, jars of precious gems, and gold in all its forms, from ingot to urn.

"Redecorating?" asked Remo as Chiun settled into the low throne which sat in the center of the main room.

"I was taking count."

"I never noticed these before," Remo said, walking to a group of ornate panels stacked against one wall.

"They are nothing," said Chiun disdainfully. "Too recent."

"I read about these," Remo went on. "These panels are known as the Room of Gold. They're some kind of European treasure. I remember reading an article about them once. They're a national treasure of Czechoslovakia or Hungary or some place like that. They've been missing since the war."

"They have not," Chiun corrected. "They have been here."

"The Europeans don't know that. They think the Nazis took them."

"They did."

"Then what are you doing with them?"

"The Nazis were good at taking things that were not theirs. They were not good at keeping them. Ask any European."

"I will, if any drop in for tea."

"Do you miss America, Remo?" Chiun asked suddenly.

"America is where I was born. Sure, sometimes I miss it. But I'm happy here. Really, Little Father."

Chiun nodded, his hazel eyes bright.

"Our ways are strange to you, even though now you, too, are a Master of Sinanju."

"You will always be the Master in my eyes, Little Father."

"A good answer," said Chiun. "And well spoken."

"Thank you," said Remo, hoping it would head off another one of Chiun's endless complaints about the frail state of his health in these, the ending days of his life.

"But I, being frail and in my ending days, will not always be the Master of this village," said Chiun. "You are the next Master. This we have agreed to."

"I hope that day is far off," said Remo sincerely.

"Not long ago it seemed that you would take my place much sooner."

Remo nodded, surprised that Chiun would bring up that subject himself. Remo was convinced Chiun's recent illness had been an elaborate con game designed to get them out of America. His miraculous recovery was suspicious, but Remo had not pressed the issue. He was too happy now that he had found Mah-Li. If it was one of Chiun's guilt trips that had brought that about, Remo reasoned, well, why not? Some people met through classified ads.

"We are both still young, you and I," said Chiun. "But I have suffered much in America, working for Mad Harold, the non-emperor. Too long have I breathed the foul, dirty air of your birthplace. It has robbed me of some of my years, but I have a good many years left. Decades. Many decades."

"I am glad," said Remo, wondering where this was leading.

"Even though you are soon to wed, which is the next important step toward assuming responsibility for my village, we must observe succession."

"Of course."

"You must learn to live as a Korean."

"I'm trying. I think the villagers like me now."

"Do not rush them, Remo," Chiun said suddenly.

"Little Father?"

"Do not force yourself upon them. In their eyes, you are strange, different."

"I'm just trying to get along," Remo said.

"You are to be commended for that. But if you truly wish to get along, you must do so according to rank."

"Rank?" asked Remo. "What rank? Everybody's a peasant. Except you, of course."

Chiun raised a long-nailed finger. It caught the mellow candlelight like a polished blade of bone. It looked delicate, but Remo had seen it slice through sheet metal.

"Exactly," said Chiun.

"I don't get it."

"If you desire to get along, your first priority should be to get along with me."

"Meaning?"

"Throw off the last of your American whiteness. In your former life, you were a caterpillar, a lowly green caterpillar."

"I thought you said I was white."

"You are."

"Which is it, white or green?"

"Honestly, Remo," Chiun said. "You are so literal-minded. I was speaking in images. You are white, but you are like the green caterpillar. And I am asking you to emerge from the cocoon of your whiteness. In the fullness of time, you will emerge as a butterfly."

"What color?" Remo asked.

"Why, yellow, of course. Like me."

"You?"

"Yes, me."

"I never thought of you as a butterfly before."

"How could you? Caterpillars do not think. Heh-heh. They do not think, but instead squirm in the mud wishing to be butterflies. Heh-heh."

"You're unhappy that the villagers are paying so much attention to me, is that it?" Remo asked.

"Of course not," said Chiun. "I merely ask that you do not fraternize with them excessively. You are a Master of Sinanju. They are the villagers. They must look up to you. They cannot look up to you if you are squatting in the dirt with them every night, eating the same food, sharing in their peasant jokes."

"The communal meals were your idea, Little Father. Don't you remember? You wanted the village to be one happy family."

"It has gone on too long. You are too happy. It is not good to be too happy."

"I could be a lot happier," said Remo.

"Name the thing that will increase your happiness, Remo, for your happiness is mine."

"Let's cut this engagement period down to something reasonable."

"Such as?"

"One week."

"It is too late for that," said Chiun sternly.

"Why?"

"You have already been engaged for eight weeks. Even a Master of Sinanju cannot roll back time."

"I meant one more week. I don't see why I can't marry Mah-Li sooner."

"Tradition forbids it," said Chiun. "A Master of Sinanju marries for life. He must marry wisely. You must get to know Mah-Li better."

"A nine-month engagement is too much. I respect your wishes, but it is too much."

"As a matter of fact, Remo, I have been reconsidering the formal engagement period."

"Oh?"

"I have been thinking that five years is more appropriate."

"Five—!"

Chiun waved Remo's outburst aside. "I said reconsidering. I have not made up my mind. I will keep your request in mind as I give this matter more thought."

Remo relaxed. "When will you let me know?" he asked.

"Two, perhaps three years."

"Chiun!"

"Hush, Remo. Do not shout. It is unseemly. What if the villagers hear us quarreling?"

"No chance. Not even an air-raid siren could pierce through these tapestries and stacks of gold."

"You cannot marry too soon. It would be wrong."

"I've been asking around. The normal engagement period is only three months."

"That is for Koreans," reminded Chiun. "You are not a true Korean."

"I will never be a Korean. You know that."

"We will work on that. Put yourself in my hands, Remo."

"And another thing, what about the village?"

"What about it?"

"I have some ideas that will make it better," said Remo, taking a piece of paper from his trouser pocket. Remo looked it over.

"Better? Better than what?" asked Chiun, genuinely

puzzled. "This is Sinanju. It is the center of the universe. What could make it better?"

"Running water, for one thing."

"We are by the ocean. We have all the water we need."

"Not to drink," said Remo.

"Sinanju is blessed with the sweetest rain," Chiun said, making fluttering motions with his fingernails. "You have only to set out your pots to collect your fill."

"I was thinking about putting in toilets."

Chiun made a disgusted face. "Toilets are a European confidence trick. They promote sloth and laziness."

"How so?"

"They are too comfortable. They are indoors, where it is warm. This encourages people to sit on them too long, reading mindless magazines, ruining their minds and posture."

"There isn't even a decent outhouse in the entire village. Everybody uses chamber pots or goes behind a rock. After a big feast, the air is unbreathable."

"It is the natural way. Fertilizer. It helps the crops."

"The only crops in Sinanju are mud and rocks," Remo said flatly. "The people are so lazy even the rice has to be trucked in."

"Do not insult my people, Remo," Chiun warned.

"What's insulting about good hygiene? I know you have a toilet in this house," Remo pointed out.

"This house was built by the finest Egyptian architects," Chiun said loftily, "back when Egyptians were good for something more than losing wars and dusting the ruins of their ancestors. It contains many curiosities. Somewhere in it there is a European water closet, I am sure. An antique."

"I hear it flush from time to time."

"It is necessary to keep even antiques in proper working order," Chiun sniffed.

"Chiun, you've got tons of gold just sitting here doing nothing and your people are living like . . . like . . ."

"Like Koreans," supplied Chiun.

"Exactly."

"I am glad we understand one another."

"No, we don't," Remo said. "If I'm going to live here

the rest of my life, I want to do something constructive. These people don't need more gold, or more security. They need a better standard of living."

"The people of Sinanju have food," said Chiun slowly. "They have family. they have protection. Even Americans have not that. Americans are subject to all manner of brutality from other Americans. In Sinanju, as long as there is a Master of Sinanju, no one need fear theft."

"That's because no one has anything worth stealing."

"They have me. I am their wealth. They have the protection of the awesome magnificence that is Chiun, reigning Master of Sinanju. They know that. They appreciate that. They love me."

Just then there was a knock on the door.

"Enter, beloved subject," said Chiun loudly.

Pullyang, the caretaker, scuttled into the room. He came to Remo's side and whispered into his ear. He took no notice of Chiun.

"Three," said Remo.

Pullyang doubled over with laughter. He ran out into the night. Remo heard him repeat his answer over and over. Other laughter welled up into the night.

"He didn't wait for the punch line," said Remo. "That wasn't even the funny part."

"What did Pullyang ask of you?" demanded Chiun.

"He wanted to know how many Pyongyangers it takes to change a light bulb."

"That was my joke!" Chiun hissed. And with a furious swirl of sleeves and skirts he leapt to his feet and bounded to the door.

"It takes three Pyongyangers to change a light bulb," Chiun shouted into the night. "One to change the bulb and two to shout encouragement while he does this!"

The laughter died abruptly.

Chiun slammed the door and returned to his throne.

"I don't understand the Korean sense of humor," said Remo.

"That is because you have none yourself. You are like all Americans, who turn the relieving of bodily wastes into a leisure activity. If I let you get your way now, you will next litter my poor village with condoms."

"What's this?"

"Condoms," repeated Chiun. "They are another American confidence trick. The tall buildings in which there are many rooms and each person owns a different room. But actually they own only the empty space within those walls, which is to say they own nothing."

"Those are condos," Remo corrected.

"And this is the treasure house of Sinanju. The house of my ancestors, and the house of all future Masters of Sinanju. Including you. Is it not good enough for you, toilet-loving American white?"

"I like it fine."

"Good. Then you will live here."

"When I am head of the village, yes," said Remo. "But until then, Mah-Li and I will live in the house I am building with my own hands."

"So be it," said Chiun, coming to his feet. "I have given you everything and you have spurned my best. Take your filthy belongings and go sleep on the beach."

"What belongings?" said Remo. "I'm wearing everything I own."

Chiun's fingernails flashed to the mahogany floor and speared the slip of paper on which Remo had written his list of improvements for the village of Sinanju.

"This filthy belonging," said Chiun, lifting it to Remo's hurt face. "I will have no toilets or condoms in Sinanju."

"Have it your way, then," Remo said unhappily.

He plucked the list and walked out of the House of the Masters without a backward glance.

5

Dr. Harold K. Smith was a simple country doctor.

The people of Oakham, Massachusetts, liked Dr. Harry, as he was called. He made house calls. No doctors made house calls anymore. Not when there was so much money to be made off the sick, and the most efficient way was to jam them into the office waiting room with plenty of waiting.

Dr. Harry had been making house calls for nearly forty years. He liked the homey touch. It was a nice, stress-free way to practice medicine. It filled his sixty-nine-year-old soul with peace. And even at his age, peace was what he most yearned for.

Dr. Harry might never have taken this route in life, but upon his graduation from Tufts Medical School, he was drafted. That was in 1943. Dr. Harry spent the next two years as a combat medic with the First Attack Squad, A Company, as they liberated France.

He had seen young men running one minute and screaming in muddy ditches—their legs chopped to hamburger by .50-caliber machine-gun bullets—the next. Crouched in foxholes, he had watched them being blown to ragged chunks of meat by grenades, crushed under panzer treads, and snuffed out with such appalling suddenness that even today he still had nightmares and woke up in cold sweats.

It had not been the best way to first practice medicine, but it had meant something. For some of the wounded Dr. Harry had treated, it had meant the difference between life and death, between walking back on the troop ships to America and hobbling on one leg and two crutches. Dr. Harry had absorbed everything it was possible for a physician to learn about wound cavitation, traumatic amputation, and human endurance, but after returning home in 1946, he went into family medicine and put the war out of his mind. Almost.

And so, on a particularly bitter winter's day, when a triple amputee was wheeled, unannounced, into his shabbily genteel office, Dr. Harry didn't hesitate to greet him. Even though the sight of the man brought back shuddering memories.

The man's age was impossible to guess. His face was rilled like a topographical map of the mountains of Mexico. His skin was unnaturally pale, and the thin red blanket that rested on his lap, covering the front of the motorized wheelchair, hung slack. There were two blunt bulges under it where his legs stopped.

The man's right arm ended in a steel claw, one of the new appliances which were such a boon to the amputee population. Dr. Harry had read about them, but had never seen one. His medical curiosity overcame his war memories and he found himself looking forward to examining this patient with unexpected eagerness.

"I'm Dr. Smith," said Dr. Harry to the old man and his beautiful blond companion. "What seems to be the trouble?"

"I'm Ilsa," the blond said. "He's having trouble with his good arm. I think it's the sciatic nerve. It's acted up before."

"You are his nurse?"

"His companion," said Ilsa.

She is so young, thought Dr. Harry, and so beautiful. He could tell by the solicitous way she hovered over him that she was intensely devoted to this shattered shell of a human being.

"Follow me into the examination room, and we'll have a look," Dr. Harry suggested.

"Ilsa, you will wait here," the man said. His voice was as dry as his eyes were bright. And they were very bright, unnaturally bright.

"Yes, of course."

Behind the closed pine door, Dr. Harry opened the stainless-steel drawer containing his instruments and said, "Please remove your shirt."

Dr. Harry watched the man unbutton his shirt with

his good hand. The fingers, gnarled and scarred, fumbled at the buttons. Dr. Harry nodded. Dexterity was impaired, but not as bad as all that. Probably the nerve was just inflamed.

When the shirt was off, Dr. Harry saw that from the neck down the man's body was a striated mass of scar tissue. Burns, horrible ones, had done that a very long time ago.

"I hope my appearance does not disturb you," said the old man. Dr. Harry suddenly remembered that he'd not asked the patient's name. Normally he left that to his receptionist, but she had already gone home for the day.

"I saw as much and worse in my time. During the war."

The patient seemed to tense as Dr. Harry approached with the blood-pressure cuff.

"You were in the war, World War Two?" the patient asked.

"Medic. European Theater of Operations."

"Those were terrible times, for both sides."

Dr. Harry nodded absently as he fitted the blood-pressure sleeve about the patient's bicep. "Do you think you could work the pump?" he asked.

The patient took the bulb and began squeezing rhythmically. The sleeve began inflating.

"I have never seen an appliance like yours," Dr. Harry said. "Bionic?"

"Yes. It is a boon to me, especially after all these years. You see, I, too, was in the war. My life ended there, for all intents."

"A terrible thing," said Dr. Harry sympathetically, looking at his watch, but surreptitiously examining the claw. It fitted onto the wooden stump of the man's wrist, the joining sealed in a plastic sleeve. Tiny wires led from the base of the appliance to the man's intact shoulder muscles. Electrodes. Brain impulses to those muscles produced twitches which in turn sent electrical signals to the artificial hand. The signals produced humanlike finger movements.

Even as Dr. Harry watched, the steel claw tensed.

The machinery whirred briefly. It was fascinating. He couldn't take his eyes off it.

"Medical science is making remarkable strides," the patient said, noticing the doctor's gaze.

"They're way ahead of this country doctor. I understand they'll be making bionic legs one day."

"Yes, but those are for men who still have one good leg. I know, I have looked into this. They cannot make them strong enough to support a man on two metal legs."

"Interesting that you should say that," said Dr. Harry, taking the inflating bulb from the patient's hand. "I was reading about a new process someone has invented for forging titanium. You know, it's stronger than steel and lighter as well. They've had excellent luck using it for implants, artificial joints and the like."

"So?"

"Well, steel is too heavy for some uses, and lighter metals, like aluminum for example, are too weak. They can't take the stress. If this man's process works as they say it does, I can see the day when they'll build bionic legs of titanium to help men like yourself to walk."

"I am intrigued. I must look into this. My doctors told me that there was no hope for me."

"There is always hope. We just have to hang around long enough for science to catch up to our problems."

"You are a great believer in hope, Dr. Smith."

Dr. Harry laughed. "I imagine so."

"Were you ever in Japan, Dr. Smith?" asked the patient.

"After the war, I came home. I haven't left Massachusetts since."

"I meant during the war. Were you there?"

"No."

"Perhaps you do not remember?"

"I'm sure I would," Dr. Harry said absently, reading the sphygmomanometer. "Your blood pressure is high. Hmmm, it seems to be rising even as you speak. When did this trouble come on?"

"Forty years ago. In Japan."

"Forget Japan. I meant the nerve."

"It all started then." The steel claw whirred open like

a venus flytrap preparing to catch a meal. "I have longed to meet you, Dr. Smith."

"Really?" said Dr. Harry Smith, taking his eyes off the claw with difficulty.

"Yes. Ever since that day in Japan, June 7, 1949."

The man's voice had dropped to a growl, and Dr. Harry took an involuntary step back. The man's arm—his good one—shot out, catching his open wrist. The grip was firm.

"Excuse me," said Dr. Harry, wriggling free. But pulling free was a mistake, because with the touch of a lever, the grizzled old man sent the wheelchair surging forward. Dr. Harry felt something clamp onto his right thigh. He looked down.

It was the steel claw. It bit through the cloth of his smock, which was reddening. Had he spilled some mercurochrome? But of course, he had not, and that voice was growling close to his ear.

"You thought I was dead, Dr. Smith. Harold K. Smith. You thought you had killed me that day. You did kill my future. But you did not kill my spirit. I live. I lived for you. All these years for you. And this moment."

Dr. Harry groped for the man's wrist. Maybe if he snapped the connection at the wrist sheath. Maybe. But the claw dug deeper with that damnable whirring, and Dr. Harry slipped to his knees.

"Ilsa!"

Dr. Harry heard the throaty bark through ringing ears. The pain was intensifying.

The blond bounced in through the door.

"He's not dead yet," she said. Her voice was disappointed.

"I would not have called you if I did not need help," the old man snarled. "Hold him down."

Dr. Harry felt soft fingers clamp his rounded shoulders, keeping him down on both knees. He tried to fight, but could not. And then through the ringing in his ears, he heard the whirring of the steel claw as it found his throat. The last words he heard were the girl's.

"I hope this one doesn't wet all over me too."

Dr. Harry fell onto the legless lap of the man in the wheelchair and slid off, taking the thin red blanket with him. On the underside, the crooked black cross of the swastika blazed like a blackened ember in its white circle.

"Was it him?" Ilsa asked breathlessly.

"No, it was not him. I could tell the first time he spoke. It was not his voice."

"Then why did you kill him?"

"His name was Harold Smith. It was reason enough. Pick up the flag and let us depart."

"Are we going to Boston next? There must be a lot of Harold Smiths there."

"No. Boston must wait. This doctor told me something important. We must return home, immediately. I must speak with my doctor about an important new discovery in metals."

6

The Master of Sinanju was unhappy.

Seated amid the opulence of the treasures of his ancestors, he hung his head low. He could not sleep. He lacked appetite—not that it mattered to the people of his village.

When Chiun had not joined the communal evening meal, no one had come to inquire of his health. No one had offered so much as a bowl of cold rice. Not Pullyang, the formerly faithful, nor Mah-Li, to whom he had bestowed a dowry of gold so that she could marry Remo—a dowry that had been the last shipment of gold from the mad non-emperor Harold Smith.

The Master of Sinanju picked up the goosequill that would inscribe this day's infamy in the personal daily records of Chiun, whom history—he hoped—would call Chiun the Great.

Dipping the quill into the black ink in a stone receptacle, Chiun began to transcribe, not for the first time, the story of how he had taken a white, a homeless unwanted white, and bestowed upon him the great art of Sinanju. He paused, pondering how best to describe Remo.

In past years, he had avoided the obvious: Remo the White. Too indelicate. Remo the Fair seemed a good compromise. But for this scroll, Chiun decided, he would be called Remo the Ingrate.

Chiun wrote "Remo the Ingrate" in the complicated ideographic language of his ancestors and, satisfied, wrote on.

He recorded how the village, dazzled by the coming of the ingrate, Remo, had turned against Chiun. Not in obvious ways, he hastened to scribble—for he did not wish his descendants to call him "Chiun, the Master who lost the respect of the village"—but in subtle ways, insidious ways. They paid attention to Remo. And in paying attention to him, there was less attention paid to the proper person. Chiun decided not to mention who the proper person might be. Better that future Masters learn to read between the lines, where truth usually lay.

Chiun wrote of his pride—a pride now sullied by ingratitude—in bringing the white to Sinanju. For this fair-skinned Korean had taken to Sinanju better than any pupil before him. He had grown through the phases of Sinanju, from the night of the salt to that glorious day when the spirit of Wang, greatest Master of Sinanju, had visited him. It had been only last year, but the boundless pride of it still filled Chiun's aged heart. Remo had seen the great Wang and was now a full Master of Sinanju. It was only meet that the villagers accord him due respect, despite his deficiencies of pigment. But even the great Wang would have been the first to say that in Remo's case, less is more.

"Less is more," cackled Chiun aloud. He had heard the phrase on an American TV commercial and liked it. In a few centuries, when America had gone the inevitable way of the Roman Empire and slipped into history, no one would know that the aphorism was not Chiun's own.

Remo, Chiun wrote, was the fulfillment of the greatest legend in the history of Sinanju. He was the night tiger who was white, but who in coming to Sinanju would be revealed as the incarnation of Shiva, the Destroyer. Chiun had known Remo was Shiva for many years. But there had never been proof, other than the clues the legends had foretold.

But in the American city of Detroit, Chiun wrote on, a city so unhappy that on certain religious holidays the inhabitants attempted to burn it to the ground, Chiun had confronted, not Shiva the Destroyer, but Shiva Remo.

Remo had been injured in a fire. Chiun had pulled him from a tangle of wreckage. When Remo had come to life, he spoke not in Remo's voice. He said words that were not words Chiun had come to expect from his former pupil. They were cruel words. For Remo had not recognized Chiun. Not at all. Not even after all they had been through together.

Even now, months later, Chiun had difficulty suppressing the shock he had experienced seeing Remo under the spell of the Hindu God of Destruction. In one accident, all that Chiun had worked for, the training of a new Master, one who would one day return to Sinanju, marry, and raise yet another Master, had been dispelled like a fragile soap bubble.

Remo's spell had been temporary, but Chiun could not know how long it would be before Shiva repossessed Remo's mind once more. And so Chiun, to save the years of training he had poured into the ungrateful white, to ensure the continuation of his line, had contrived to break the bonds that tied Remo to his homeland. The nature of this subterfuge, Chiun wrote on the scroll, was not important—except perhaps to note in passing its brilliance. After a pause, Chiun inserted the word "unsurpassed" before the word "brilliance." Some truths did not belong between the lines.

It had worked, Chiun wrote on. He and Remo had returned to Sinanju, no longer bound to work for the client state of America. Remo had agreed to succeed Chiun and had fallen in love with a Korean maiden. And now they were to wed. In time, there would be grandchildren. And Chiun's lifework would be complete. Chiun, who had married unwisely and had no living heir to call his own. Chiun, who was forced to take a white pupil to continue the line of Sinanju, and although his misjudgment might have been catastrophic, had in fact produced the greatest Master of Sinanju, Remo the Fair.

Chiun stopped and crossed out the word "Fair," substituting "Ingrate." Then he crossed that word out and tried to think of a word that somehow meant both. He could think of none.

And in thinking, he was reminded of his sadness. All of his dreams for Remo—and for Sinanju—had come true. Yet he was unhappy. The treasure house of Sinanju was bursting with new gold and old treasure. Yet he was unhappy. He need never work in a foreign land again. Yet he was unhappy. Remo had promised to remain with him in Sinanju, taking no outside work without mutual agreement. And Chiun was unhappy.

But he dared not admit this. Remo had always complained about Chiun's constant carping, as he had called it. Chiun thought the choice of words unfortunate, even harsh, but understood that there was a grain of truth in them. Chiun had for years beseeched Remo to abandon America and work for more reasonable empires. Like Persia, now fallen into disgrace and called Iran. Chiun had hoped that working for another country would be the first step toward making Remo a Korean.

Now Remo had done better. He had come to Sinanju and had won over its inhabitants. Chiun had never thought it would happen, much less happen this easily.

And still Chiun was unhappy.

He would have liked to complain openly, but he dared not. If Remo thought that Chiun was unhappy, as much as Remo loved Chiun, he might do something rash. Like insist that they return to America, where Chiun had been happier. Comparatively.

A peculiar look crossed the wrinkled features of the Master of Sinanju at that thought.

He set aside his scroll to dry, and from a low table took a square piece of parchment. It had been manufactured during the reign of Thutmosis II. By Western standards it was priceless. To the Master of Sinanju it was notepaper worthy of the greatest house of assassins in history.

Chiun addressed the note to Remo, suddenly thinking of a word that meant both "fair" and "ingrate," and began to write.

A green outline of the United States of America filled the right-hand side of the computer screen.

Dr. Harold W. Smith tapped a key and the borders of the forty-eight contiguous states appeared within the outline. On the left-hand side of the screen, separated by a dotted line, was a vertical list of Harold Smiths, along with the dates and places of their deaths. Smith had called up the list after a new man, a Dr. Harold K. Smith, had been found murdered in his Massachusetts office. His was the last name on the list, which was arranged chronologically by date of death.

Dr. Smith's fingers flurried across the board, tapping in a keying sequence.

One by one, a number was assigned to each name on the list. And one by one, a corresponding number appeared on the map. Each time a new number appeared on the outline, a solid green line ran from the previous number to its location, like a child's connect-the-dots game.

When the program ceased running, Dr. Smith had a zigzag line running from Alabama to Massachusetts. The line meandered in a winding but definite progression. That probably meant the murderer—if there was only one—traveled by road.

Smith tapped a key and all major U.S. highways appeared on the map.

The zigzag line seemed to correspond to the major highway systems in the states in which the murders had been committed. It was a confirmation; there was a pattern. And the line, which had headed in a northerly direction from Alabama up through the Great Lakes region and into New England, was now moving south. The next Harold Smith to die, Smith deduced, would be in Massachusetts, Rhode Island, or Connecticut. And after that?

The traveling killer could not drive east into the Atlantic Ocean. Thus he could continue either south into New York, or west, into upstate New York. Either way, Smith realized with a queasy feeling, the killer's path would bring him, eventually, inexorably, to Rye, New York.

And to himself, Harold W. Smith.

7

An accident of seating had made Ferris D'Orr one of the leading lights in his field.

Ferris D'Orr was in metals. Some who could make that claim speculated in gold or platinum, others in silver. Ferris D'Orr was in titanium. He didn't buy it, sell it, or trade it. He worked it. He was, at age twenty-four, one of the leading metallurgists in a field where practical application, not scarcity, created value.

As he tooled his silver-gray BMW into the parking lot of Titanic Titanium Technologies, in Falls Church, Virginia, Ferris D'Orr thought again of that portentous day when it had all begun.

D'Orr had been a high-school student, and not a very good one incidentally, dating Dorinda Dommichi, the daughter of a dentist who thought Ferris was a likable enough fellow, but not much more. That was because Ferris lacked ambition. Totally. He had no plans for college, no particular career direction, and a vague hope of winning the state lottery.

Ferris also had hopes of marrying Dorinda. If for no other reason than that her folks had money. Ferris liked money.

It had all come crashing down one night on the front seat of Ferris' gas-guzzling Chrysler. Ferris had decided that it was time that his relationship with Dorinda, in his words, "ascend to a new plateau of intimacy."

"Okay," said Dorinda, not exactly understanding, but liking the sound of the words.

"Excellent," said Ferris, pulling her sweater up over her head.

"What are you doing?" asked Dorinda.

"We're ascending. Remember?"

"Then why are you pushing me down on the seat?"

"How do you unlock this thing?" Ferris asked, tugging on her bra strap.

"Try the front."

"That's where I'm headed. Your front."

"I mean it unlocks in front."

"Oh. Why didn't you say so?"

It had not been the exciting, pleasurable experience Ferris D'Orr had always dreamed of. The front seat was too cramped. After Ferris got one leg tangled in the steering wheel, they tried the back seat.

"That's better," Ferris grunted. He was sweating. It seemed like a lot more work than he expected.

"This is icky," said Dorinda, her brows knitting.

"Give it time. We're just getting started."

No sooner were the words out of his mouth than Ferris was done.

"That's it?" asked Dorinda in a disappointed voice.

"Wasn't it wonderful?" asked Ferris, dreamy-eyed.

"It was icky. Let's go see a movie and forget this ever happened."

"Dorinda, I love you," Ferris said, taking Dorinda in his arms. And in his passion, he spilled his greatest secret. "I want to marry you."

"Maybe," said Dorinda. "I'll have to ask my father first."

"My mother might object too," said Ferris. "She's got some crazy idea of me marrying a nice Jewish girl."

"How come?" Dorinda asked, closing her jeans.

"My mother is Jewish. But I'm not."

"That's nice," said Dorinda.

"I'm only telling you this because I don't want any secrets between us now. Not after tonight. Promise that this will be our little secret?"

"I promise," said Dorinda, who at breakfast the next morning asked her father a simple question.

"What's Jewish?"

"A person who is a Jew is Jewish. It's a religion. You've heard Father Malone mention them at Mass."

"Oh," said Dorinda, who skied in the winter, sailed in the summer, and rode horses the rest of the year, but otherwise didn't get around much. "I thought they only existed in the Bible. Like Pharisees."

"Why do you ask?" said Dorinda's mother.

"Because Ferris said he wasn't one."

"Of course not. He goes to church with us, doesn't he?"

"But his mother is, though."

Mrs. Dommichi dropped her coffee. Dr. Dommichi coughed violently.

"When did he tell you this?" asked Dr. Dommichi casually.

"After," said Dorinda, buttering a muffin.

"After what?"

"After we ascended the new plateau of intimacy."

Ferris D'Orr noticed a definite coolness in the Dommichi family's attitude toward him the next time he happened to drop in at suppertime. At first, he thought it was something he had said, but when they stopped inviting him on the weekly family boat outings, he knew he was in deep trouble.

He asked Dorinda what was wrong one night while she was resisting his attempts to unclasp her bra.

"My dad says you're a Jew."

Ferris stopped. "You told him!"

"Of course."

"But that was a secret. Our secret."

"Isn't that what secrets are for, to tell other people?"

"I'm not a Jew. My mother is a Jew. My father was a Catholic. I was raised Catholic. Even after my father died, I stayed Catholic. Despite my mother's nagging."

"My father says a Jew is a Jew."

"What else does he say?" asked Ferris dejectedly, giving up on Dorinda's snow-white brassiere.

"He says that I shouldn't count on marrying you."

"Damn," said Ferris D'Orr, realizing his meal ticket was slipping out of his fingers.

Despite that, Dorinda's family had invited him to Thanksgiving dinner. It was a typical Italian Thanksgiving, with a lot of wine, garlic bread, homemade ravioli, and linguine in clam sauce. And as an afterthought, a very small turkey. You didn't eat much turkey with all that pasta. Ferris suspected that Dorinda had to throw a tantrum to wangle the invitation.

His suspicions were confirmed when, instead of seating him at the family table next to Dorinda, her parents, and the seven Dommichi children, he got stuck in a satellite table with a gaggle of cousins.

Ferris made the best of it. He was there for the food, mostly. And so he struck up a conversation with a short-haired cousin not many years older than he.

"Ferris D'Orr," he had said, sizing up the man.

"Johnny Testa. Happy to meet you." He had the polite air of an Eagle Scout about him. In fact, Ferris found him too nice. Maybe the guy is a priest or a seminary student, Ferris thought.

"You from around here?"

"Originally. I'm on leave at the moment from the Navy."

"Oh yeah? Submarines and aircraft carriers and that stuff?"

"Actually, I only get out on the water when Uncle Dom invites the family out on his sloop. I'm with the Naval Research Laboratory in Washington. I'm a metallurgist."

"You work with metal?" said Ferris, recognizing half of the word. "Like a welder?"

The Navy man laughed good-naturedly.

"No, not exactly. My team is experimenting with titanium applications. It's a metal," he added, seeing Ferris' blank look.

"What's so great about titanium?" asked Ferris, tasting a rubbery substance that he realized, too late, was squid.

"Titanium is a crucial defense metal. We use it for critical parts of aircraft, submarines, satellites, surgical implants, and other high-tech applications. On the one hand, it's great. It will withstand corrosion, stress, and high-speed punishment. But it can't be worked the way steel or iron is worked. You have to form it in cold state and then machine it. It's expensive, and you lose a lot of it in the process. They call that the 'buy-to-fly' ratio. How much titanium do you have to buy to make that aircraft part? Usually the ratio is 1.5 to 1, which means you lose one-third of the metal in fabrication."

"You're really into this stuff?" said Ferris.

"Titanium has other problems. Its melting temperature is too high. Makes it tough to weld—you have to do it in an inert-gas chamber—and practically impossible to forge. When it reaches its melting point, it absorbs nitrogen, causing embrittlement."

"That makes it no good, right?" asked Ferris D'Orr, who thought he was catching on.

"Right. Exactly."

"So what do you do?"

"We're trying to find a way to make titanium take ordinary welding. If we can weld it, we can build aircraft from titanium. Right now, we can only use it for the most critical machine parts."

"Anybody see any pork?" Ferris said loudly, looking in Dr. Dommichi's direction. "Boy, I could really go for some juicy pork chops right about now. Yum yum, my favorite."

The head table pointedly ignored him and he settled for a pasta dish he didn't recognize.

"The metallurgist who can figure it out will make billions," Johnny Testa continued.

"Billions? Maybe that guy will be you," Ferris suggested, secretly hoping it would not be.

"If I succeed, the Navy will get the money. I'll just get the credit."

"That's kinda unfair."

Johnny shook his head. "I won't crack it. All I'm doing is taking high-speed camera films of welding checks. We analyze the way the solder droplets fly off the titanium forms. The real breakthrough will be in solving the hot-forging problem. They're years away from real progress."

"How many years?"

"Five, maybe ten."

"How many years does it take to become a metallurgist?"

"Four. But it's been done in less."

"Can you be a metallurgist without joining the Navy?"

"Absolutely. I'll bet some private firm pulls off this coup. Those are the boys who'll make the bucks."

"Where do you go to learn this stuff?" asked Ferris D'Orr, who right then and there was motivated into a career decision.

"I went to MIT."

"That's in Boston, isn't it?"

"Near Boston, anyway."

"Can you be more exact?" asked Ferris D'Orr, scribbling furiously on his linen napkin. "And spell 'metallurgy' for me, will ya?"

The next day Ferris D'Orr broke off with the lovely Dorinda and started hitting the textbooks with a vengeance. He had two years of high school left and he was going to make the best of them. In his spare time he read all he could about metallurgy so that when he got to MIT he'd have a head start. With his luck, some joker was going to beat him to all those billions of dollars.

But no one did. Ferris got to MIT and completed the four-year metallurgy degree in three years. In his senior year, working entirely on his own, he discovered a method of annealing bronze that experts speculated was similar to the method once known to the ancient Egyptians, but now lost. Ferris immediately fell into a top position with Titanic Titanium Technologies of Virginia, one of the most important defense-industry metallurgy firms.

That had been five years ago, thought Ferris D'Orr as he stepped from his car. In those five years he had risen to the position of vice-president of exotic-metals applications at Titanic Titanium. All that time, he pursued his goal in his personal lab. He kept plugging away during the superplastic forming scare, which drastically simplified titanium forming. He had squeaked through the revolution in bonding titanium with space-age plastics, and the quartz-lamp forging experiments. Still the industry had not solved the ultimate problem of forging titanium.

This morning, Ferris D'Orr thought to himself, he was about to render all those advancements obsolete.

"Good morning, Mr. D'Orr," said the security guard.

"Good morning, uh, Goldstein," said Ferris, squinting at the guard's nametag. He made a mental note to have the man fired. He didn't like Jews. They reminded him of his mother.

Ferris D'Orr slipped his plastic keycard into the proper slot and the security door buzzed open, then clicked shut behind him.

In his private laboratory, Ferris got to work. He was excited. This was the day. Or maybe tomorrow would be. He wasn't sure, but he knew he was close. Very close.

Three round billets of grayish-blue titanium stood on a worktable. They bore the Titanic Titanium triple-T stamp. They looked like ordinary lead bars, except for their rounded corners and high finish. If you saw one lying on the street you wouldn't give it a second look.

But Ferris knew that in their way, they represented the ultimate in titanium technology. To get pure titanium in bar form, the metal had to be consolidated from its mined granule form. Even then, the billet was only the raw material. It had to be painstakingly ground, cut, or machined into usable parts, and a lot of valuable titanium was ground away in the process. It could be welded only with difficulty and it could not be melted. With its high melting temperature, heating titanium turned it into a pourable, but brittle, slag that was useless for commercial applications.

The problem seemed insoluble, but Ferris D'Orr had hit upon a solution that was as perfect as it was obvious. In other words, it was brilliant.

If heating titanium to get it into a desired shape created more problems than it solved, then the trick was to melt the metal without heating it.

Ferris D'Orr had explained his idea to the president of Titanic Titanium Technologies, Ogden Miller.

"You're out of your mind," Miller said. Ferris reminded him of how he had discovered the method of annealing bronze while still in college. Miller gave him a private lab and unlimited funding.

The result was the titanium nebulizer. Ferris D'Orr wheeled the prototype over to the worktable where the three billets stood on separate trays.

The titanium nebulizer looked like a slide projector on wheels. There were no high-tech dials, frills, or gimcracks. It was simply a black box with a stubby tubelike muzzle mounted on a mobile stand. Ferris pointed the muzzle at one of the billets, which sat in a tray labeled A. Another rested in a tray labeled B. The third lay on the middle tray, which was labeled AB.

He turned on the nebulizer. It hummed, but otherwise there was no indication that it was working. Ferris adjusted two micrometer settings until the numbers matched.

"Vibration frequencies attuned," he sang happily. "Ready, set, go."

He pressed the only other control, a microswitch button.

The billet in the A tray melted like a dropped ice-cream bar.

"That's A," Ferris hummed.

He readjusted the micrometer settings and hit the microswitch.

The billet in the B tray wavered and swam, filling the tray like poured coffee.

"That's B," Ferris sang. "Here comes the hard part."

Ferris fiddled with the micrometer settings. Each time he thought he had the vibration settings he wanted, he hit the button. Nothing happened. The melted titanium in the A and B trays shimmered liquidly. The middle billet just sat there.

"Damn," said Ferris. "I'm so close."

"You're close to being shut down," said a voice at his side.

Ferris jumped.

"Oh, Mr. Miller. I didn't hear you."

"Ferris, what's this about your secretary leaving in tears yesterday?"

"We had an argument," said Ferris absently, removing a panel on the side of the nebulizer to get at the inside workings.

"She claims you tried to get into her pants."

"Actually, I succeeded."

"In this very room, from what I hear."

"She enjoyed it. Or so she claimed at the time."

"So you fired her after you had your way with her? Is that it? Stop fiddling with that thing and look me in the eye when I talk to you."

"Can we discuss this later? I think I'm almost there."

"You're almost out the door, is where you are, Ferris."

"Since when is sleeping with my secretary a crime? Almost everybody in this company sleeps with some other worker. At least I don't sleep with members of my own sex."

"We can live with that," Ogden Miller said hastily. "What we can't live with is a discrimination suit. She claims you fired her for religious reasons."

"She was Jewish. She admitted it. If I'd known it beforehand, I wouldn't have slept with her. Or hired her in the first place."

"You'd damn well better have a stronger excuse than that. We have big government contracts that can be taken away over something like this."

"It's not my fault," said Ferris forlornly. "Her last name was Hart. What kind of a Jewish name is that? Somebody ought to give them badges, so we can tell them apart or something."

"Someone tried that. I think his name was Hitler. What's gotten into you?"

"Could you stand aside? I think I have the setting synchronized again."

"You're out of sync, Ferris. That's your problem."

"Out of sync," Ferris said, closing the panel. "Maybe that's it. In sync for A and B, out of sync for AB. It might work."

"What might work?"

"Watch," said Ferris D'Orr, replacing the A and B trays with identical trays and placing new billets in each tray.

"The tray marked A is alpha-phase titanium," Ferris said as he hit the button.

The billet liquefied.

"So what?" said Miller. "We already know you can melt titanium with a laser. It doesn't matter. The metal's too brittle to use now. It's been exposed to air."

"This isn't a laser."

"Yeah?"

"It's a nebulizer. It doesn't use heat."

"No heat," said Miller thoughtfully, taking a cigar out of his mouth.

"Do you feel any heat?"

"Now that you mention it, no."

"Put your hand in front of the nozzle."

"No, thanks."

"Then hold this button down while I put my hand in front of the thing."

Ferris waved his hand in front of the nozzle. He grinned.

"Microwaves?" asked Ogden Miller.

Ferris shook his head. "They'd cook my hand to hamburger. It's sonic."

"No heat at all?"

"Watch," said Ferris, walking to the A tray. He dipped his index finger in and brought it out dripping liquid titanium.

"Oh my God," said the president of Titanic Titanium Technologies. "I'll get a doctor."

He was halfway out of the room when Ferris got in his way.

"Touch the metal," he said, holding his metal-coated finger under Miller's nose.

Gingerly Miller felt the metal. It was hard, cold. And as Ferris pulled the thin covering off his fingernails, malleable. Definitely malleable.

"Not brittle?" asked Miller incredulously.

"Not brittle at all." Ferris grinned.

"Do you realize what this means? No more superplastic forming. We can pour the billets directly into molds. Like steel."

"Better," said Ferris D'Orr. "We can skip the mill stage altogether. The nebulizer will leach the raw titanium from rock. We can melt and remelt it like it was taffy."

"This thing will do that?"

"That's not all," said Ferris, pulling a square block off a shelf. He handed it over.

"What's this?"

"Yesterday, it was two rectangular forms. Pure titanium."

"I don't see any weld seams."

"Weld seams are yesterday. Like the 78 RPM record. Or dry-box welding."

"No more dry-box welding?" Ogden Miller's voice was tiny, like a child's.

Ferris nodded. "You can throw them all out—as soon as I lick the alpha-beta-phase titanium problem."

"Can you?"

The two men walked over to the nebulizer.

"Something you just said makes me think I can," Ferris D'Orr said as he played with the micrometer settings. "As you know, titanium in the alpha phase has its atoms arranged in a hexagonal formation. When the metal is heated above 885 degrees Centigrade, it's transformed into body-centered cubic beta titanium."

"I don't know that technical stuff. I don't have to. I'm the president."

"But you do know that alpha-beta titanium is the best for commercial use?"

"I've heard it said, yeah."

"This device, through focused ultrasound, causes the metal to vibrate so the atomic structure is, to put it in layman's terms, discombobulated. It falls into a liquid state without heat or loss of material."

"Just like that?"

"Just like that. But alpha-beta titanium won't respond to the nebulizer. I've spent the last two weeks trying every possible vibratory setting to get the same reaction. It's like trying to crack a safe. You know the tumblers will respond if you hit the right combination. You just have to keep searching for that exact number sequence."

"Well, keep searching."

"If alpha titanium **discombobulates** when exposed to synchronized frequencies, then might not alpha-beta-phase titanium respond to out-of-sync vibrations?"

"You're the whiz kid. You tell me."

"No, I'll show you."

And Ferris D'Orr got to work.

Ogden Miller, president of Titanic Titanium Technologies, Inc., pulled up a stool and lit another cigar. His face shone like a wet light bulb; his eyes glazed in thought. He had visions of his company dominating America's defense and aerospace programs into the twenty-first century. Perhaps beyond. This was big. It was bigger than big. It was a metallurgical revolution. He had visions of a two-page ad in the next *Aviation Week* announcing the first one-to-one buy-to-fly ratio in metallurgical history. And it had been created on Titanic Titanium company time. Which meant that Ogden Miller owned it. If it worked on alpha-beta titanium, that is.

Under his superior's watchful eye, Ferris D'Orr worked through lunch. He worked past five o'clock. And he worked well into the evening, setting and resetting the micrometer dials and triggering the nebulizer, without result.

At exactly 9:48 eastern standard time, the billet in the AB tray liquefied.

The two men, their eyes bloodshot from hours of staring at that stubborn chunk of bluish metal, blinked furiously.

"Did it melt?" whispered Miller.

"My eyes tell me it did."

"I don't trust them. Mine neither."

"Do you want to dip your finger into it, or should I?"

"I want the honor this time."

Ogden Miller walked to the AB tray and carefully touched the cool surface of the bluish material in the tray. It shimmered. It felt cool to his touch, like a very dense pudding. When he lifted out his finger, it gleamed silvery-gray and the puddinglike stuff blopped down into the tray, one fabulous drop at a time.

Ogden Miller looked back at Ferris D'Orr.

"AB titanium. You're certain?"

"We did it!" Ferris howled. "We can pour titanium into molds like steel."

"We can forge it, weld it. Hell, we can practically drink it!"

"I think that would be going too far, Mr. Miller."

"Well, Ferris, we can drink champagne, can't we? Get those out-of-sync settings down on paper and we'll celebrate."

"What about that matter?"

"What matter?"

"The secretary."

"Hell with her," said the president of Titanic Titanium Technologies. "Let her sue. We'll settle out of court and still be billions in the black."

"Billions," said Ferris D'Orr under his breath. "Billions."

8

Remo Williams awoke with the rain.

Or rather, the rain woke Remo Williams. He had spent the night in his unfinished future home, sleeping on the hard floor and collecting a few splinters from the unplaned wood. The rain started shortly after dawn, a light sprinkle, and pattered on his sleeping form.

A fat droplet splashed on Remo's high cheek and rilled into his parted mouth. He came to his feet, tasting the cool, sweet drop. It was different from the rain in America, which tasted brackish and full of chemicals. He threw his head back to catch more drops.

Today, Remo decided, he would thatch the roof. Then he remembered that he didn't know how.

Remo reluctantly made his way through the mud to the House of the Masters, which shone like a slick jewel in the rain.

Remo knocked first. There was no answer.

"C'mon, Chiun."

He knocked again, and receiving no reply, focused on his breathing. A Westerner, straining to hear better, concentrates on his ears. But that tenses the sensitive eardrums and is counterproductive. By focusing his breathing, Remo relaxed his body and attuned it to his surroundings.

Remo's relaxed but very sensitive ears told him that Chiun was not inside the house.

"Anyone see Chiun?" Remo asked of the two women walking by with burdens of cordwood.

They smiled at him and shook their heads no.

Remo shrugged. He tried the door. It was not locked and he went in.

Everything was as before; heaps of jewels and bowls of pearls were scattered across the floor. On the taboret beside Chiun's low throne there was a piece of parchment. Even across the room, Remo recognized his name, written in English.

Remo snatched up the paper.

To Remo the Unfair:

Know that I do not fault you, my son, for the misfortune that has recently befallen me, the Master of Sinanju, who has lifted you up from the muck of a foreign land and raised you to perfection. That you have never thanked me for my sacrifices is of no moment, I do not hold this against you. Nor do I fault you for the manner in which you have stolen the affection of my people. It is their affection to give, and how could they resist the insidious blandishments of one who has been trained by Chiun—whom I know you will refer to in the histories that you will write as Chiun the Great. Not that I am telling you your business. Write the histories as you see fit.

Do not worry about me now that I have gone from Sinanju. I am in the evening of my life, and my work is done. I would stay in the village I have selflessly supported, but no one wants an old man, not even to honor for his great accomplishments. But I did not do the work of my House to be honored, but to continue my line. And now you will take up that burden from my drooping shoulders. May you bear many fine sons, Remo, and may none of them visit upon you the ingratitude and indignities which have been my sorry lot.

The village is yours. The House of the Masters is yours. Mah-Li is yours—although I expect you to honor the traditional engagement period. I do not blame you for casting me aside like an old sandal and lavishing your fickle affections upon Mah-Li—formerly known as Mah-Li the Beast—for she is young like you, and youth never appreciates the company of the stooped and the elderly, for it reminds them of the loneliness and infirmities that lie in store for them. Sometimes deservedly so.

Build your toilets, Remo. As many as you like. Make them big enough to swim in. I grant you my permission. And condoms. Build those too. May the shoreline of Sinanju boast condoms taller than any known in the modern world, as a true testament to the glory of Remo the Unfair, latest Master of Sinanju.

I go now to live in another land—the only land in which I have known contentment and the respect of a fair and generous emperor.

P.S. Do not touch capital. Spend all the gold you wish, but do not sell any treasure. The gold exists for the use of the Master, but the treasure belongs to Sinanju.

P.P.S. And do not place your trust in the villagers. Not even Mah-Li. They are fickle. Like you. And they do not love you, you know, but only covet your gold.

The note was signed with the bisected trapezoid that was the symbol of the House of Sinanju.

"Oh, great," said Remo in the emptiness. He plunged into the next room, where Chiun kept his most personal effects. They were stored in fourteen steamer trunks, all of them open. There were no closets in Sinanju. It was another improvement Remo had hoped to make.

All fourteen steamer trunks were still there. The note, therefore, had to be a bluff. Chiun would never leave without his steamer trunks. Remo checked Chiun's kimono trunk. There were three garments missing, a gray traveling robe, a sleeping robe, and the blue-and-gold kimono favored for wear when Masters met with former emperors.

"He really has gone," Remo said dully.

And it was true. Remo turned out the whole village. Every hut, every hovel, was checked. Chiun was nowhere to be found.

"What does this mean?" asked Mah-Li, after the truth became clear.

"Chiun's gone," Remo said. "He left during the middle of the night."

"But why would he leave? This is his home. He has longed for Sinanju ever since he departed for America."

"I think he felt left out," Remo said at last.

The villagers of Sinanju were distraught. The women wept. The men howled their anguish to the sky. The children, frightened by the sounds, ran and hid. All had the same plaintive cry. All asked the same burning question. All feared the answer.

It was Pullyang, the caretaker, who addressed it to the new Master, Remo.

"Did he take the treasure with him?"

And when Remo barked, "No!" joy filled the village like the lifting of storm clouds.

"Shame, shame on you all," scolded Mah-Li. "The Master Chiun has protected us and fed us for as long as most of us have lived our lives. Shame that you should be so uncaring."

"Thanks, Mah-Li," said Remo, as the villagers slinked away.

"But where would the Master go?" she asked in a quieter voice.

Remo was standing in the mud outside of Chiun's house when the question was asked. The light rain was steadily obliterating any possible trace of footsteps, and the Master of Sinanju, whose step would not wrinkle a silk-sheeted bed, never left a discernible trail anyway.

But, oddly, there were traces visible in the melting mud. A deeper footstep here, a faint thread of gray kimono silk there. Could Chiun be so upset, Remo wondered, that he did not take the usual care in walking?

With the curious villagers trailing behind him, Remo retraced Chiun's path out of the village and up the lone trail through the rocks to the one road leading in and out of the village.

At the crest of the hill, Remo looked down the dirt road, which, at a respectful distance, widened into three black highways, built by the leader of the People's Republic of North Korea, Kim Il Sung, to atone for a transgression against Sinanju made not long ago. One highway ran east; the others veered north and south.

Chiun's sandaled footsteps led as far as the end of the dirt road. Remo saw faint wet imprints of his steps at the beginning of the south highway.

Chiun had gone to Pyongyang, capital of North Korea. And from there, who knew?

What was it Chiun had written? "I go now to live in another land—the only land in which I have known contentment and the respect of a fair and generous emperor." Normally that would have been Persia, but even Chiun admitted that Persia was a mess these days, ruled by priests, not true rulers. China, then. No, the Chinese were thieves, according to Chiun. Japan? Worse. When Remo had eliminated the Pacific rim and Europe from his mind, only Africa and North America were left.

Could Chiun have meant America?

The farmer from Sunchon would have been glad to give the elderly wise man with the stovepipe hat a ride, he said.

"Then why do you not stop?" Chiun asked, walking alongside.

"I have no room in my cart," was the reply. The cart was drawn by a lone bullock. "See? It is full of barley, which I am taking to market."

Chiun, without breaking stride, peered into the square back of the two-wheeled cart. Heaps of barley lay there, soaking up the light rain.

"It is good barley. Do you mind if I walk with you?" asked Chiun innocently.

"If you wish, stranger."

"I am no stranger," corrected Chiun. "Every man knows me."

"I do not," the farmer said reasonably.

And because Chiun was traveling incognito, he did not tell the farmer who he was. Any who wished to follow him would have to work at it. Not that anyone would.

After a time, the farmer noticed that the tired bullock was stepping more smartly. The shower had tapered off and the clouds were parting in the sky. It was going to be a good day after all. Then, realizing that the old wise man had been silent too long, he looked back to see if he still walked beside the cart.

He did not. He was placidly sitting in the rear of the cart. The empty cart.

"Where is my barley?" the farmer screeched, pulling the bullock to a halt.

"You have a defective cart," said Chiun evenly. "It sprang a leak." The farmer then noticed the trail of barley beans—a single ragged line extending down the highway back to the West Korea Bay.

"Why did you not tell me?" The farmer was fairly jumping up and down. His conical hat fell to the asphalt.

Chiun shrugged. "You did not ask."

"What will I do?" wailed the farmer. "I cannot pick them up one by one. I am ruined."

"No, only your cart is ruined," said Chiun. "Take me to Pyongyang airport and I will give you a gold coin."

"Two gold coins," said the farmer.

"Do not press your luck," warned Chiun, arranging his traveling kimono so that it covered the fingernail-size hole that had appeared in the bottom of the cart, just wide enough to let one barley bean at a time fall out, like the grains of sand through the neck of an hourglass. "It is fortunate that I happened to be traveling with you at this unhappy time."

The Master of Sinanju was informed at the People's Democratic Airport that, no, he could not book a seat on a flight to the West. The North Korean airline did not fly to the West. If he wanted to go to Russia, and he had the proper documentation, fine. If he wished to fly to China, that, too, was possible. From Russia or China, he could obtain connections to any other proper destination in the Communist world.

"Seoul," said the Master of Sinanju, still refusing to identify himself. "I can change for a Western flight in Seoul."

The airport guards arrested the Master of Sinanju as soon as the words were out of his mouth. They called him a defector and a lackey of the West.

Chiun's arrest lasted about as long as the epithets hung in the air around him.

The two security guards found their rifles had jumped from their hands and embedded themselves, muzzle-first, in the ceiling. Plaster fell on their bare heads. While they were looking up, they required major surgery. Very suddenly.

The head surgeon at the People's Democratic Emergency Ward wanted to know how the two guards had managed to enter military service despite their obvious congenital defect.

They were not believed when they explained that they were not really Siamese twins, born fused at the hip, but the victims of a particularly vicious Western attack. After surgery, they were court-martialed for concealing medical disabilities.

By that time, Chiun had been deposited at Kimpo Air Base in South Korea in a North Korean military craft which had its markings removed. The pilot and copilot, who had volunteered for the mission, swallowed poison upon landing in Seoul, capital of South Korea.

Chiun, oblivious of the fact that he had precipitated a major international incident, stepped off the aircraft and disappeared into the drizzle and fog of midmorning. He was one step ahead of the South Korean and American troops who converged upon the plane.

Hours later, a Strategic Air Command bomber took off from Kimpo on a routine flight back to the United States. Over Hawaii, the pilot and copilot were more than a little astonished when they heard a knocking on the cabin door.

They looked at one another. As far as they knew, the rear of the craft was empty. There shouldn't be anyone in back.

"Maybe a maintenance worker fell asleep," the pilot suggested.

"I'll take a look," said the copilot, removing his earphones.

When he opened the sealed door, he saw a little Korean in a gray robe.

The little Korean smiled pleasantly.

"You speakee English?" asked the copilot.

"Better than you," retorted Chiun. "I have been waiting patiently for many hours. When are meals served on this flight?"

9

In 1949 they had told him there was no hope.

He did not believe them, not even in those early months in the green room. He was in an iron lung then. He was in an iron lung a long time, staring up at the angled mirror in which his seared face stared back as pale and bald as that of a new hatchling.

The doctors had told him there was no hope of his ever leaving that mechanical barrel which kept him breathing in spite of his weakened lungs.

But the face of the brutal Harold Smith stared back at him from the inescapable mirror. His hair grew back, in patches. His eyebrows resprouted. The plastic surgeons—paid for by benefactors from the old days—recarved his melted ears until they were like any normal person's ears, if smaller.

And in time, they pulled him from the iron lung. He had demanded it. At first they refused, insisting that he would die. But he ordered them. In the name of the old days, of the Reich that was now never to be, he ordered it. Finally they relented.

And he breathed on his own.

They had not told him he had lost both legs.

"We thought it unnecessary to burden you," the doctor told him. "It is a miracle you are out of that damnable machine at all." His accent was of the old country, of the undivided Germany. He was the only one of the doctors he trusted. The others were good, but they were mongrels, with greasy black hair and skin the color of heavily creamed coffee. They spoke the debased Spanish tongue of Argentina.

"I should have been told," he had railed at them. "Had I known, I would not have allowed myself to survive. Had I known, I would have gone to my grave in peace. What good is my freedom if I cannot walk? I have one good arm. With one arm I could strangle that assassin, Smith. One arm is all I would need. But no legs . . ."

The German doctor had shrugged helplessly.

"You are fortunate to live at all. Be grateful for that."

It had taken many years of therapy before he had the strength to sit up in a wheelchair. That was the second step. The third was the year the motorized wheelchair was put on the market. With that, there was no need to be pushed around by nurses. But that wasn't what he wanted.

He wanted to walk. Erect, like a whole man.

The years passed in the hospital outside of Buenos Aires. They gave him a wooden arm with a hook at the end of it. The hook had lasted barely a week. He would wake up in the middle of the night, sweating and screaming, trying to beat back the flames. The hook shattered the night-light, tore the bedclothes, and ripped open the cheek of one of the yelling nurses as she tried to hold him to the bed.

They replaced the hook with a black plastic cap. It was as blunt and impotent as the smooth scar tissue of his groin, where the surgeons had, in those early days, removed the dead, gangrenous organ, and inserted a tiny plastic flange to keep the inflamed opening of the urinary tract from sealing over.

It was an indignity that seemed inconsequential compared with the others Harold Smith had visited upon him in one red-lit evening. It did not matter that he was no different from a woman in that respect. He was still a man in his heart. And his heart lusted for a man's vengeance. An Aryan's vengeance.

They told him there was no hope of walking. Ever.

When they introduced the first bionic arms in the 1970's, he demanded one. And got it. He was no longer in the green room he had come to loathe, but in a stucco home near Salta that was paid for by donations from those of Germany who still believed and remembered.

"If they can do this with arms, they can do it with legs," he had told his doctor at the time.

"They are working on it," the doctor had told him. "I

think they will succeed. It will be a boon for those missing one leg, yes. But for those with none . . ." The doctor had just shaken his head sadly.

"There is no hope?" he had asked.

"There is no hope."

And he had believed him. But the face of the hated Harold Smith kept staring back from every mirror, every pane of glass touched by the Argentinian sun, and taunted him. Eternally young, he had taunted him.

By that time he had established contacts throughout the world. There were people, good Germans, who had left the dismembered ruin of their native country and resettled in America. Some had visited him in his stucco home, to reminisce, to speak of the old days and old glories, glories that might still shine.

"Find Smith," he had begged them. "Do not approach him. Do not touch him. Just find him."

They had not found Smith. The old Office of Strategic Services had been disbanded. Smith had been an employee to the end, but there the trail ended. There was speculation that the man might have transferred over to the new intelligence organ of the United States government, the Central Intelligence Agency, but the old CIA records were impossible to access. There was no Harold Smith listed in the newer records.

"Perhaps he is dead," they suggested.

"No," he had spat back. "He lives for me. He lives for the day my hands clutch his throat. He is not dead. I would feel it if that were true. No, he is not dead. And I will find him. Somehow."

It was then that he finally came to America, back to America. It was a changed place, but all the world had changed. Even he had changed.

In America he had found many Harold Smiths. And so he had set out to kill them all.

He had killed several. It had been easy, but oddly disappointing. None was the right one. And there were so many Harold Smiths. He had begun to despair once more.

Until today.

Now the doctor was speaking words that brought him back to the present.

"There is hope."

"Are you certain?"

"If what you tell me is true, there is hope," the doctor said. He was the latest doctor. Young, brilliant, loyal, and one of the finest bionics experts in the country. The doctor had created his three-fingered claw that was superior to anything available from the best American medical-supply houses.

"I have heard about this man D'Orr's discovery. If he's solved the titanium problem, then I can see the day when this method could be applied to bionic legs."

"When?"

"Three years. Perhaps less."

"I cannot wait three years," he said.

He was lying on an examining table, a sheet covering his stumps and the obscene nudity between them. Ilsa stood off to one side. He was not ashamed to let her see him like this, lying like a piece of wrinkled meat on the table. She had seen him like this many times. She dressed him, fed him, and bathed him. She helped him when he had to use the bathroom. He had no secrets from Ilsa—except perhaps his desire for her.

He smiled at her, and she gently soothed his brow with a cool damp cloth.

"We're so close to finding him," Ilsa told the doctor.

"I cannot stop now," he told the doctor. "I have begun my search. What can you do for me?"

"Nothing."

"What do you need? I will obtain it."

"The technology exists," the doctor said. "The trouble is, it exists in two parts. I can give you anything that modern bionic engineering can provide. But you know the problem. Steel is too heavy for the powering mechanisms that would have to be built into each limb. Aluminum is too light. The legs would buckle under the strains you propose. I could give you legs tomorrow, but they would not be equal to the task. If I had D'Orr's nebulizer, it would be possible to create titanium parts that would work. Otherwise, we must wait for the device to come on the commercial market."

"Then we will get D'Orr's secret," he said, and Ilsa squeezed his real hand tightly.

"I will leave that up to you," said the doctor, replacing his stethoscope in his black bag. "Contact me when you have succeeded. I want to leave here while it is still dark. A man of my reputation cannot be seen coming and going from this place."

"You are a good German," he told the doctor.

There was hope. After all these years, there was hope.

10

In his office at Folcroft Sanitarium, Dr. Harold W. Smith rubbed his eyes furiously. Replacing his steel-rimmed glasses, he returned to the mocking video screen.

A light snow was falling on Long Island Sound. Smith had no eyes for its quiet beauty.

Moment by moment, unusual reports flashed onto the silent screen. Tapped off wire-service and network newsfeeds, only CURE-potential events showed on the screen. Smith had long ago worked out a system that enabled the dumb, unthinking computer to separate human-interest and other miscellaneous events—the chaff of the daily news—from the wheat, possible CURE priority material. Buzzwords were the key to the program, buzzwords like "death," "murder," "crime." When the computer found those words, it filed those reports.

Smith read each time the screen flashed a new paragraph.

In Boston, a twenty-two-year-old girl was shot twice in the chest in a drug-related murder. The previous week she had escaped a similar attack by unknown persons brandishing an Uzi machine gun.

In Miami, two undercover vice cops were missing for the third day and presumed dead.

In San Francisco, military police surrounded an Air Force transport upon its arrival from the Far East. The pilots claimed they had a mysterious Oriental stowaway, but when the plane was boarded, no trace of the stowaway was found.

And for the fourth day in a row, no one named Harold Smith had been found murdered anywhere in the United States.

Smith brought up the U.S. map on which the trail of the Harold Smith killings was plotted. The line stopped in Oakham, Massachusetts. Cold. No other Harold Smiths had died in that state, as Smith had projected. Or in Rhode Island. Or in Connecticut.

What did it mean?

Had the killings stopped as mindlessly as they had begun? Or was the unknown killer simply still traveling to his next victim? In four days, he could have entirely covered Rhode Island, the smallest state in the Union. Or Connecticut, for that matter.

Unless, of course, the killer intended to bypass those states. Unless he was already in New York State. Unless he was in the vicinity of Rye, New York.

Smith had ordered the security guards attached to Folcroft on high alert, but they were not equipped to handle anything this serious. Folcroft was an ordinary institution, and the guards believed they were guarding an expensive health facility. Smith, with the resources of the United States government at his command, could have ordered Folcroft surrounded by crack units of the National Guard. Navy helicopters could, in less than an hour, be deployed in the air over the grounds.

And by the seven-o'clock news, CURE's cover would be exposed to the harsh spotlight of the media, if not blown entirely. There was no way to hide Smith's intelligence background. A cover-up of his past had been considered during the formative days of CURE, and rejected.

Instead, Smith had simply retired from his CIA position and taken a dull but well-paid job in the private sector. It was done all the time. No one would have suspected Smith's new position as director of Folcroft masked America's greatest secret.

So no helicopters flew the skies to protect Harold W. Smith.

For the same reasons, Smith dared not bring the still-undiscovered pattern of killings to the attention of law-enforcement agencies. In fact, he had spent a good part of the last four days pulling strings to make certain that local police reports on the killings did not enter the interagency police intelligence networks. Computer files were mysteriously erased. Paper files disappeared from locked cabinets.

No, there must be no headlines detailing the killing of Harold Smiths. It would draw attention to every Harold Smith in Smith's age group—the age group of the thirteen murder victims to date.

And so, Harold W. Smith, with the might of the entire United States military at his command, but unable to call the police like any other citizen, worked in his Spartan office, his only protection a Colt .45 automatic in his upper-right-hand desk drawer. His eyes remained fixed on the busy computer terminal. It would tell him when the mysterious killer struck again.

Unless, of course, he struck at Folcroft. In that case, Smith would know in a more immediate way. Because Smith would be the next victim.

The phone rang and Smith scooped it up.

"Harold?"

It was Smith's wife.

"Yes, dear?"

"It's six o'clock. Aren't you coming home tonight?"

"I'm afraid I'm going to be working late again. I'm sorry."

"I'm worried about you, Harold, about us."

"There's nothing to worry about," Smith said in an unconvincing monotone.

"We're slipping, aren't we? Back into our old ways."

"You mean I'm slipping, don't you?" said Smith, his voice warming.

"I wish you were here."

"I wish I was home too." Out of the corner of his eye Smith saw an entry flash on his video screen. "I have to go now. I'll be in touch."

"Harold—"

Smith hung up abruptly. Turning to the screen, he saw the name Smith. He relaxed when he saw that the item was a news report about a politician, last name Smith, who had been arrested on a bribery charge.

False alarm. Smith thought about calling his wife back, but what did it matter now? She was right. He was slipping back into his old habits, his cold manner.

They had a good marriage, but only because she put up with his long hours, his constant preoccupation, his dry manner. Smith was a good provider, a stable husband, and a churchgoer, but that was as far as it went. A lifetime of public service had crystallized him into the ultimate bureaucrat. A lifetime of responsibility for America's defense had boiled the juices from him.

When Remo and Chiun were set free from CURE, Smith had found freedom himself. Freedom had made a new man of him. He had grown closer to his wife. After forty years of complacent marriage, they were like newlyweds again.

And it had lasted barely three months, Smith thought bitterly, forcing his thoughts to refocus on the here and now.

Smith did not know who the killer was. He did not know for certain that his rampage through the ranks of Harold Smiths was a hit-or-miss attempt to snuff out Smith's own life. But he had to assume so.

First there was Smith's background. His OSS/CIA history was full of old enemies. There had been CURE-related enemies, but thanks to Remo and Chiun, none of them had lived. No, this matter could not involve CURE. Anyone knowing of Smith's link to CURE had to know enough to locate him with ease.

That made the killer, inevitably, someone from Smith's pre-CURE days. But who? Whoever it was did not know certain important facts.

He did not know where Smith currently lived or worked.

He did not know Smith's full name, otherwise only Harold W. Smiths would be targeted.

But most important, he did not know he was stalking a man who could fight back.

11

Boyce Barlow had single-handedly made the town of Dogwood, Alabama—population 334—racially pure.

Boyce was very proud of his accomplishment. Dogwood, Alabama, was his hometown, not far from the big city of Huntsville. There were no Jews in Dogwood. Never had been. There were no Asians in Dogwood, although there were a few in Rocket City. As long as they stayed in Rocket City, Boyce Barlow didn't much care about them.

Boyce Barlow was the founder of the White Purity League of Alabama. He had founded it one night in Buckhorn's Lounge, about two weeks after his unemployment checks ran out, while a string band played bad country music on the jukebox.

"This country is going to hell," Boyce told his cousins Luke and Bud.

Luke and Bud each lifted a bottle of Coors in salute to Boyce's righteous sentiment. Luke burped.

"It's getting so a man can't count on worthwhile employment in the land of his birth no more," said Boyce.

"There are other gas stations," said cousin Luke.

"Not in Dogwood, there ain't," Boyce complained. "I can pump gas as good as anyone, but I ain't pumping gas in Dogwood no more."

"Move."

"Shoot, man. I was born here. Can you beat Old Man Shums up and firing a native son like that? I was with him, hell, all of a year and three months. I had seniority."

"Old Man Shums said you also had your hand in the till."

"So what? I worked there, didn't I?"

"He said you had your hand in the till after closing," Luke pointed out.

"I was drunk," said Boyce. "How the hell's a man supposed to know what he's about when he's drunk? It ain't natural."

"I hear Old Man Shums got himself a replacement," Luke offered. "Some Indian fella from Huntsville."

"Indian! Damn! That's what's wrong with this country. Too many damn furriners."

"I don't think he's that kind of an Indian."

"What other kind of Indian is there?" asked Bud, who had dropped out of Dogwood Elementary School after the fifth grade.

"There's two kinds. The turban kind and the bow-and-arrow kind," said Luke, who'd come within two months of graduating from high school. "Neither damn one of them any damn good."

"Damn straight," said Boyce. "They're lazy, don't like to work, and they sponge off this great nation of ours."

"Sounds like you, Boyce," the bartender called over.

Boyce threw the bartender a surly look.

"When I want your attention I'll piss on the floor."

"You did that last week."

"And this week I'm considering the other option."

"I had no idea you took in solids," the bartender said dryly.

"Which kind stole my job?" Boyce wondered aloud. "The turban kind or the other?"

"I hear the guy's name is Eagle," said Bud. "John Eagle."

"Must be the bow-and-arrow kind. If it were the other, his name would be John Cow," offered Luke, the historian. "They're big on cows over in India."

"It's un-American," Boyce complained to no one in particular. "Him taking my job like that."

"It's very American," said the bartender, polishing a glass. The bartender polished his glasses to get some use out of them. No one drank beer out of a glass in Dogwood. "The Indians were here before us. That guy's more American than any of you."

The revelation seared into the brains of the drunken trio.

"I think he's right," Luke whispered. "I heard something like that on *The Rifleman* once."

"Well, he's not white, is he?" demanded Boyce.

"That's right. They're red. They call 'em red men."

"Communists," said Bud, spitting on the floor.

"No, but they're no good neither," said Luke.

"I think we should do something," said Boyce Barlow.

"Do what?" asked Bud.

"Like let's take Dogwood back from the Indians."

"How many Indians we talking about?" asked Luke, who was a cautious soul.

They looked at Bud.

Bud shrugged. "I think there's only one of them."

"Good. We outnumber him."

"Not from what I hear. Them Injuns, they're tough mothers."

"We'll bring a bat with us," said Boyce Barlow, pulling his baseball cap with the Confederate flag down low over his mean eyes.

And that night, the three cousins pulled into Old Man Shum's gas station and yelled for service.

"No need to shout," a deep, rumbling voice said very close by. "I'm right here."

"Where?" demanded Boyce, sticking his shaggy head out the driver's window of his four-by-four pickup.

And then he saw John Eagle. The man stood nearly seven feet tall. He was as wide as a gas pump. In fact they had mistaken him for a gas pump in the darkness, which was why his sudden appearance was so unnerving.

"You John Eagle?" asked Boyce Barlow.

"That's right," said John Eagle, leaning down. He smiled. It was a big, friendly smile, but it made John Eagle's wide Indian face look like the front of a Mack truck. "Something I can do for you?"

The three cousins stared at John Eagle with their mouths open and spilling beer fumes.

"He's whiter than us," whispered Luke.

"And he's bigger than us," added Bud. "All of us. Put together."

"Fill 'er up, friend," Boyce said good-naturedly, vainly trying to match the big man's smile.

Driving off, Bud Barlow broke the strained silence.

"It was a good idea, anyway."

"It still is," said Boyce Barlow. "We gotta make Dogwood a fit place for white Americans."

"And Indians. White ones," added Bud, looking back furtively.

"Who else lives in Dogwood who ain't white?" asked Boyce.

"There's that pumpkin farmer at the edge of town," Luke said. "What's his name? Elmer something."

"Elmer Hawkins," said Boyce. "He's a nigger. Yeah, we can run him off."

"What'd he do?" demanded Bud.

"He ain't white, is he?" said Boyce. "Ain't this the idea? We gotta run off the ones what ain't white."

"But Elmer, he's pushing seventy. And who'd he ever bother?"

"You let one nigger in, soon you got a townful."

"Shoot, Elmer's been living here going on fifty years. He come into town by himself. He's the only nigger we got."

"He's leaving town. Tonight," Boyce said firmly.

They crept up on Elmer Hawkins' neat shack by moonlight, Boyce Barlow in the lead. It was easy going. There was no kudzu to tangle their feet. Elmer Hawkins' place was about the only open part of Marshall County that wasn't overrun with the indestructible weed.

They knocked on Elmer's front door. The windows of the shack were unlit.

"Elmer, open up," Boyce called drunkenly.

When there was no answer after ten minutes of furious knocking, they gave up.

"Must be minding someone's kids," said Bud. "Elmer's always doing nice stuff like that."

"Shut up!" yelled Boyce. "I ain't coming back tomorrow night. I'm in a mean mood now. Tomorrow I might not be."

"Well, I ain't waiting all night, neither," said Luke.

"Who's got a match?" asked Boyce. "We'll burn this nigger out of Dogwood."

"I don't like this," said Bud, but it was too late. Boyce was holding a butane lighter under one corner of the dry wood shack.

The corner darkened, caught, and a line of yellow flame climbed the unpainted wood until there was no chance of putting it out.

Elmer Hawkins came running up the road not many minutes later.

"What's goin' on? What you doin' to my house?" he yelled. He was a lanky old man with peppercorn hair.

Boyce Barlow yelled back at him.

"We're running out all the niggers in Dogwood."

"This ain't Dogwood, you fool. This is Arab."

"Ay-rab?" said Luke dazedly.

"The Dogwood town line is up the road. What you want to go and burn down my house for?"

"We're getting rid of all the niggers in Arab too," Boyce said smugly.

And he did. But not the way he thought. Elmer Hawkins watched the shack he had lived in for most of his life burn to the ground. He did not get mad. He did not call the police, nor did he press charges. Instead, he hired a lawyer and got even.

The county judge at the trial awarded Elmer Hawkins seven hundred dollars in punitive damages for his shack and an additional fifty thousand dollars for emotional distress. Because Boyce Barlow was dirt poor and unemployed, he could not pay. So the judge ordered Boyce's house—which had been in his family since the Civil War—auctioned off and the proceeds given to the victim. Elmer Hawkins took the money and bought himself a modest home in Huntsville. There was enough left over to put a down payment on a diner near the Marshall Space Flight Center, where Elmer Hawkins lived out the rest of his days in busy contentment.

"At least I won," Boyce Barlow said when it was over. He was back at his usual table at Buckhorn's.

"But you lost your house, Boyce," Luke pointed out glumly.

"Dogwood is racially pure, though, ain't it?"

"Always was. Elmer lived in Arab, remember?"

"We're not stopping with Dogwood anymore," Boyce said, staring into the dark Coors bottle like a man gazing into a crystal ball. "We're going to expand."

Expanding was not easy. The White Purity League of

Alabama picked up a few new members who thought it was a crying shame that Boyce lost his house that way, which brought the ranks to exactly six. Because all six were temporarily out of work, dues were a problem.

"How can we expand without any money?" Boyce complained one night at Buckhorn's.

"We could all go out and get jobs," Bud suggested. He was ignored.

The bartender, who had long ago grown tired of the White Purity League of Alabama holding meetings in his establishment and forgetting to pay its tab, made a fateful suggestion.

"Go on cable TV," he said. "They let any group on the air now. It's called local access or something like that. It's free."

"We don't have cable TV in Dogwood," Boyce said reasonably.

"They do in Huntsville," the bartender countered.

And so the *White Purity League Hour* was born. Within three months its message, "Take Back America," was reaching viewers in twenty-nine states and the District of Columbia. Membership rose from the founding six members to nearly three thousand nationwide. Boyce Barlow bought himself a nice white frame house in suburban Huntsville, a short drive from the national headquarters of the renamed White Purity League of America and Alabama, a former Boy Scout campground Barlow had purchased and converted into Fortress Purity, a barbed-wire compound off Route 431.

Barely a year after the groundbreaking of Fortress Purity, a man showed up at the electrified fence. The man was in a wheelchair.

"I want to join your worthy group," the man said. He was old, too old. And he had no legs.

"Go 'way," said Luke Barlow from the gate. "We got standards."

"Ilsa!" the old man called.

A blond girl stepped out of a bronze van.

"Hi," she said breathily. Then she smiled sunnily.

"Hi!" Luke said, staring at her chest.

"Can we come in? Please?"

"Sure," said Luke, who realized that recruitment among single women was distressingly low.

After he had unlocked the gate, he said, "Pleased to meet you. I'm Luke. I'm vice-corporal in charge of security."

"I've never heard of such a rank," said the old man in the wheelchair.

"I made it up," said Luke proudly. "It was either that or admiral of the gate. I liked that one best, but the other was longer."

The old man smiled. His smile was hideous. It was the smile of a rot-toothed corpse. "Of course."

When the old man was brought to Boyce Barlow, Boyce was three thousand dollars in the hole to his poker partners and welcomed the interruption.

"I'm calling the game. We split the pot," he announced suddenly, scooping up two handfuls of money. "What can I do for you folks?"

"You are Boyce Barlow. I have watched your program. We are kindred spirits, you and I."

"You and me is kin?"

"In spirit. I, too, believe as you do. America for Americans."

"Who're you?"

"This is Herr Konrad Blutsturz," said Ilsa proudly. "He is an Aryan. He is like you."

"The hell he is. I got both my legs," said Boyce Barlow. "No offense," he added.

"I have a gift for you," said Konrad Blutsturz, tossing a book onto the poker table.

Boyce Barlow picked up the book and read the title. "*Mein Kampf*," he said aloud.

"The first word is pronounced 'mine,' as in 'yours or mine,' " Konrad Blutsturz corrected. "Not 'main.' "

"Main's how they say it at the China Dragon. You know, chow mein."

"A different language altogether. The words mean 'My Battle.' A great man wrote it."

"Adolf Hitler," Boyce read aloud. "Wasn't he a bad guy?"

"The losers are always called that. Had Hitler won the war, there would now be no Jews, no blacks, no inferior peoples living in America, taking American jobs from true Americans and draining the vitality out of this once-strong nation."

"Is that so?"

"His ideas are your ideas," said Konrad Blutsturz. "He was espousing them before you were born. You, Boyce Barlow, have reinvented the wheel. Read this book and see for yourself. When you are done, call me at the number I have written on the flyleaf and we will talk."

Boyce Barlow had read the book. The old man without legs had been right. Boyce Barlow found that the old man was right about many things.

Konrad Blutsturz told them he could triple the membership of the White Purity League of America and Alabama. Overnight.

"You have only to do three things."

"What are those?" Boyce had asked suspiciously.

"Starting today, fly this flag from your highest building."

Boyce Barlow took the flag. It was red. In the center was a twisted black cross in a white circle. Boyce recognized the flag; he had seen it in World War Two films.

He showed the flag to Luke and Bud.

"What do you guys think?"

"It would look better if it were green," said Luke.

"I like red," said Bud, thinking of the Confederate flag.

"Me too," said Boyce. "Done."

"Excellent. Second, change the name of your organization to the Aryan League of America."

"What's an Aryan?"

"We are Aryans," said Konrad Blutsturz. "Aryans are the master race, descendants of the racially pure warrior Vikings. Like Ilsa, here."

They all looked at Ilsa. Ilsa looked back. She smiled sweetly.

"We're all Aryans, ain't we, boys?" Boyce said. "Especially me. How about we call it the White Aryan League of America, though? So the dumb ones don't get confused."

"I will agree to that," said Konrad Blutsturz.

"And the third thing?"

"Appoint me your second-in-command."

Boyce Barlow had done this too, and, true to the old man's promise, the membership rolls swelled. That they swelled with people who had German last names was at first troublesome to the ruling triad of the newly renamed White Aryan League of America and Alabama. Boyce had insisted on retaining the "Alabama" part, in his words, "to remind folks this great movement began in the heart of Dixie."

One night, while counting up the month's dues, Boyce asked the old man, "Isn't our slogan supposed to be 'America for Americans'?"

"That is our slogan," admitted Konrad Blutsturz.

"Then what are those damn furriners doin' here?"

"They are not foreigners. America is a melting pot. The best of all white nations have come to these shores. German-Americans are as American as any. More so. It is the blacks, the Jews, the Smiths who are to be eradicated."

"The Smiths?" asked Boyce. "Aren't they white too? I mean mostly?"

"They are the worst of all. They look white. Their skins appear to be white. But their souls are black, and evil. We will rid America of the blacks and the Jews and other inferior peoples. But first we must crush the Smiths."

Boyce Barlow didn't quite follow Konrad Blutsturz on that last point, but the dues kept coming in and so he did everything that Konrad Blutsturz suggested.

Konrad Blutsturz had showed how to get the White Aryan League of America publicity. Instead of just preaching the word over cable TV, or on street corners where they were hooted and booed, he showed that marching down the streets of American towns, shouting racial epithets, usually brought media coverage. Free media coverage. And when you shouted racial slogans, the races you insulted always shouted back. Sometimes they threw rotten fruit and bottles.

"Do this and we will get sympathy. Provoke the blacks and Jews and Orientals to attack us. We will look good and they will look bad because the networks cannot spend more than three minutes of footage on any news event. They will omit our slogans and show our enemies attacking our peaceful march."

And it had worked. All of it had worked. That man Konrad Blutsturz was a genius. He knew everything.

And when Blutsturz had insisted that he be called Herr Führer, Boyce Barlow had made it White Aryan League policy. And when Herr Führer Blutsturz had made the finding of one man named Harold Smith the League's top priority, Boyce Barlow had not questioned him. After all, Harold Smith was a black-souled Smith, possibly the secret leader of the coming Smith uprising that threatened to undermine the racial purity of America.

And when Herr Führer Blutsturz ordered Boyce Barlow and his cousins Luke and Bud to personally go to Falls Church, Virginia, after a scientist named Ferris D'Orr, Boyce Barlow asked only one question.

"You want him alive or dead?"

12

At first, Dr. Harold W. Smith thought he was hallucinating. He had not gone home the night before. He dared not. First, there was the fear that he would miss some critical report coming over his computers. And then there was the shame. He did not want to face his wife in his current state, as the old Harold Smith, the lemony-faced, cold-blooded Harold Smith who had been ground down by a lifetime of intelligence work. Last, there was the fear that if he went home, he would lead the unknown killer straight to his door, and to his wife.

"Could you repeat that, please?" Smith asked, thinking that lack of sleep had caused him to hear things.

Mrs. Mikulka patiently repeated herself, speaking slowly and distinctly through the office intercom.

"I said a Mr. Chiun is here to see you. He's very insistent, and the guards at the gate don't know what to do."

"You did say Chiun?"

"Yes, Dr. Smith. Chiun. What shall I tell the guards?"

"Tell them to escort Mr. Chiun to my office. Carefully. Tell them not to touch him, provoke him, or otherwise get in his way."

"My goodness, is he an escaped patient?" asked Mrs. Mikulka, placing a plump hand to her well-cushioned chest.

"Just do it," said Smith, one harried eye on his computer console.

Minutes later, the guards left their charge outside Smith's office door.

"Oh, hello." said Mrs. Mikulka, recognizing the Master of Sinanju. She had seen the elderly Oriental before. He had visited Smith on other occasions.

"Greetings, lady-in-waiting to the Emperor Smith.

Please inform the emperor that the Master of Sinanju, formerly his royal assassin, has arrived."

"I'll do just that," breathed Mrs. Mikulka, wondering if this man was not a candidate for a Folcroft rubber room.

"That man is here, Dr. Smith."

"Send him in. And take an early lunch."

The Master of Sinanju, resplendent in his blue-and-gold greeting kimono, entered the room with dignified ceremony.

"Hail, Emperor Smith," he called, bowing slightly. "The House of Sinanju brings you greetings and felicitations. Great is my pleasure in beholding your wise, your magnificent, your robust countenance once more."

"Thank you," said Smith, whose eyes were red-rimmed and bloodshot, and whose ashen face looked like a dead man's. "I am surprised to see you."

"Your joy is returned a thousandfold," said the Master of Sinanju.

"Er, you're not working for anyone at the moment, are you? I mean, this is a social call—isn't it?"

"I am between employers at present," admitted Chiun.

Smith relaxed slightly. The loyalty of a Master of Sinanju, he knew, stopped at the termination of each contract. There was no telling what Chiun wanted. He might even be here to assassinate Smith himself.

"You're not here about that unresolved matter in Sinanju?" asked Smith cautiously.

"And what unresolved matter is that?" asked Chiun innocently.

"When the Russian business was concluded, I asked you to terminate my life, and you refused."

"Ah." Chiun nodded. "I recall I refused because you had not enough coin to pay. Oh, I am ashamed, Emperor Smith, ashamed to the very core of my being. I should not have refused so minor a boon. In truth, I am here to atone for my error."

"I no longer require your services," Smith said hastily.

"No?" The Master of Sinanju looked disappointed, nearly stricken. "Are you certain?"

"Quite certain. The President has authorized CURE

to continue. This releases me from my duty to commit suicide."

Chiun lifted a long-nailed finger.

"This is good," he said. "For the atonement I wish to make has nothing to do with killing you—although I would gladly do so if this were your command. I would do anything the Emperor Smith, in his inexorable wisdom, commands."

"You would?" said Smith, dumbfounded. "Anything?"

"Anything," Chiun said placidly.

"But our contract has been voided. You told me so yourself."

"Clause Fifty-six, Paragraph Four." Chiun nodded. "Which stipulates that contracts between emperors and the House of Sinanju may not be transferred to third parties. You did this, committing the Master of Sinanju to service to Russia. You did this under threat of blackmail by the Russians. Remo has explained these details to me. I bear you no ill for your oversight, for that is surely all that it was. Emperors, of course, cannot be expected to remember all the niceties and details, especially the fine print."

"I'm glad you feel that way, Master Chiun, but I still don't quite understand what you're doing in America."

"Clause Fifty-six, Paragraph Ten." Chiun smiled. "Under the rubric 'Refunds.' "

"As I recall, a shipment of gold accompanied you on your last submarine crossing to Sinanju. Under the circumstances, I didn't assume we were due a refund. Are you here then to return the gold prepayment?" asked Smith.

"Would that it were in my power," said the Master of Sinanju sadly.

"Then what?"

From the folds of his robe the Master of Sinanju extracted a gold-edged scroll tied with a blue ribbon. Chiun delicately untied the ribbon, causing the scroll to roll open.

"Allow me to read. 'In the event of termination of services, the House of Sinanju is obligated to refund all prepayments, prorated to the term of unfulfilled service.'

"Alas," continued the Master of Sinanju, "Remo, my

adopted son, is to wed a Sinanju maiden, and because that maiden was an orphan bereft of family and dowry, and because Sinanju law forbids the House of Sinanju to retain gold that it has not truly earned, I was thrown into a dilemma. I did not know what to do," said Chiun, because emperors sometimes did not know simple words like "dilemma." "I could not keep the gold. And you had already returned to America when I discovered my lapse. Poor Remo, my son, could not marry his chosen bride because she had no dowry. It was a difficult time. But in my wisdom, I saw a solution to all our problems."

"You gave the gold to Mah-Li," Smith said wearily.

"I gave the gold to Mah-Li," said Chiun triumphantly, in almost the same breath. And he smiled. "Truly, you are a mind reader, as well as generous and understanding."

"You came all the way to Sinanju to tell me that you can't return the gold?"

"No, I have come all the way to the wonderful land of America to atone for my error, as I have said."

"Meaning?"

"Meaning my new dilemma," said Chiun. "I cannot return the gold, for I have given it away."

"You have a great deal of gold, Master of Sinanju," reminded Smith.

"True," said the Master of Sinanju. "But I do not have a submarine. Only a submarine is capable of transporting such generous quantities of gold from Sinanju to these happy shores."

It was true, thought Smith. Annually, he had shipped enough gold ingots to Sinanju to pay off the debts of many small nations. And Chiun never spent that gold, according to Remo.

"I can make arrangements for one of our nuclear subs to pick up the repayment," Smith said.

"I cannot allow that," said Chiun.

"Why not?"

"It would be unfair. The expense you would incur in sending that vessel would detract from the value of the repayment." Chiun shook his aged head. "No, I would not do that to you."

"We can work something out," said Smith.

"No," said Chiun hastily. "For Sinanju law dictates that all repayments be made in the same coin. No substitutes."

"I would not mind," said Smith.

"But my ancestors would," returned Chiun.

"Then what?"

Chiun paced the office. "I cannot repay in the same coin. It is regrettable, but I am stuck. Therefore, as difficult as it will be, as much as I desire to remain in Sinanju with my adopted son and my people who wept bitterly when I left them, I must fulfill my contract with you."

"I'm sure we can come up with an alternate solution," Smith said.

"I have thought long on this," Chiun said firmly. "This is the only way."

"Things have changed, Master Chiun. CURE is no longer set up for operations."

Chiun waved a dismissive hand. "A mere detail. A trifling of no moment in the magnitude of this event. Lo, my descendants will sing in praise of this hour for generations to come," Chiun said loudly. "After too long a time, the House of Sinanju has been reunited with the most kind, most generous, most able client it has ever known, Smith the Wise."

"It has been only three months," reminded Smith.

"Three long months," Chiun corrected. "Each day a year, each month an eternity. But at last it is over."

"What about Remo?"

Chiun's pleased expression fled. "Remo is happy in Sinanju. We do not need him. Or he, us."

"I see."

"You see all." Chiun smiled.

"This could work out," said Smith slowly. His mind was racing. Only days ago, the thought of having to deal with the mercurial Chiun would have sent him reaching for his Maalox, but now, with this Smith-killer matter, Chiun's reappearance might be the best thing that could happen.

"Do I understand that our last contract is now in force once more?"

"Not quite," said the Master of Sinanju, settling on the floor in front of Smith's heavy desk.

And Smith—who knew that when Chiun sat on the floor like that it meant that it was time to renegotiate—grabbed two extra-sharp pencils and a yellow legal pad and joined him on the worn hardwood floor.

"Remo will not be considered a part of this negotiation," began Chiun.

Smith nodded. "That would mean a reduction, retroactive, on the prepayment due to the loss of his services."

"Not quite," said the Master of Sinanju.

"What then?"

"It requires an additional payment above the prepayment."

Smith snapped the pencil in his hand. "How do you figure that?" he said angrily.

"Without Remo, I will have to work twice as hard as before. And I am an old man, frail and in my declining years."

"How much more?" Smith asked tightly.

"Half. Half would be fair."

Smith, who was facing death from an unknown assassin, balanced the cost of Chiun's demands against the probable expense of finding a new CURE director and decided they were roughly equal.

"Done," he said, writing it down.

"And I further require other amenities—lodging and clothes."

"Clothes?"

"Because I came by air, I was unable to carry my possessions with me. I have only a kimono or two, nothing more."

Smith, suddenly remembering the news report of the Air Force transport that had the mysterious stowaway the day before, understood completely.

"I don't know where we're going to find a clothier who specializes in kimonos, but I'll see what I can do."

"Do not trouble yourself. Introduce me to a worthy tailor, and he and I will work out the details."

"Done. Anything else?"

"One last item. Traveling expenses."

"How much?" Smith asked, bracing himself.

"Seven dollars and thirty-nine cents."

"You traveled from Sinanju to America and spent only seven-thirty-nine?"

"It was the strangest thing. No one asked me for money. But the American flight did not serve meals for some reason and I was forced to dine in a restaurant before sojourning here to Fortress Folcroft."

And the Master of Sinanju smiled innocently.

"I imagine you'll require living expenses until I requisition the gold," Smith said wryly.

"I was not going to mention it, but yes," said Chiun.

"I'll get you an American Express card."

"American . . . ?" said Chiun, puzzled.

"Gold card, of course."

"Of course." Chiun beamed. He had no idea what Smith was babbling about, but was willing to agree to anything that involved gold.

When they had finished amending the old contract and initialing the changes, the Master of Sinanju signed with a flourish.

"And now you," he said happily, turning the contract over to Smith.

Smith scrawled his signature, wondering why Chiun seemed so delighted. Usually upon signing even the most generous contract, he acted like he had been victimized by Smith's sharp trading. And why had Chiun willingly left Remo back in Sinanju? Could there be a problem between the two of them? As soon as the thought entered his head, Smith dismissed it. Remo and Chiun were inseparable. But then, why were they separated?

When Smith finished, Chiun rose to his feet like smoke arising from an incense burner.

"I am at your service, O just one. Merely point and I will cut down your enemies like the wheat in the field."

"As a matter of fact, I do have a problem."

"Name it," said Chiun.

"It's difficult. It involves another assassin."

"There is no other assassin," retorted the Master of Sinanju. "Speak the wretch's name and I will place his head at your feet by the setting sun."

Just then the phone rang. Smith looked up. It was the

direct line to Washington—the dialless phone which connected the President of the United States with CURE.

Smith reached up stiffly and pulled the red receiver to his ear.

"Yes, Mr. President?"

"We have a problem, Smith. I don't know what you can do without operatives, but maybe you can advise me."

"Excuse me, Mr. President, but we do have an operative."

"We do?"

"Yes, the old one."

"Older one," Chiun whispered, tugging on Smith's sleeve. "I am older than you and Remo, but I am not old."

Smith coughed noisily. "Yes, Mr. President. You heard me correctly. We have just finished negotiating for another year of service."

"I thought he had retired," said the President, "and that he was upset with us over the matter with the Soviets. After all, his pupil did die during that one."

"He's sitting before me even as we speak," said Smith uncomfortably.

"Younger than ever," Chiun said loudly.

Smith clapped a hand over the receiver. "Hush. The President still thinks Remo is dead."

"Stricken by grief at the loss of my only adopted son, I will nevertheless bear up under my burdens and deal with the enemies of America," Chiun added.

"That's enough. Don't overplay it." Having lied to the President about Remo's supposed death, there was no way Smith could admit to the truth—that he had fudged the facts to cover for Remo. As long as this President served in the Oval Office, he must never learn that Remo still lived. That discovery would expose Smith as unreliable and could pull the CURE operation down around Smith's head.

"All right," said the President. "I won't ask questions. Here's our problem. A fellow named Ferris D'Orr has just escaped a kidnapping attempt. D'Orr is important to America. He's discovered a remarkable way of cold-forging titanium. I think you know how important that is to our Defense Department. Why, this process could cut so much from next year's defense budget that we could fund a lot of the programs that Congress is now trying to stifle."

"Who is responsible?"

"That's just it. We don't know. The Soviets, the Chinese, hell, it might even be the French. They've got a pretty fair space program going now. Who is behind this doesn't matter so much. We've just got to protect D'Orr."

"I'll put our special person right on it."

"Good man, Smith. D'Orr is being transported to a safe house in Baltimore. It's the penthouse of the Lafayette Building. Keep me informed."

"Yes, Mr. President," said Dr. Harold W. Smith, hanging up the phone. To Chiun Smith said, "That was the President."

"So I gathered," said the Master of Sinanju, who, now that he was under contract, felt no pressing need to gush over Smith. "Something was said about work."

"What I began to tell you can wait," said Smith, knowing that the threat to his own life was a personal matter, but that national security was CURE's prime directive. "I'm sending you to Maryland."

"A lovely province," said Chiun.

"Yes. Someone has attempted to kidnap Ferris D'Orr, a metallurgist."

"The fiends," cried Chiun, "kidnapping a sick man like that."

"Sick?"

"He is a metallurgist, correct? He is allergic to metals. The poor wretch. Imagine never being able to touch gold, or hold coins in his hand. He must be beside himself."

"A metallurgist is someone who works with metals," said Smith, getting to his feet.

"Ah, an artisan."

"Not quite. He's invented a process for melting titanium, an important metal."

Chiun shook his head slowly. "There is only one important metal, and that is yellow."

"Titanium is important to America."

"Is it yellow?"

"No. I believe it is bluish, like lead."

Chiun made a face. "Lead is not a good metal. Lead killed the Roman Empire. They used it for their plumbing. Romans drank water from their lead pipes and lost first their wits, and later their empire. No doubt they had lead toilets too. Toilets will bring down a civilization faster than pestilence. Even the mighty Greeks would not have been able to survive the onslaught of toilets."

"Titanium is important to America," Smith repeated, ignoring Chiun's outburst.

"Oh? It is valuable?"

"Very," said Smith. "It is used for jet-engine parts and in space-age technologies."

"If it is valuable, why waste it on machines?" Chiun asked. "Why not make beautiful urns of titanium instead? Or statues of worthy persons? I am certain I would look wonderful in titanium."

"Protect D'Orr, and if anyone comes after him," Smith said wearily, "eliminate them."

"Of course," said the Master of Sinanju. "I understand perfectly."

13

Remo Williams had walked most of the way to Pyongyang, capital of the People's Republic of Korea, before he saw his first automobile.

It was an imported Volvo. Remo stepped out into the middle of the highway and waved his arms for the car to stop.

The car slowed. The driver took a long look at Remo and drove around him.

Remo ran after the Volvo. The Volvo picked up speed.

The driver of the Volvo looked at his speedometer. It read seventy. But the white man in the black T-shirt was still in his rearview mirror.

When the running white man drew up alongside the Volvo, there were tears in the driver's eyes. There was no way this could be happening. The white man must not be a Western spy, as he had first thought. He had to be an evil spirit.

"I need a ride into Pyongyang," Remo yelled at the driver.

It was then that the driver knew of a certainty that the white being must be an evil apparition. Not only was he keeping pace with a seventy-mile-an-hour automobile, but he spoke Korean. Western spies did not speak Korean. Korean ghosts spoke Korean, however. Among other things they did, like pass their intangible hands through solid objects and pluck out the hearts from the chest cavities of the living.

"I said I need a ride into Pyongyang," Remo repeated. When the Korean did not reply, Remo tapped the window on the driver's side until the glass spiderwebbed and fell out.

The Korean had the gas pedal to the floorboards by that time. The white ghost was still running even with the car. There was no escape.

The white ghost had said something about needing a ride. Why a ghost who could run in excess of seventy miles an hour would need an earthly vehicle did not matter. Nor did the fact that the Volvo had cost eight years' salary. The ghost was demanding the car, and there was no escaping him. Therefore there was only one thing to do.

The driver braked the Volvo, plunged out through the passenger's side, and stumbled into the tall grass. The white ghost did not pursue him.

"I only wanted a ride," Remo Williams said to himself. He shrugged as he got behind the wheel of the Volvo. The keys were still in the ignition. He got the car going.

Remo drove slowly, his eyes on the road. The faint images of sandaled feet showed from time to time. A mile down the highway, the trail of footprints abruptly stopped. It was replaced by a string of barley beans that seemed to stretch, single file, all the way to the capital city.

"Chiun," Remo said under his breath.

An hour later, Pyongyang was framed in the bug-splattered windshield. It was a city of imposing white buildings with a stone torch—the North Korean version of the Statue of Liberty—dominating the skyline.

Remo drove through the checkpoint because he was in a hurry. Red tape always annoyed him anyway. He was not stopped, because he was driving a foreign car. Only high-ranking members of the North Korean government drove foreign cars. Or any cars, for that matter.

Pyongyang was not like Moscow. It was not like Peking. It was not one of the drab Communist capitals that give the Eastern bloc a bad name. The buildings were immaculate. Gorgeous trees lined the banks of the Taedong River. Happy children marched, singing, to school. Workers marched, singing, to work. Nobody walked anywhere in Pyongyang. Everyone marched and sang. The difference was, the children sang because they enjoyed it. The adults sang because not to sing carried criminal penalties. Many marble statues of the Great Leader, Kim Il Sung, dotted the spacious parks, and dozens of posters of him smiled benignly from the sides of buildings.

Remo, who had met Kim Il Sung, knew the statues and posters were a lie. They showed a black-haired and rosy-cheeked politician, when in fact Kim Il Sung's cheeks had fallen in, he wore spectacles, and his hair was the color of soiled cotton.

As Remo drove around the city looking for the airport, he was amazed at the wide and very modern street system. There were five lanes, but very few cars. The only cars were occasional Volvos or Toyotas. For some reason, none of the autos used the center lane. To save time, not that there was much traffic in the first place, Remo drove down the center lane.

He had not gone very far when one of the little white military police cars began to chase him. The officer waved him over to the side of the road.

"Where's the airport?" asked Remo in Korean.

"Over! Over!" the officer yelled back.

Remo, figuring he could get directions to the airport faster by obeying, obliged.

The officer came up on him with a drawn pistol.

"I wasn't speeding, was I?" asked Remo politely.

"Out of the car," the officer said. "Out!"

Remo got out. The officer got a clear look at him for the first time. He yanked his whistle free of his tunic and blew on it furiously.

"What's the problem?" Remo wanted to know.

"You are under arrest. Driving down the lane reserved for the official use of the Leader for Life, Himself, Kim Il Sung."

"You gotta be kidding," said Remo. "He's got his own freaking lane?"

"And for being an unregistered foreigner," the officer added, blowing on the whistle again.

The officer nudged Remo with the muzzle of his pistol. That was a mistake.

Remo plucked the pistol from the man's fingers before he could react. He held it up before the man's widening eyes.

"Watch," said Remo. "Magic." He closed one hand around the pistol barrel and rubbed it very fast, and when he took his hand away, the muzzle began to droop like a limp rubber hose.

Remo handed the man back his weapon.

The officer blinked incredulously. If he pulled the trigger now, he would unquestionably emasculate himself.

"Sinanju?" he stammered.

Remo nodded. "I'm the new Master."

"White?"

"Not entirely. It depends on who you ask."

The officer bowed. "I am at your service."

"I like your attitude. I'm looking for the older Master, my teacher."

"He has been here. There was great trouble at the airport. He caused difficulty with the officials there. No one knows why. He had only to ask, and we would have obliged him. But he refused to identify himself."

"Where is he now?" Remo asked.

The officer shrugged. "They say he was flown to the unfortunate South. No one knows why. Paradise is here in the North."

"If you're the Leader for Life, it is," said Remo. "How about a police escort to the airport?"

"At once," said the officer.

At the airport, they were more than delighted to assist the new Master of Sinanju, white or not.

The chief of airport security smiled his delight until a nerve in his cheek started to twitch. He softened the smile into a less stressful expression.

"When's the next flight out of here?" Remo asked.

"Moscow or Peking?"

"Neither," Remo said. "I'm heading for America, I think."

"You should know," said the head of security, "but I regret I cannot accede to your wish, as much as I would like."

"Why not?"

"The People's Democratic Republic cannot afford to lose any more pilots transporting Masters of Sinanju to unfriendly places."

"Did Chiun kill them?"

"No, they committed suicide upon landing. They knew that the South is a terrible place. They chose to extinguish their lives rather than live without the beneficence of Himself, our glorious leader."

"Tell you what," Remo offered. "Give me one pilot and I'll make sure he comes back. Fair enough?"

The security chief shook his moon face.

"Not possible," he said. He knew that the next pilot might not believe the official propaganda and decide that South Korea was a place worth living in, after all.

"What is possible?"

"A land escort to, say, ten miles north of the thirty-eighth parallel. You could walk from there."

"I'm used to curb-to-curb service," said Remo, picking up a brass spittoon from beside the security chief's desk and squeezing it until it squeaked. He placed the mangled remains in the security chief's hands.

"I will drive you personally," the Korean decided suddenly, feeling the sharp metal edges cut his palms.

Hours later, the security chief's enclosed jeep came to the barbed-wire fortification that North Korean policy claimed was designed to keep the devils of the South out of the People's Republic. In fact, it was there to keep the people of the North from spilling down to freedom.

"I leave the rest to you," said the security chief.

"Thanks," said Remo.

"I wish your teacher had been so reasonable. If only he had identified himself, we could have come to some realistic accommodation."

"I think he wanted to be followed."

"Then why maim two of our soldiers instead of revealing himself?"

"I think he wanted to be subtle," said Remo, melting into the trees.

14

Everyone knew that Ferris D'Orr was in hiding. The whole world knew that the federal government had placed him in a safe house ever since the first announcement that Ferris D'Orr, discoverer of the secret of cold-casting titanium, had been the target of a kidnapping attempt.

And the whole world knew, thanks to the ever-present news media, that the safe house was not a house at all, but a penthouse in downtown Baltimore.

"This is correspondent Don Cooder, reporting from outside the Lafayette Building, the probable—but not definite—location of the safe house where FBI agents have secreted metallurgical genius Ferris D'Orr, the man who may revolutionize defense applications of titanium. Can you confirm any of that for me, Field Agent Grogan?" the newsman asked, shoving his microphone into the face of a big stone-faced man in a blue jacket with the yellow plastic letters FBI on the back.

"No comment," said the FBI man. He cradled an automatic rifle in his arms. Behind him, the glass entrance to the Lafayette Building was sealed off by wooden sawhorses. Other men, all wearing FBI jackets and brandishing firearms, loitered outside the doors. Overhead, a helicopter flew in noisy circles. The letters FBI were stenciled on it too.

The whole FBI team had been moved into the street only an hour ago.

"Our information is that Ferris D'Orr has set up a laboratory in the penthouse suite, where he is continuing his work," the newsman persisted. "Can you confirm that?"

"No comment," the FBI man said laconically.

"Then explain for me, if you can, Agent Grogan, why

there is a highly visible FBI presence in front of this building at this particular time."

"To control the media. We weren't called in until you people practically stormed the place."

"Are you saying that you are not here to protect Ferris D'Orr, possibly the most important scientist in America today?"

"I know what Ferris D'Orr is," Agent Grogan said testily. "You don't have to give me the man's whole history. And yes, I am categorically denying that my team is guarding Ferris D'Orr. I just finished explaining to you. Here it is again. We're on station to control the media. You don't muster a force like this to guard a safe house. That's like hanging out a shingle that says 'Hostage for Rent.' "

"But you're not denying that Ferris D'Orr is hiding twenty floors above our heads in fear of his life?"

"No comment," said FBI Agent Grogan, rolling his eyes heavenward.

"How about the attempted kidnapping of Mr. D'Orr? Are there any leads on that?"

"You'd have to talk to the district supervisor on that one."

"But you expect another attempt, do you not?"

"No comment."

The newsman turned toward his cameraman and fixed the videocam with a steely gaze.

"There you have it, ladies and gentlemen of the audience. Not quite proof positive, but certainly a revealing indication, that scientist Ferris D'Orr is being held in protective custody on this very block. What does this say about our government's ability to protect important members of the defense community? Is security so lax that just anyone can uncover a so-called 'safe' house? A discussion on these disturbing questions and a special background feature, 'Titanium and Your Taxes,' will air on a CableTalk Special tonight at eleven, ten central time. Until then, this is Don Cooder, CableTalk Network News, Baltimore."

After the news crews had gone home, confident that they had satisfied the American people's pressing need to know that a man crucial to America's defense future was safely—if no longer secretly—protected by the FBI, a taxi pulled up before the Lafayette Building and a man stepped out.

The man was barely five feet tall, Oriental, and wore a gray kimono, and he informed the FBI agents that they could go home.

"You are no longer needed now that I am here," the little man said in a pleasant, squeaky voice.

When FBI Agent Grogan politely requested the citizen's name, the citizen waved him away. And when the FBI man attempted to lay hands on the Oriental, he found himself clutching air.

"Stop that guy," he yelled to the guards at the door.

Five FBI agents barred the door. There was a sudden flurry of movement, a flash of gray, and a sound similar to that of coconuts being cracked together.

Five highly trained FBI agents sank to the pavement, their eyes glazing, their heads bobbing on their unsteady necks after the old Oriental had knocked their heads together in sets of two.

Agent Grogan lunged for the old Oriental. The Oriental turned, and Grogan had a momentary glimpse of two yellowish fingers coming at his eyes. That was usually enough time for the human blinking reflex, one of the fastest reflexes in nature, to react. In this case, the fingers were swifter than the blink and Agent Grogan found himself sitting on the street clutching his face. Tears streamed between his fingers and he could not see.

The squeaky voice called back, "Remind me to kill you later."

A few minutes later, the district supervisor arrived, trailed by a battery of camouflaged agents.

"What happened here?" he demanded.

Agent Grogan stumbled to his feet, stabbing at his tearing eyes with a handkerchief.

"I think he poked me in the eyes," he said. "A little guy. An Oriental. Did you get him?"

"No—but he obviously got you. All of you."

"We've got to stop him."

"No, we don't. We've got to go home. We're relieved."

"Relieved! By who?"

"By the little Oriental who played Moe to your Six Stooges. Don't ask me to explain. I don't understand it any more than you do. But the word came from the top. Let's call it a night."

The next morning, when the network news returned for more no-comments, it found every trace of FBI presence mysteriously gone. They instantly assumed Ferris D'Orr had been removed to an even more secure safe house, and frantically scattered to chase it down, so that the American people would sleep better in the knowledge that he was still in safe hands. In their quest for truth and a higher ratings share, they neglected to do a simple thing. They forgot to enter the building to confirm that Ferris D'Orr had, in fact, been moved.

Ferris D'Orr could not believe his ears.

"One man?" he yelled. "One man is supposed to protect me? Are you crazy? Do you have any conception of how valuable I am to our Defense Department right now?"

"Yes, sir," said the FBI field supervisor. "I understand my superior received word of the change from the Secretary of Defense himself."

"Why would he do a crazy thing like that?" cried Ferris. "Wait a minute. What's his name—Somethingberger, right? He must be Jewish. That's it! This is a Zionist plot, isn't it?"

"I'm sure the Secretary of Defense knows what he's doing," the FBI man said.

"Are you Jewish?" Ferris asked suddenly, suspiciously.

"Sir?"

"I asked you an important question."

"Well, actually, no."

"You probably wouldn't admit it if you were."

'I have my orders," the FBI supervisor said stiffly. "Now, if you'll excuse me . . ."

The FBI supervisor led his men away, shaking his head. It had been a while since he'd seen such rabid religious hatred. Funny thing was, the guy looked Jewish himself.

After he had left, Ferris D'Orr dazedly sank into a chair. His face was drained of color.

"You poor man," said the Master of Sinanju, entering the room. "Let me help you."

"Who? What? How did you get in here?"

"The elevator," said the Master of Sinanju, pushing the titanium nebulizer into another room.

Ferris jumped to his feet. "What are you doing? Where are you going with that?"

The Oriental stopped momentarily. "I am Chiun, reigning Master of Sinanju. You are Ferris?"

"Ferris D'Orr."

"You are a metallurgist?"

"That's right."

Chiun nodded. "I am removing the offending metals from this room. It is a good thing I am here. Those who guarded you before me should have known better than to leave you alone with the cause of your illness."

"What illness?" demanded Ferris D'Orr, blocking Chiun from leaving the room with the nebulizer.

"You are a metallurgist. You said so."

"We've been through that."

"You are allergic to metal. I am removing the metals."

"I didn't ask for a cleaning person," said Ferris D'Orr haughtily. "Certainly not one who can't speak the language."

"I was speaking English before you were born," Chiun said. "But I will not hold your insult against you. You are obviously in a weakened mental state from this cruel exposure to metal. Look at this room. It is filled with blocks of metal, all ugly and dull and useless."

"This is my laboratory,' said Ferris D'Orr, trying to shove the nebulizer back into the room. For some reason, it would not budge, even after he pushed with all his might. It was as if the device was bolted to the floor.

"You are beginning to sweat, poor man. Come. It will be better if I take you into the next room."

"I don't want to go into the next room!" said Ferris D'Orr, and although the old Oriental only took his wrist between two delicate fingers, Ferris found himself pulled into the next room as if by a tow cable.

"I have a very dangerous guard coming to protect me," Ferris warned after he was gently but firmly deposited on an overstuffed chair. "This man is so dangerous he's replacing a crack team of FBI agents. So you better get outta here, pal."

The Master of Sinanju, receiving a compliment, bowed and allowed the faintest of satisfied smiles to etch his features.

"I am Chiun. I have only today returned to your wonderful land, which I see with new eyes. I will therefore allow you to call me Chiun, as other Americans familiarly call one another by their first names."

"Wonderful. But my warning still goes. This guy is a killer."

"I am that guy, the killer," said Chiun.

"You?"

"Me."

"I never saw a killer who looked like you."

"You never saw a killer who killed like me," Chiun said reasonably.

"What do we do now?"

"You have a television set?"

"Right behind you."

The Master of Sinanju turned. "I see no such thing," he sniffed.

"The cabinet. It's a projection TV. You lift it by the handle."

Puzzled, the Master of Sinanju walked over to a false wood table with a hand slot on the top. He reached in, and the hinged top lifted, exposing not the glass tube of the usual TV set, but a large white screen. Then the Master of Sinanju saw the familiar knobs. He pressed the On button.

The news appeared on the screen and Chiun quickly changed the channel.

"What are you doing?"

"I am trying to find one of my beautiful dramas of happier days. I did not bring my tapes with me, alas."

"Beautiful dramas?"

"Is *Edge of Darkness* still shown?"

"I think it was canceled."

Chiun's face wrinkled. "It was probably the violence.

It had fallen far from the heights of Mrs. Lapon's hysterectomy, and the unfortunate drug addiction of her son, who she mistakenly believed was fathered by her ex-husband, and not Darryl, the doctor."

"Who's going to protect me while you watch the soaps?"

"Me, of course."

"And what am I supposed to be doing?"

"Sitting here recovering from your unfortunate exposure to ugly metal objects."

"You're going to guard me and watch soaps at the same time?"

"Masters of Sinanju are ambidextrous," said Chiun, flipping the channel selector in search of something familiar.

"Masters of what?"

"Sinanju."

"Sinanjew? You don't look Jewish," said Ferris D'Orr.

"That is because I am not Jewish."

"Good. I don't like Jews."

"My ancestors would agree with you. They never got any work from the House of David. Herod was another matter."

A round balding face appeared in the big TV screen just in time to receive a thrown grapefruit.

"Ah, they are on TV too," Chiun said pleasurably. "I saw them before in a movie. They must be very popular."

"Them? Those are the Three Stooges, aren't they?"

"They are wonderful," said the Master of Sinanju, settling onto the couch. He arranged his kimono skirts modestly so that they covered his legs.

Ferris D'Orr watched as the three men on the screen hit one another over the head with an assortment of blunt objects, chased each other through a house, and climaxed their antics with an ink-squirting duel.

The Master of Sinanju cackled happily. "I love them. They are so . . . so . . ."

"Stupid," Ferris supplied.

"So American," said Chiun.

"You like American stuff, huh?" asked Ferris D'Orr.

"American stuff is an acquired taste, I know, but I am trying."

"Well, if I were you, I'd get a change of clothes. You dress like a sissy."

The Master of Sinanju restrained his anger at the white metallurgist. No doubt he was still suffering from his exposure to the laboratory.

"Alas," he said. "I have only one decent kimono left. Do you know a good tailor?"

"There's gotta be at least one decent one in this city."

"After this is over, we will visit him."

"Can't," said Ferris D'Orr. "I'm supposed to stay here. This is the safe house, remember?"

"Where would you feel safer," countered Chiun, "alone in this house where killers can walk through the door with impunity, or on the street with the Master of Sinanju?"

Ferris D'Orr remembered his inability to budge the nebulizer and how the funny little Oriental had dragged him out of the lab with no apparent effort.

"No contest. I'll call a cab," he said.

15

The phone rang on the desk of Dr. Harold W. Smith.

Smith jerked away from his video screen. It was the regular line, not the direct connection to the White House. Smith looked at his watch. It was after eleven P.M. That meant his wife.

He decided to ignore it.

But when the phone continued to ring, shattering his concentration, Smith relented.

"Yes, dear?"

"Who is she?" Mrs. Smith demanded, her voice clogged with emotion.

"Again?"

"The other woman. You can't hide it anymore, Harold. First you develop a sudden interest in me, now you're out at all hours. Is it your secretary? That Mikulka woman?"

In spite of himself, Harold Smith burst out laughing.

"Harold? What is it? Are you choking? If you're choking, hand this phone to whoever the tramp is. Maybe she knows the Heimlich maneuver."

"I . . . I'm not choking," Harold Smith said uproariously. "I'm laughing."

"You sound like a machine gun having convulsions. Are you sure that's laughter?"

"Yes, dear, I'm sure. And there's no other woman in my life. But thank you for thinking that. You've made my day."

"It's night, Harold. Almost midnight. I'm in bed. Alone. Just as I've been alone for the last week. How long can this go on?"

"I don't know, dear," Smith said in a more sober tone. "I really don't."

"Stop tapping those infernal computer keys when I'm talking to you."

"What? Oh, I'm sorry."

"You really are working, aren't you?"

"Yes, dear," said Harold Smith, turning away from the screen. But only slightly.

"It's serious, isn't it?"

"Yes," said Harold Smith. "Very serious."

"Do you want to talk about it?"

Relief surged through Harold Smith. "Yes, I do. I really do. But I can't."

"You know that I know. You don't have to pretend anymore."

"Shhh, this is an open line," said Harold Smith.

"I'm sorry. But you know what I'm talking about."

"Yes, I do. And honestly, if I could talk about it, you would be the one I'd be talking to. But the nature of my work—"

"Harold, there's a big wide-open space right beside me. I'm patting it, Harold. Can you hear me patting it?" Her voice was low and soothing.

"Yes, I can," Harold Smith said uncomfortably.

"I wish you were in this big wide empty space right now."

"I will be soon. Please believe me. I will be home as soon as I possibly can. It will be like it was."

"Like it has been—or like it used to be? It feels like we're settling back into old patterns. Me the undemanding wife and you the upright husband whose work comes first—always first. I'm not sure I could stand going back to that life, Harold."

"No, that isn't happening. I promise."

"I love you, Harold."

"I know. I feel the same way."

"But you can't say the words, even after all these years. Those three simple words. Can you, Harold?"

"Some things don't have to be said."

"Call me. Soon."

"Good night, dear," said Harold Smith quietly, and hung up. He wished she hadn't used that sexy voice. It made him yearn for her again. But to protect her, Harold Smith had to keep his distance.

Smith returned to his computer. He felt a renewed burst of stamina. It had been so hard these last days, cooped up in his office, shielded by the Folcroft security guards, who were starting to wonder if they were truly on alert to keep a deranged patient from escaping—as Dr. Smith had told them—or to keep someone out.

Talking to his wife, Smith had felt his pent-up frustration drain away. He returned to his computer terminal, a faint smile tugging at the dryish corners of his mouth. His wife thought he still secretly worked for the CIA. For years, he had kept the true nature of his job at Folcroft from her. But intuitively she knew. She had known for a long time. She didn't, however, suspect CURE's existence. As long as she didn't, Harold Smith would continue to let her believe she was merely the long-suffering wife of a dedicated CIA bureaucrat. And admire her for that.

Smith pushed the thoughts of her from his mind and returned to the problem at hand.

Over and over, he had run test programs on the pattern of the Harold Smith killings. Over and over, there had been no correlations—no common background features, no family relationships, no patterns of criminal activities. Nothing tied the Harold Smiths together except that they were all named Harold Smith, were males over sixty, and had disappeared or died in grisly circumstances.

The evidence was circumstantial, but it was compelling. It looked like the work of a possibly insane serial killer. Certainly normal law-enforcement agencies, if they ever learned of the pattern, would come to that conclusion.

Dr. Harold W. Smith knew that he was the killer's real target. He knew it with a certainty that bordered on the psychic. He knew it because of who he was, and he knew he was next on the killer's route.

The waiting was becoming a problem. Smith wished the killer would find him, just to get it over with. Just to learn the identity of his enemy.

Smith decided to attack the problem from another angle. He ran a logical extraction program and began entering facts.

Fact 1: Unknown killer knows name of target.

Fact 2: Unknown killer knows approximate age of target.

Fact 3: Unknown killer selects targets as he travels, probably by road.

Query: How does unknown killer locate his targets?

The computer busily searched its files, correlating data faster than any machine but the number-crunching supercomputers owned by the Pentagon. After a minute, answers began to scroll up the screen, each rated by probability factors. Smith selected the least likely probability for a control test.

The least likely probability indicated that the unknown killer selected his targets from local phone books.

Smith asked the computer to sort the names of the murdered Harold Smiths into two categories: those who were listed in local phone directories and those with unlisted numbers. As an afterthought, he added a third category, those who did not own phones or were not listed under their own names.

Smith stared for a long moment at the computer's answer.

All thirteen victims were listed in the local phone directories.

"It's too simple," Smith told himself. "It can't be."

But it was. Smith had been operating on the assumption that the killer was some highly trained intelligence agent who would use sophisticated resources and experienced methods to execute his goals. This was too crude, too amateurish, too random. It would take months, even years, before the unknown killer reached his objective. Conceivably, he might kill every Harold Smith in the target group before reaching the right one. If then.

Smith entered the Social Security files in Washington—the greatest repository of data on U.S. citizens in existence—and pulled out the addresses of all Harold Smiths in the target group currently living in Massachusetts, Rhode Island, Connecticut, and upstate New York—the states where the unknown killer was likely to strike next.

There were only three Harold Smiths in that geographical area who were over sixty. The only one listed in the telephone book was Dr. Harold W. Smith of Rye, New York, listed as the director of Folcroft. Smith did not have a listed home number.

The sweat began pouring from Smith's body so hot and so fast his glasses actually steamed. He wiped them off hastily.

If the killer was indeed picking his victims out of telephone directories, he should have been to Folcroft by now. He was overdue.

At that critical psychological moment, gunfire erupted outside Smith's office.

It was a short volley of shots, like a string of firecrackers going off. It barely penetrated the walls of Smith's office, but to a man trained to recognize gunfire, there was no mistaking it.

Smith grabbed the desk phone and punched the front-gate extension.

"What's happening down there?" he demanded.

"There's someone trying to get in, Dr. Smith. I think we chased him off."

"What did he look like?" Smith demanded. "Describe him."

"Wait. There he goes. He's gone over the fence."

"The fence! Is he on the fence or over it?"

"I dunno. He moved too fast."

"Describe him, please," said Dr. Smith, gaining control over his voice. Calmly he reached into his desk drawer and removed his old OSS-vintage .45 automatic.

Gunshots came through on the receiver.

"Guard? Guard?" called Dr. Smith, cradling the receiver between shoulder and ear. He sent a round into the automatic's chamber with a hard pull on the slide. He was ready, but for what?

Smith heard the guard shouting. "Inside, he's inside!" the guard was saying.

Then there was only a clattering noise. The guard's phone had been dropped. Suddenly.

Dimly the sounds of squealing tires, ragged gunshots, and angry shouting men filtered in through the walls and were echoed through the phone. Smith hung up, getting to his feet.

A loud knocking came at his door.

"Yes?"

"Hastings, Dr. Smith. We have a problem out here."

"I know," Smith told the guard. "I think we have an intruder."

"Orders, sir?"

"Keep him out at all costs. And shoot on sight. To wound if possible. To kill if necessary."

"Yes, sir," called the guard. Smith heard his footsteps fade away. He extinguished the lights in his office.

Bitter moonlight poured through the spacious picture window. There would be no danger from that quarter. The glass was bulletproof, unshatterable.

Standing behind his desk, Smith was a resolute, ragged figure. Men who had stood and fought at Lexington and Concord looked as he did, simple Yankee stock fighting for their farms and their families. Smith, despite his high-tech resources and his awesome international responsibilities, was at heart a Vermont Yankee who firmly believed in his country and its principles—and was willing to lay down his life for both.

The automatic felt cool in his moist palm.

Who? he thought for the thousandth time. Who was this man who knew only his name and age and with a murderous, obsessive single-mindedness had killed and killed in a blind brutal pattern designed to eradicate him? Why had the killer waited so long to seek him out?

"He's in the elevator!" Hastings' voice called faintly.

The moon went behind a cloud, plunging the room into abject darkness. Smith gripped his weapon more tightly. He cut the video terminal, its greenish wash of light distracting him at this crucial moment.

More gunshots came, too many. It was a firefight. It had to be. However, the intruder did not sound as if he were heavily armed. No rapid firing from a machine pistol or other high-velocity weapons ricocheted in the corridors. There was only the ragged bark of handguns.

"Here he comes," a voice yelled. "The elevator door's opening. Take him now."

Bullets stormed in the outer hall. Then there was silence.

"Did you get him?" Smith called. He was not leaving the room. Not that he was afraid. But there was only one way into his office. That one door would give him a clear shot. And one clear shot was all that Harold Smith wanted. Or needed.

"Did you get him?" Smith repeated.

"He musta tricked us," Hastings called through the door. "He's not in the elevator."

And suddenly Hastings howled in fright.

"There he is! There he is!" The bullet sounds began again. Briefly.

They stopped one by one, until Smith could hear only the nervous clicking of a gun hammer dropping on empty chambers.

"Don't hurt me!" a guard screeched. "Don't hurt me." And his voice choked off. Smith heard the mushy thud of a body falling to the floor.

Smith swallowed hard. One clear shot, that was all.

Light footsteps approached. The door was outlined in yellow light from the foyer. At the bottom crack, the light was intercepted by moving feet. It seemed like one man. One man, one bullet. Smith was ready.

"The door is unlocked, whoever you are," Smith called out.

The door whipped open. A lean shadow stood framed in the doorway. Smith fired once coolly.

And missed.

The lean shadow faded off to one side, and the door slammed shut, returning the room to darkness.

Smith listened for footsteps, his gun held two-handed before him. He swept the room with its muzzle, one eye on the big window, made faintly visible by cloud-screened moonlight. If he passed in front of the window, Smith had him.

The intruder did not pass before the window. He came the other way.

Suddenly Smith felt a vise clamp around his weapon. It was no longer in his fingers.

He was helpless, and for the first time, a sob racked his throat. It was all over. He would never see his wife again.

"I just want to see your face before I die," Smith said chokingly.

Light blazed suddenly in the room and Smith looked into a pair of the coldest, deadliest eyes he had ever seen.

"Don't break up, Smitty," Remo Williams said. "I missed you too."

16

Boyce Barlow wasn't going to make the same mistake twice.

He had been outwitted the first time, he and his cousins Luke and Bud. He admitted it. He told the Führer Blutsturz straight out, "I screwed up."

Konrad Blutsturz' voice crackled over the receiver. "I know. It is all over the evening news. What happened?"

"Me and Luke and Bud snuck in that building, like you said. We asked at the door for Ferris Wheel."

"D'Orr. Ferris D'Orr."

"Ferris Door. That's a funny name, Door. We asked if the guy was working late. It was late on account of we took a wrong turn outside of Roanoke and lost three hours. It's hard getting good directions from folks out here. They all talk funny."

"Go on," said Konrad Blutsturz.

"Well, when the guard fella said that Ferris guy was inside, we asked real polite if we could see him. We said we were big admirers of his. When the guard said no, we weren't sure what to do so we shot him."

"You shot him. Good."

"We couldn't get the door open, though. It was locked, but there wasn't no keyhole. The guard had a bunch of keys, but there was no keyhole in the door. Can you beat that?"

"Then what?"

"We busted a window."

"Which set off an alarm."

"Hey! How'd you know that?"

"Never mind," said Konrad Blutsturz. "Continue."

"Well, we looked and we looked and finally we found one guy hiding in a big room with all this science-looking stuff. He kinda looked like the newspaper picture of the Ferris Wheel guy and so we asked if he was him."

"And he said no," Konrad Blutsturz said tiredly.

"Hey, that's right. How'd you know?"

"Please continue."

"Well, when he said no, naturally we kept on looking. But we couldn't find the guy. I think he musta gone home. About that time, the cops showed up and we cut out of there. Barely made it, too. I think Luke shot one of the cops. I dunno. Are we in trouble?"

There was a long silence. The receiver hissed.

"Herr Führer?" said Boyce Barlow. He pronounced it "Hair Fairer." He couldn't help it. It kept coming out that way. It always annoyed Herr Führer Blutsturz, but he couldn't help it.

"Everyone knows you're looking for Ferris D'Orr now," said Konrad Blutsturz slowly. "They will move him. It will be more difficult now."

"Can we come home now? Bud is homesick. And you can't find country music on any of the radio stations around here."

"No. You screwed up. You admitted so yourself."

"The guy who said he wasn't this Ferris guy really was, wasn't he?"

"He was."

"Hey, you were right, Bud," Boyce called. "It was him, the stinker."

"Boyce Barlow," said Konrad Blutsturz, "find a place to hide your truck. Find some woods. Stay there. Sleep there. Call me in the morning. I will have new instructions for you."

"We gonna try to get him again?"

"Exactly."

"Well, okay. I'm kinda scared, but the way that guy up and lied through his teeth at us, well, it sets my boil to boiling."

"Hold that thought," said Konrad Blutsturz, and hung up.

Ilsa Gans came into the office carrying a stack of letters.

Konrad Blutsturz looked up from his desk. He wore a terrycloth robe for comfort. Rougher cloth scratched his ravaged skin. Another scourge visited by that devil Harold Smith.

"More goodies," Ilsa said brightly.

She perched herself on the armrest of the wheelchair. Her perfume filled his nostrils.

"From the members?"

"Yes, this one is from St. Louis," she said, razoring the envelope open with a multiblade letter opener in the shape of a swastika. It spilled thin folded pages torn from a phone directory into her lap.

"There are lots and lots of Harold Smiths on this page," Ilsa breathed happily.

Konrad Blutsturz made a disgusted sound in his throat.

"Why couldn't his name have been Zankowski or Boyington?" he said miserably.

"It's not that bad. The over-sixties are circled. There's only . . . one-two-three . . . um, twelve of them. According to the letter, our man in St. Louis pretended to be a pollster and got their ages."

"Twelve is too many, Ilsa. I am not young. I cannot drive around this country killing Harold Smiths for the rest of my days."

"Oh, but I'll be with you. You know that."

Konrad Blutsturz patted Ilsa's hand warmly. "I know that, *liebchen*, but look how few we have done in two months."

"You're not giving up!" Ilsa said, jumping to her feet. There was fire in her eyes. "I was counting on having his skin. I want to cover my diary with it. Don't you think that would be neat? On the last page I could write, 'We finally caught him and used his skin to cover this book.' "

"No, Ilsa, I am not giving up. It is just that I have been thinking. This way is not working. Instead of going to them, they should be coming to us."

"How are we going to do that?"

"We will invite them. We will send out invitations to every Harold Smith we can find."

"You mean a party?"

"No, I mean a massacre."

Ilsa dropped to her knees before Konrad Blutsturz.

"Tell me more."

"No, it is just an idea forming. I must talk to Dr. Beflecken first. I am going to ask him to do more for me than just provide legs of titanium. Much more," he said, eyeing the gently rising valley of her cleavage. And he smiled.

"Oooh, I can hardly wait. Does this mean that Boyce captured Ferris?"

"No, he failed. He is a fool. But only a fool would have allowed me to gain so much control over so many blindly obedient followers so quickly."

"Oh, poo. Can't we do something? You just have to have legs."

"You are so eager, Ilsa. You have no patience. I admit my patience is wearing, as well. But our time is coming soon, I promise."

"I was thinking," said Ilsa slowly. "After we get Harold Smith—the real one, I mean—do you think we could go after the Jews next?"

"The Jews?"

"I mean, really go after them. Not just picket them and insult them."

"Why would you want to do that, my child?"

"Don't you remember? They murdered my parents. You told me so."

"Ach, I had forgotten. Yes, the Jews hacked them to pieces with machetes."

"I thought they beat them to death," Ilsa said puzzledly.

"They beat them first. Then they hacked them. I neglected to tell you the whole story. You were too young in those days to hear the whole story," said Konrad Blutsturz, gently stroking her blond hair. "But why do you wish to kill all Jews, when only a handful committed that heinous deed?"

"To carry on, of course. Just because we lost the war doesn't mean we give up. You didn't give up. No matter what they did to you, you didn't give up."

"I am after one man," said Konrad Blutsturz, flexing his steel claw.

"What about after that? I mean, we'll have this wonderful organization and all these guns and bombs and soldiers. We have to do something with them. We just have to."

"After Smith . . ." Konrad Blutsturz said. "After Smith we will discuss this. You are so young and trusting, Ilsa. That is what I like about you." And he gave her a squeeze that just happened to crush one breast. Ilsa didn't seem to notice. In fact, she smiled.

Boyce Barlow took a last swig of breakfast, and crushing it, threw the Coors can into a ditch.

"Paugh!" he said. "That's good."

"You gonna call Hair Fairer now, Boyce? Are you?" asked Luke.

"Yeah. There's a pay phone up the road. I'll walk."

Boyce Barlow got the secretary at Fortress Purity on the second ring. He winced slightly at the sound of her voice. It was so thickly Germanic it bothered him.

"Yes?" the secretary said.

"Put me though to Hair Fairer," Boyce said.

The line clicked and the dry voice of Konrad Blutsturz came on.

"Hair Fairer? It's Boyce."

"They have moved Ferris D'Orr to a safe house, as I anticipated," Konrad Blutsturz said without preamble. "The news media have discovered the location. It is in Baltimore."

"Where's that?"

"In Maryland."

"Never heard of it."

"Get in your truck and drive north. Go through Washington, D.C."

"I've heard of that one."

"Good. Keep going through Washington and you will see the signs saying Baltimore. The address is 445 Lafayette Street. Ferris D'Orr is in the penthouse, the top floor."

"Sounds simple enough," said Boyce Barlow.

"It is simple. That is why I am trusting this important task to you."

"We're on our way, then."

"Don't forget the nebulizer."

"I won't."

"And throw away your wallets. Just in case."

"Just in case of what?"

"Capture," said Konrad Blutsturz.

"Shoot, Hair Fairer, there's three of us. I got a twelve-gauge shotgun and Luke and Bud got good mail-order rifles. Who's gonna capture us? We got just about everybody outgunned."

"D'Orr will be protected. Go in shooting if you have to, but do not shoot him and do not get captured. If you are captured, say nothing. Tell the others to do the same. Keep your mouths shut like the proud Aryans that you are and we will take care of you. Now, do as I say. Get rid of everything in your wallets."

"The money too?"

"No, not the money. Just your personal papers."

"Good. I figger we might need the money for gas."

"Call me as soon as you have succeeded," said Konrad Blutsturz.

Boyce Barlow trudged back to his truck, which was parked behind a massive stand of magnolia trees.

"Hair Fairer says we gotta get rid of our personal papers," he told Luke and Bud.

"Why?" Bud and Luke asked in unison.

"In case we get captured, he said."

Boyce got behind the wheel of the truck and turned the ignition.

"Who's gonna try and capture us?" Luke said, climbing in beside him while Bud vaulted into the truck bed. "You got a double-barreled shotgun."

"I tried tellin' the man that, but you know how he is—extra cautious."

They dug out their wallets, tore their Social Security cards and the papers to tiny bits and, as Boyce Barlow set the pickup in motion, released them, piece by piece, down the highway, where they joined the lightly falling snow.

At Fortress Purity, Herr Führer Konrad Blutsturz hung up the phone and turned to Ilsa.

"They are trying again."

"Think they'll get it right this time?"

"No, I do not."

Ilsa's face pouted. "Then why send them?"

"Because they might. If they do, it will save us more exertion. If they do not, then the White Aryan League falls entirely into our hands, Ilsa."

"Oooh, good thinking."

"And then, Ilsa, you and I will get Ferris D'Orr."

"And Harold Smith," said Ilsa. "Don't forget him."

"I will never forget Harold Smith," said Konrad Blutsturz, his black button eyes reflecting the light of the fireplace. "Never."

17

Remo Williams took the big automatic in one hand and shuttled the ejector slide with the other. The mechanism spewed shells like quarters from a slot machine.

He tossed the empty gun onto the desk.

"Remo," Dr. Harold Smith said, ashen-faced, "what on earth are you doing here? You're supposed to be in Sinanju."

"I'm delighted to see you too, Smitty," Remo replied sarcastically.

Smith sank into his leather chair, threw his gray head back, and closed his eyes. A long sigh escaped his thin lips.

"At this moment, even your flip remarks are welcome."

Remo noticed Smith's corpselike face and detected the furious pounding of his heart, which, as Remo listened, slowly calmed.

"What's going on, Smith? I'm gone a couple of months and this place is an armed camp."

"I'm in trouble," Smith said, opening his eyes. "Serious trouble."

"Is there any other kind?" Remo asked. And when Smith didn't react, he added: "The operation?"

"CURE is secure—I think. I'm being stalked by a killer."

"Anyone I know?" asked Remo coolly.

"I don't know who he is. But I'm the target of an assassin. Your showing up now may be the solution to my problem."

Remo's shoulders fell a little.

"I guess that answers my next question," he said. "If Chiun were here you wouldn't need me. Funny, I figured Chiun would have come here first thing."

"He was here," Smith admitted.

"Yeah? What did he say? Did he tell you where he was going? I'm trying to catch up with him."

"Is there a problem between the two of you?" Smith asked.

"Nothing I can't handle. So where is he?"

"In Baltimore. On assignment."

Remo's eyes narrowed. "For who?"

"Whom. For whom," Smith corrected absently.

"I asked a question, Smitty. I don't think I'm going to like the answer, but let's just get it over with, shall we?"

Smith sighed. "All right. I've rehired him."

"Unhire him."

"Believe me, I wish I could. I had no desire to see either of you ever again. Life has been peaceful these last weeks. Then this Harold Smith killer business, and then—"

"The which killer?"

"Let me rephrase that. Someone is killing men named Harold Smith all over the country. I believe he's after me."

"What is he doing, saving you for dessert?"

"Don't be smart, Remo. This is serious. I don't have many facts. Thirteen men named Harold Smith have been murdered since last November. All were over sixty years old. I have reason to suspect their killer is an old enemy from my past—apparently someone who knows my name, my age, but not my current whereabouts. He is therefore attempting to kill every Harold Smith in my age group he can locate. It's only a matter of time before I'm next."

"Only you, Smitty, could upset someone so much he'd go to all this trouble to settle a score."

"Remo," Smith said levelly, "I could use your help."

"If you think I'm hiring back on, forget it. I'm back in town to find Chiun. Period. He's a big enough problem without my adding another."

"Then there *is* a problem," Smith said.

"I don't know," Remo admitted. "He's been acting strange, more so than usual. The other night he walked off. Left his steamer trunks and a note. Something about being an old sandal. I figured he had to come here. You mean he actually volunteered for work?"

"He didn't put it that way exactly, Remo. He said he owed me a year's service to replace the gold prepayment from last year."

"I'll give it back," Remo said hastily. "With interest."

"I suggested that, believe me. Chiun refused. He claimed he couldn't do it. He had to repay in services. I tried to talk him out of it, but he wouldn't hear of it. If you want my opinion, Remo, he sounded lonely."

"Great. Well, tell me where he is and I'll try to talk some sense into him. When we come back, I'll see what I can do about your problem. For old times' sake."

"Go to Baltimore, the penthouse of the Lafayette Building. He's guarding a metallurgist named Ferris D'Orr. It's too complicated to explain now, but it's important to America that D'Orr and his titanium nebulizer do not fall into unfriendly hands."

"Titanium nebulizer?" said Remo. Then he held up his hands. "Forget I asked. I don't want to know. I just want to find Chiun and talk sense into him."

"Were you happy in Sinanju, Remo?"

Remo paused. "Yeah, kinda. I wasn't unhappy. I was still settling in. It takes some getting used to."

"Married yet?"

"No, that's another problem I'm having. Chiun is trying to stall the wedding."

"Marriage is a wonderful thing, Remo. I recommend it."

"How is Mrs. Smith?"

"She's fine. Lonely. I haven't been home in a week. If this killer finds me, I want him to find me at Folcroft, not at home where my wife could be hurt."

"Sounds like you're hurting too, Smitty."

"I am, Remo. I feel like a big piece of my life was replaced, only to be ripped out just when I was adjusting to being whole."

"Yeah. I feel that way about Mah-Li. Funny how that is. What do you want me to do about these guards?"

"They're not dead?"

"No, I just put them to sleep. They'll recover."

"I'll handle this as an internal problem. I must keep the police out of this. Entirely."

"Your call, Smitty. Catch you later."

The flight from New York's La Guardia Airport to Baltimore, Maryland, was advertised as fifty-five minutes. It was accurate if you didn't include the thirty-six-minute boarding delay, the approximately two hours in which the plane sat on the runway with its air conditioner off to save fuel and increase passenger irritability, and the forty-two minutes stacked up over Baltimore-Washington Airport.

It was dawn before Remo Williams found himself in downtown Baltimore, and he considered himself lucky. The other passengers were delayed another five hours while their luggage was rerouted from Atlanta, where it had accidentally been sent. Remo had no luggage.

A cab deposited Remo in front of the Lafayette Building. He tried to pay the driver.

"What's this?" the cabby demanded.

"Look, I don't have any American money on me, all right? Don't give me a hard time."

"Don't give *me* a hard time. The fare is twenty-three-eighty-seven. Pay up."

"This is a genuine gold coin. It's worth over four hundred dollars."

The cabby took the coin in his hand and hefted it.

"It's heavy like real gold," he said slowly.

"It is real gold," said Remo wearily, wishing he had thought to ask Smith for a cash loan. Remo had made his way from Seoul, South Korea, to the United States on a handful of ounce-weight gold ingots he had taken from the treasure house of Sinanju. He overpaid outrageously for every fare, but because he paid in gold, the true item of value behind the world's paper-money supply, he had received nothing but a hard time. People were willing to accept cash, checks, or credit cards, but not gold. Not the one thing that was of true value in the world.

"If it's real gold, why are you overpaying me by over three hundred and fifty dollars?" the cabdriver wanted to know.

"I'd appreciate change," Remo said sweetly, and he smiled.

"Nothing doing," said the cabby, who was beginning to suspect the gold was genuine. Especially after he bit into the yellow ingot and saw toothmarks. "I get cash or I keep the whole thing."

"Then keep the whole thing," Remo said in a pleasant tone while he rubbed a finger against the lock on the driver's side. A wisp of smoke came out of the lock aperture. When the driver next tried to open the door, he would find he couldn't. He would learn that the door would have to be replaced, but that it could not be removed for replacement without dismantling the taxi.

It wasn't as good as exact change, Remo thought as he took the elevator to the penthouse, but true satisfaction is without price. He decided to write that down somewhere. It would be the first thing he wrote in his histories of Sinanju when he got around to writing them.

The elevator took Remo to the penthouse floor. When the doors opened, he found himself confronted by an unusual sight.

A man stood facing the elevator, as if he had expected visitors. The man was short, very short. He wore sunglasses. A bowler hat sat on his head, canted at a rakish angle. The hat was green, Christmas-package green. So was the tiny man's neat jacket. The pants, however, were canary yellow, as was the man's shirt. He wore a purple tie. Silk.

"Excuse me, I'm looking for Ferris Wheel."

"D'Orr," the voice said, pitched very low.

"Which door?" asked Remo, looking around. The little man followed him.

"Not door. Not wheel. D'Orr. Ferris D'Orr," the little man said, his voice rising to a squeaky pitch. "Honestly, Remo, have you so soon lost command of your native tongue?"

Remo spun as if on a pivot. He looked closer. The little man beamed, and Remo noticed for the first time the wisps of white hair on the little man's face and the Korean sandals peeping out from the trouser cuffs.

Remo lifted the green hat and exposed a balding head with tufts of white hair over the ears.

"Chiun?"

The Master of Sinanju removed his sunglasses and did a delicate pirouette to show off his new American attire.

"Brooks Brothers," said Chiun happily. "Only the best. How do I look?"

"Like a lemon-lime sherbet," Remo said, hardly believing his eyes.

"You must have searched far and wide to find me," said Chiun with satisfaction. "You must have covered all of Asia before you knew I was not there. Africa's sands must have known your implacable step before that continent, too, was eliminated from your arduous search. Lo, in the generations to come, future Masters will sing of how Remo the Unfair shunned his bride, telling her she was no longer important, bade his villagers a tearful farewell, and said to the heavens, 'I must go, though it take me to the end of my days, and seek out the Master who made me whole, and throw myself at his feet to beg his forgiveness. Though it take me decades, and Chiun the Great spit upon me when I find him, I will do this gladly, for I owe him everything.' "

The Master of Sinanju stepped back a pace to allow his pupil groveling room.

Remo frowned, putting his hands on his hips.

"You left a trail a pig could follow. A blind pig," he said.

The countenance of the Master of Sinanju assumed a hurt expression.

"You are not here to grovel?"

"I'm here to take you back. To Sinanju."

"Impossible," said the Master of Sinanju, turning on his heel. "I am under contract."

"We'll break it. You've done it before."

"I have a new appreciation for America," Chiun said.

"You didn't ever have an old appreciation for America. It was a barbarian land, remember? It was full of round-eyed whites who smelled of beef and pork fat and had feet so big it was a miracle they could walk."

"I was younger when I said those things. Much younger. I have grown in wisdom since those long-ago days."

"Since last week?"

"What's that racket?" asked Ferris D'Orr, poking his head out of his laboratory.

"Who's he?" asked Remo peevishly.

"That is Ferris. Do not mind him. He always gets irritable when he is around metals. He is a metallurgist, poor fellow."

"Is that the kidnapper?" asked Ferris, looking at Remo.

"No, this is my son. The son I told you about. Allow me to present Remo to you. He is in condoms. And toilets."

Ferris looked Remo up and down. "Keep him away from me, then. I don't swing that way."

"Can we have a little privacy, please?" Remo asked.

"Sure thing," said Ferris D'Orr, hanging a Do Not Disturb sign on the lab door and slamming it behind him.

"The treasure house?" Chiun asked low-voiced. "Did you lock it behind you?"

"Double-locked. I left Pullyang in charge."

"Pah! Better you had staked one of the village dogs at the door. A dog does not bray at lame jokes."

"What's eating you? Will you tell me that?"

Chiun reached into his breast pocket and extracted a red leather wallet. "Look," he said.

Remo looked.

"A woman's wallet. So what?"

"It is a woman's?" asked Chiun, surprised. "I chose it because it was the most appealing in color."

"A man's wallet is never red. Black or brown. Never red."

"I almost bought a green one," Chiun said hopefully, "with a silver clasp."

"Woman's."

"Oh," said Chiun. "Then show me your wallet."

"I don't have one. I threw it away when I knew I wasn't coming back to America. Or so I thought."

"Then do not insult my fine American wallet if you do not have one of your own. This will serve me well, for it carries something that is priceless."

"Gold?"

"Better than gold," said Chiun.

"Am I dreaming, or did you say better than gold?"

The Master of Sinanju extracted a gold-colored plastic card from the otherwise empty wallet. "Behold."

Remo took the card.

"American Express," he said. On the card was embossed the name M.O.S. Chiun. "M.O.S.?"

"Master of Sinanju," Chiun replied. "I wanted it to read 'Reigning Master of Sinanju,' in acknowledgment of your current status as subordinate Master, but there was not enough room on the card, so I had to settle."

"I didn't know I was supposed to be subordinate Master. Is that my title?"

"I just made it up," Chiun admitted. "But let me explain how this wonderful American invention works."

Remo was about to say that he already knew, but realized that Chiun would go on anyway, so he shut his mouth to save time.

"Instead of money, you give this card to merchants in return for services."

"Oh really?" Remo said.

"Oh, I know that does not seem like much," said the Master of Sinanju, lowering his voice to a conspiratorial whisper. "But that is not the wondrous thing."

"What is?"

"They always give the card back."

"They always give—"

"Shhhh," said Chiun. "I do not want this to get out. Then everyone will go to Smith for one of these wondrous cards."

"Can't have that," Remo said.

"It is better than gold. You give a merchant gold and what happens?"

"He bites it to see if it's real," said Remo, thinking of the cabdriver who had brought him to this precious moment in life.

"Exactly. Because he has your gold. But unlike gold, merchants in America do not get to keep this card. They put it through crude machines or copy down the unnecessary numbers which for some reason are on my wondrous card. And then they give it back. Some of them even say thank you."

"Imagine that. They must not know how you're putting one over on them."

The Master of Sinanju drew himself up haughtily. "I am doing nothing of the kind, Remo. I give them the card. They give it back. How am I at fault if the merchants of America are so feeble-witted that they cheat themselves at every turn?"

"You have a point there, Little Father. But maybe it isn't what you think."

"Do you know something I do not, Remo?"

"Let's go see Smith. He'll explain it."

"I cannot. I am here on important service to the Generous Emperor Smith, Dispenser of American Express."

"Last week he was Mad Harold."

"He has changed, Remo. Surely you noticed."

"He did look grayer, at that."

"He has many burdens. Burdens whiten the hair." And the Master of Sinanju made a point of stroking his snowy beard.

"I was talking about his face."

"He is not ill?" squeaked Chiun.

"He has problems. But never mind that now. What's this about your returning to service?"

"It is true. I am bound to serve Generous Harold another year."

"Mah-Li will give up the gold."

"But then what will you do?" asked Chiun. "You can't marry her without the gold for a dowry. It is contrary to Sinanju law. Unless you wish to break the engagement. If you wish to break the engagement, I will be disappointed, but I will try to bear up. Yes, if that is what you must do, let us sit down now and write to the poor child and inform her of your decision while there is still strength in our breaking hearts."

"Nothing doing," Remo said flatly. "We're getting married. As for the dowry, I'll go earn a new dowry for her."

"That is forbidden," said Chiun. "The husband does

not provide the dowry. It is as foolish as the American merchants returning the wonder card."

"I'm not going back to Sinanju without you, Chiun. You know that."

"Maybe Smith has a place for you in the organization," said Chiun thoughtfully. "I cannot guarantee this, but I will put in a good word for you, if that is your wish. I cannot promise you a magic card, for obviously only assassins with seniority get these, but perhaps there is such a thing as a silver card. Or a titanium card. I understand titanium is a very valuable metal in America."

"Forget it. I'm not working for Smith. Those days are gone."

"But their pleasantness lingers in the memory, does it not?" Chiun asked.

"Right," said Remo. "It does not."

Just then the elevator doors slid open.

"Expecting company?" Remo asked.

"Not such as these," said Chiun disdainfully.

The three men who gingerly stepped from the elevator cage wore goosedown jackets, stained bluejeans, and plastic baseball caps decorated with Confederate-flag decals. Their pores reeked of beer.

"We're lookin' for Ferris Wheel," said Boyce Barlow, pointing a double-barreled shotgun at Remo and Chiun.

"Try a carnival," said Remo.

"Do you mean Ferris D'Orr?" asked Chiun.

"Yeah, that's him," said Boyce Barlow. "Trot him out, hear?"

"I am not deaf," said the Master of Sinanju. "One moment."

"What are you doing?" Remo asked Chiun, who was calmly walking to the door with the Do Not Disturb sign on it. Chiun knocked.

"What?" Ferris D'Orr called angrily.

"A moment of your time, O metallurgical one."

Ferris stuck his head out the door.

"Are these the bandits who attempted to kidnap you?"

"Yeow!" said Ferris, slamming the door.

"I think that was a yes," Remo pointed out.

"I think it was too," said Chiun, walking up to the three men. "Watch this," he added under his breath.

Remo leaned back against the wall. He yawned.

The Master of Sinanju stopped before the three men. They pointed rifles at his head. The Master of Sinanju smiled and bowed from the waist, first unbuttoning his coat.

The three men looked uncertain. When they did not bow in return, the Master of Sinanju kicked them in their shins, producing the required bowing action.

With fingers so fast they blurred, the Master of Sinanju sent the first two fingers on his right hand into the eyes of the man on the end.

The man dropped his rifle. His hands started to reach for his eyes, but he fell backward before completing the motion.

Boyce Barlow heard his cousin Luke fall over. The closing elevator doors vised his head. Then he heard Bud, on the other side, do the same. Boyce tightened down on the double triggers of his shotgun. He stopped squeezing because, suddenly, two fingers pushed his eyes back into his brain with such force that the pressure cracked his skull. That crack was the last sound Boyce Barlow ever heard.

Chiun returned to Remo's side, dry-washing his hands.

"I've never seen you do moves like that before, Little Father," Remo said.

"I learned them from Moe Stooge," said Chiun happily.

"Never heard of him."

"Really, Remo, he is very famous in America. He is one of the Stooge Brothers. They are excellent entertainers. Possibly brilliant. I would like to visit them as soon as possible. I may be able to help them refine some of their moves."

"No chance," said Remo.

"You would deny me such a tiny request?"

"I'm sorry to be the one to break this to you, but they all died years ago."

Chiun trembled. "Curly too?"

"He was the first to go."

The Master of Sinanju bowed his head in sorrow. "The good die young," he said.

Remo went over to the three bodies and tested their carotid arteries.

"They're dead," he said.

"Of course. They are the vicious would-be kidnappers of Ferris the Metallurgist. They did not deserve to live. What are you doing?"

"Checking them for identification."

"Why bother? The dead have no need of their names."

"But Smith might. Nothing. Their wallets are empty."

"What color?" asked Chiun.

"This one's black."

"I will take it, seeing he does not need it any longer."

"Okay, let's go," said Remo, straightening.

"Where?"

"Back to Smith. We're going to get you unhired."

"But, Remo, what about Ferris?"

"Smith sent you to protect him from these guys. He's protected. Permanently. Let's go."

"I cannot. My duty is to stand guard until my emperor orders otherwise," said Chiun.

"What's going on out there?" Ferris' frightened voice called out from behind the lab door.

"It is all right, Ferris. Your assailants have been vanquished by the awesome magnificence that is Sinanju."

"Are they dead?" asked Ferris, stepping carefully into the hall.

"Of course," said Chiun, dragging the bodies into the elevator.

"Is he always like this?" Ferris asked Remo.

"Usually he makes me dispose of the bodies," Remo said. "Watch. He'll say something about being too old to lug them onto the elevator."

But when the Master of Sinanju continued piling the three Barlow cousins onto the elevator in silence, Remo was forced to ask, "Need any help, Little Father?"

"I am fine," said Chiun. "Do not trouble yourself. I will dispose of these carrion and return momentarily."

"I don't get it," Remo said in a shocked voice. "He never handles the bodies himself."

"They pile up a lot, huh?" asked Ferris D'Orr.

"Sometimes they're hip-deep."

* * *

In the alley behind the Lafayette Building, the Master of Sinanju tossed the Barlow cousins into the building dumpster. Seeing that it was nearly full, he stirred the garbage until the bodies were covered.

Chiun did not know who these men were and he did not care. Perhaps they were free-lance, possibly they worked for someone else. Smith would know. But if Smith identified them as the instigators, and not hirelings, then Chiun might be recalled to Folcroft, his mission accomplished.

The Master of Sinanju did not wish to be recalled to Folcroft, where Remo might convince Smith to release him from his contract. He did not wish that at all.

18

They welcomed Konrad Blutsturz with the straight-arm salute of the past.

As one, they came to their feet in the great auditorium of Fortress Purity, their arms shooting out and up in perfectly stiff Nazi salutes, more like robots than men and women.

"*Sieg Heil!*" they shouted, as Konrad Blutsturz, Führer of the White Aryan League of America and Alabama, sent his wheelchair buzzing down the aisle, beneath the swastika flags hanging in ordered rows. The wheelchair labored up the low inclined ramp to the podium like a wind-up toy that didn't quite work. The handicapped ramp was one of the first things Konrad Blutsturz had installed earlier in the day. By nightfall, every staircase in Fortress Purity would be replaced by a ramp.

Attired in a jet-black military shirt, Konrad Blutsturz joined Ilsa, who stood waiting, microphone in hand, and faced the audience. A huge Nazi banner served as a backdrop.

He returned the salute and lifted the microphone slowly, soaking up the cheering like a thirsty man. For a moment he knew how Hitler had felt. For an instant he felt the thrill the true Führer must have known. But then he looked hard into the faces of the crowd, these sons and daughters of Alabama and North Dakota and Ohio and Illinois, and made a disgusted noise low in his throat.

Hitler had spoken to a unified people. These were rabble. It was not the same at all. He let the noise of the crowd run its course and motioned them to be seated.

At a nod from him, Ilsa dropped to her knees so that no one sat higher than Konrad Blutsturz.

"A war is coming," he told the crowd, his dry voice rumbling over the public-address system. "A race war. You know it. I know it. Our beloved founder, Boyce Barlow, knew it. That is why he founded the White Aryan League. This is why he built Fortress Purity. That is why we have had to erect razor wire around our settlement and top it with electricity. Because the rest of America—mongrel America—resented our prophetic vision."

The crowd applauded.

"The Jews already control America. Everyone knows it. They control the media. They control Wall Street, and the corporations. If their power grows, they will control America the way they control Israel. If this goes on, we true, white, patriotic Americans will be displaced as the long-suffering Palestinians have been displaced. America will become the new Israel—an occupied land!" Konrad Blutsturz shouted, and the effort set him coughing.

Ilsa handed him a glass of water. He sipped.

"But this day may never come to pass," he went on.

The crowd cheered.

"It may never come because the inferior blacks will bring this proud nation to its knees before then. Look at the major cities of America. Once they were proud and white. Now they are dirty and black. Many people have come to these shores. Germans have come, and the English, and the French. Even the Polish. They have given to America. The blacks only take. They steal from our mouths by refusing to work. They live off welfare. Our taxes pay for their loud radios, their many children, their vile drugs. Now, the Jews are bad, but the blacks—they are like the kudzu weed you chop from the perimeter fence each day. The blacks, by their sheer numbers, are strangling this land."

"Down with the blacks!" the crowd roared, and Konrad Blutsturz had them. He grinned his skull-like grin.

"Keep it up," Ilsa whispered. "You've got them going good now."

"But the blacks are not organized," said Konrad Blutsturz, his voice cracking with exertion. "And the

Jews are patient. There is a third enemy, the Orientals. They are the more immediate menace."

The crowd hissed. Some yelled "Gook" and "Slant-eyes."

"The Orientals combine the worst traits of the others. They are becoming as numerous as the blacks, but they are as crafty and avaricious as the Jews. You have seen them coming to these shores in increasing numbers. Even here in Huntsville, there are many. It does not matter whether they are Chinese, or Japanese, or Vietnamese, or any other 'ese.' They are all the same. You know it. I know it."

The crowd cheered the words of Konrad Blutsturz as other crowds had cheered the words of Adolf Hitler fifty years ago, because the words were the same and the crowd—like all mobs—was also the same.

"How is it," Konrad Blutsturz shouted, "that when America defeated the Japanese, the Japanese ended up with economic superiority?"

"They cheated," the crowd yelled.

"When the Vietnamese defeated the Americans in the last decade, the Vietnamese flocked to these shores, to steal the jobs that the Japanese industries did not already take, and buy up the homes that true Americans could no longer afford. These people are so unfair, they work two or three jobs. For every employed Vietnamese, there are three unemployed Americans!"

The crowd screamed its anguish at the injustice of the selfish Vietnamese immigrants.

"But the Orientals are not the worst. No," said Konrad Blutsturz in a low voice that forced the auditorium to listen very hard.

"The fourth group is the worst. We cannot recognize them by the color of their skins, or by their habits. Because they are chameleons, poisonous chameleons."

"I didn't know chameleons were poisonous," Ilsa whispered.

"Poisonous chameleons," Konrad Blutsturz repeated, ignoring the girl. "For they come in all sizes and shapes. They blend into our society unsuspected and unchallenged. You know them for what they are, the Smiths." Konrad Blutsturz hissed the word.

The crowd screeched its horror at the menace of the Smiths until the walls shook.

"You know that I have just returned from investigating the Smith menace firsthand. I have seen the evidence with my very eyes. The Smiths are as numerous as the blacks, more numerous than the Asians, and craftier than the Jews. I have fought them in unreported skirmishes. I have inflicted Aryan vengeance upon their seemingly white heads."

"Aryan vengeance," howled the members of the White Aryan League of America and Alabama.

"When the race war begins, it will be begun by the Smiths. Not the Jews, not the blacks, not the Asians, but by the Smiths. Have I not always said so?"

"Yes!"

"Did not Boyce Barlow, our founder, prophesy this?"

"Yes!"

"And it has come to pass!"

"No," the crowd protested.

"They have struck the first blow."

"No!"

"A cruel blow," said Konrad Blutsturz. "They have extinguished the pure flame that was Boyce Barlow."

A low moan lifted from the audience. Faces contorted in pain.

"And his cousins Luke and Bud."

The crowd was stricken. There were shouts for revenge and, amid them, cries for the heads of the agents of this atrocity.

"But fear not," Konrad Blutsturz went on. "We are not lost. I will lift up the banner they have dropped. I will carry on in their place. If you will have me."

"Yes! Yes! Yes!"

Konrad Blutsturz let the howls of adoration continue until the crowd grew hoarse. He liked them better when they were hoarse. Their American twangs and drawls and nasal consonants offended his ears. It was a mongrel sound.

Finally Konrad Blutsturz waved for them to calm down.

The crowd quieted, their heads turned upward, their emotions spent. They believed. They believed in the purity of their skin color. They believed in the righteousness of their cause. And they believed in Konrad Blutsturz. They did not know they believed in a lie. Or that Konrad Blutsturz, who spoke so ringingly despite his many handicaps, believed none of it.

"The first blow has been struck. We will not wait long to counterstrike. I have selected men among you to become my lieutenants. They will form you into squads. You will march, you will drill, and you will learn to use the weapons we have stockpiled in secret. Instead of hiding from an impure world, we will march into it. Instead of clinging to our vision of a white America inside Fortress Purity, we will expand Fortress Purity. Fortress Purity will become America!"

"Take back America! Take back America! America for Americans!" the crowd screamed.

"I will name those I have selected as my lieutenants. They will stand as I call out their names.

"Goetz, Gunther.

"Schoener, Karl.

"Stahl, Ernst.

"Gans, Ilsa."

"Does this mean I get to run the *White Aryan League Hour?*" Ilsa whispered in his ear.

Konrad Blutsturz hushed her.

A man jumped up from the audience. He spoke in a Texas drawl.

"Hey! How come none of us good ol' boys are gettin' to be lieutenants?"

Konrad Blutsturz fixed his bright black eyes upon the protester. This was the moment he had expected. The crucial moment where his leadership would be tested.

"Your name?"

"Jimmy-Joe. Jimmy-Joe Bleeker."

"Are you sure?"

"Huh?"

"Are you sure your name is Bleeker, I asked."

"What else would it be?" Jimmy-Joe Bleeker sneered, shoving his hands into the pockets of his loose-fitting jeans.

"Are you sure your name isn't . . . Smith?"

"Naw, it ain't Smith."

"You sound like a Smith," suggested Konrad Blutsturz.

"He even looks a little like a Smith," chimed in Ilsa. "Around the eyes. A little."

"I ain't no Smith," said Jimmy-Joe Bleeker. "Smiths are poison."

Konrad Blutsturz snaked out his left hand. It glittered under the light, deformed and shining.

"There are Smiths everywhere. They are serpents in our paradise, lying, scheming, twisting facts. You have criticized the White Aryan League of America. I declare you a secret Smith, and ask the crowd to pronounce your sentence."

The crowd hesitated. All knew Jimmy-Joe Bleeker. He was a regular, one of the first members.

"Death," said Ilsa, turning her thumbs down. To Konrad, she added, "Can I kill him?"

"Death!" said the crowd.

"Aryan lieutenants, take this man out to the center of the compound and have him shot. This vile Smith will be an example to all Smiths of what is coming. Vengeance!"

"Aryan vengeance," screamed the crowd, and dragging the man, they broke open the great auditorium doors.

Ilsa ran after them. "I want to watch," she said.

Left alone on the podium, Konrad Blutsturz finished his glass of water greedily. Public speaking always wore his throat raw. He did not understand how Hitler had done it. The water accidentally went down the wrong way and he started choking. When the raw coughing fit subsided, he thought he could again taste the smoke of that night in Japan, almost forty years ago.

When the crack of rifle fire echoed back into the vast hall, he vowed again that Harold Smith would pay for his deeds on that long-ago night.

Konrad Blutsturz lay dreaming.

He dreamed he lay in bed with the hands on the clock across from him reading three minutes to midnight, but that wasn't what brought the panicky sweat to his chest. Caught between the clock hands was a severed gangrenous greenish-blue male organ. It looked familiar. And when he felt the smoothness between his legs, he knew the organ was his own. Konrad Blutsturz fumbled desperately for the clock, but it was out of reach. He tried to climb out of bed, but found he had no legs.

And then, like slicing scissors, the minute hand clicked to two minutes to midnight.

Konrad Blutsturz snapped awake from his nap. A dream, it had been a dream. But looking down at himself, he knew it was not a dream.

Reaching for his wheelchair, he maneuvered himself into a sitting position, and with simian agility, fumbled on the bluntness of his lost legs into the wheelchair, where he buckled himself in.

Konrad Blutsturz sent the wheelchair over to the balcony of his bedroom, which overlooked the grounds of Fortress Purity, and considered how easy it had been.

Below, soldiers of the White Aryan League goose-stepped in their brown uniforms. They were soldiers in name only. They were the malcontents of America, the unemployed and unemployable. They were men without hope or direction, who nursed smoldering resentments against life. Boyce Barlow had given them a place to hide from the world, but Boyce Barlow was gone.

Now, under the guidance of good German stock, they were being welded into killing teams to fight the race war they believed would inevitably come. But Konrad Blutsturz believed in no coming race war. He believed even less in the scarlet-and-white flag that flew from every building in Fortress Purity.

The Third Reich was long dead. It lived on only in the nostalgic memories of very old men, and the sons of those men, whom he had recruited to the White Aryan League of America. It lived, too, in the muddled thinking of the morbid young, like Ilsa, who even now was commanding a squad of men with the crackle and fire of a seasoned boot-camp instructor.

Good riddance to the Third Reich, thought Konrad Blutsturz. In his youth it had promised him so much, and cost him so dearly.

Konrad Blutsturz had come to the United States in

1937, a young man of nineteen. He had come with a mandate—organize the German element for the coming war. He had believed in it all then, believed in the myth of German superiority, believed in the great Jewish conspiracy, and he had believed in Hitler.

It was Hitler himself who had plucked Konrad Blutsturz from a Hitler Youth group and given him his mission. "Go to America. Succeed, and you will be the Regent of America when their government is overthrown," Hitler had told him.

It had seemed so grandiose, in those days. So possible.

Konrad Blutsturz spat over the railing a great greenish glob of expectorate at the memory of his naiveté.

In America, Konrad Blutsturz formed the Nazi Alliance. He did not build Bund camps or make inflammatory public speeches. He could have duplicated Fritz Kuhn's 1936 Madison Square Garden rally of twenty-two thousand people—if he didn't care about the quality of those people.

But he did care. Konrad Blutsturz did not want quantity. He wanted quality. German-Americans in the days before World War Two were much more American than they were German, which is to say, they were anti-Nazi, but there were those who believed in the New Germany, and Konrad Blutsturz had sought them out and organized them. They existed as a provisional government in waiting, waiting for the fall of Europe.

But Europe never fell. And Konrad Blutsturz' contacts with Berlin, over shortwave radio relayed from the German Legation in Mexico City, grew less and less frequent.

After Germany was defeated, Konrad Blutsturz fled to Mexico. And after the Allies discovered certain documents in Berlin, they sent OSS agents on his trail. His Nazi Alliance had been quietly rounded up.

Alone, unsupported, Konrad Blutsturz fled into South America, and from there he was spirited to Japan, where he had intended to offer his services to the emperor.

Then came Hiroshima and Nagasaki. It was as if the mighty fist of the Allies was following him into hell itself.

And into that hell came Harold Smith.

Konrad Blutsturz blotted out the memory. He remembered it in his dreams often enough. It was too painful to relive in his waking hours. It was enough that he had survived the hell of Tokyo. It was enough that he had returned to America at last.

Konrad Blutsturz had known Hitler himself, personally. It was that brief relationship that seemed to compel those he met. It moved the Germans of Argentina and Paraguay, as if somehow Hitler lived on through this broken wreck of a Nazi dupe. It had moved Ilsa, the American girl who was no more German—really German—than Sylvester Stallone.

And it had moved Boyce Barlow and his White Aryan League of America, who were desperate for the American dream and were willing to accept a nightmare in its place—just as long as they could call that nightmare their own.

It had been so easy.

When a day had passed and Boyce Barlow was not heard from, Herr Führer Konrad Blutsturz assumed he and his cousins had gotten lost on the way to Baltimore.

When two days passed, he assumed that they had been captured, and ordered his specially equipped van gassed up for a quick escape. If the Barlows were in FBI hands, they would spill their guts for a warm beer.

When a third day came and went without an FBI raid on Fortress Purity, Konrad Blutsturz knew they were dead and had not talked.

And all they had lived for was now his.

19

Ferris D'Orr's mother was crushed when he was christened at St. Andrew's Church in Dundalk, Maryland. She had wept on that first day when he went to Sunday school years later. At his First Communion, she was bitter, and at his Confirmation at the age of fourteen, she was inconsolable.

During the drive home, Mrs. Sophie D'Orr went on and on.

"Your father was a good man, God rest his soul," Mrs. D'Orr said. "Don't get me wrong, he was good to me. The best."

"I know, Ma," Ferris said. He sat in the back seat, slipping lower and lower into the cushions with every word. He was too ashamed to sit up front with his mother.

"We loved each other," Mrs. D'Orr went on. "We couldn't help it. It was one of those things, a Catholic and a Jew. It happens. It happened to us."

Ferris D'Orr sank even lower in his seat. He hated it when his mother raised her voice. The louder she got, the more her accent showed. The other kids always made fun of him over that. She sounded like a cartoon German. It embarrassed him. He wished he had a lemon Coke right then. Lemon Cokes always made him feel better.

"So we married. That wasn't the hard part. But your father, and the priest who married us, got together. This priest said we could marry if we promised to raise the product of our union—that was the phrase that priest used, can you believe it—the product of our union in the faith. They called it that, too, the faith. Like there's no other."

"Ma, I like being a Catholic."

"What do you know? You don't know any other way. You're fourteen now and you don't know your maftir. You've never been to shul. I should have had you bar-mitzvahed. It's too late now."

"Ma, I don't want to be a Jew."

"You are a Jew."

"I'm Catholic, Ma. I've just been confirmed."

"You can be bar-mitzvahed at any age. It is done. Ask your cousins. They will tell you how it is."

"Kikes," mumbled Ferris under his breath, using a word he had picked up in Sunday school to describe his cousins on his mother's side. Other kids called him that sometimes. When they didn't call him Ferris Wheel.

"What?"

"I'm thirsty."

"I'll buy you a lemon Coke. Will you promise to think about it if I buy you a lemon Coke?"

"No."

Later that night, his mother had taken him aside and patiently explained to Ferris what it meant to be a Jew.

"Whether you want to accept it or not, Ferris my lamb, you are a Jew. Because being a Jew is not just being bar-mitzvahed and going to temple. It is not like some of your friends who go to church every Sunday and raise hell on the other six days of the week. Being Jewish is in the blood. It is a special responsibility to keep God's covenant. It is a heritage. You are Jewish by heritage, Catholic or not. Do you understand?"

"No," Ferris had told her. He didn't understand at all.

His mother tried to explain about the holocaust.

He had explained back how his friends sometimes taunted him because his mother was a Jew, and how some of them said that it was the Jews who killed Jesus.

His mother said that they were talking about the same idea. Good Jews had died in the concentration camps of Nazi Germany because of lies like those. For no other reason, six million good people had died. She showed him picture books of the ovens and the gas chambers.

Ferris had said that had all happened in the past, and he did not live in the past. "The Nazis are dead." he told her. "They don't exist anymore."

"It will not be the Nazis next time. It might not even be the Jews next time. This is why we must remember."

"You remember," Ferris said. "I wouldn't be a kike for a million dollars."

And his mother had slapped him, later apologizing for it with tears in her eyes.

"I only wanted you to understand. Someday you will understand, my Ferris."

All Ferris understood was that his mother wouldn't stop going on about what a mistake it was to let him be raised a Catholic, and that he never, never wanted to be Jewish.

When Ferris went off to Boston to college, he never looked back. He worked through the summer just so he didn't have to return to his mother's home and the relatives who were strangers to him.

When he graduated from MIT in three years instead of four, he didn't tell his mother, because he was ashamed to have her show up at the ceremony. And when he went looking for his first job, he made sure it was as far away from his hometown as possible.

Now Ferris D'Orr was an important scientist. His face was on the cover of *Time* magazine. He was being called a genius. In a recent speech the President of the United States had called him "the keystone of America's defense future."

But his mother wouldn't stop calling him.

"Don't answer that phone," Ferris D'Orr yelled. "This is a safe house. There's only one person in the world who would call me at a safe house."

"Who?" asked Remo Williams, who, out of boredom, was watching Ferris melt little blocks of metal into little puddles of metal. When the little puddles hardened, Ferris would melt them again. Over and over. Remo thought it was like watching paint dry, but Ferris didn't seem bored by the repetition. He actually became more excited.

"Never mind," said Ferris, remelting an inch-square block for the thirty-first time. By actual count. "Just don't answer it."

"It might be important," Remo said. "They keep ringing."

"Not they, her. Only one person would keep ringing like that. Anyone else would figure out I'm not here. Not her. She'll keep ringing until I give up and answer."

Finally Remo picked up the phone because he didn't want to hear any complaints from Chiun. Not that Chiun had been complaining these last few days. In fact, he hadn't complained once, not once.

"Hello? Yes, he is," Remo said.

Remo turned to Ferris D'Orr. "It's for you. It's your mother."

"What did I tell you?" Ferris moaned. "Tell her I'm not here."

"She can hear you yelling," Remo said.

"She won't leave me alone," Ferris said. "She got the FBI on the phone and browbeat them into giving her this number. The combined efforts of the KGB and the Internal Revenue Service couldn't squeeze that information out of the FBI, but my mother did."

"He's very wrought up right now," Remo said into the phone. "No, he hasn't been kidnapped. No, ma'am, I wouldn't fib to you. Yes, ma'am, I'm one of his guards. I'm sure he'll be all right. Yes, ma'am, I will."

Remo hung up.

"What did she say?" Ferris asked.

"She said you should write her."

"I did, long ago. I wrote her off."

"That's not nice," said Remo, watching Ferris adjust his nebulizer. "What are you doing?"

"It's too complicated for a layman to understand."

"Try me," said Remo.

"I'm slagging this titanium block over and over again to see if fatigue sets in."

"I never get tired," said Remo.

"I meant the metal."

"Oh," said Remo.

At that moment the Master of Sinanju walked in.

"What transpires?" he asked.

"Ferris is avoiding his mother," Remo said.

"For shame," said Chiun. "You call her this very moment."

"Nothing doing."

"You shouldn't have said that," Remo warned.

"What is the number?" Chiun asked.

"I forget. It's been so long."

The Master of Sinanju carried the phone over to Ferris D'Orr. He picked it up delicately and placed the receiver in the metallurgist's left hand. He inserted Ferris' right index finger into the rotary dial.

"I will help," said Chiun. "As you begin to work this instrument, I am sure the number will come to you."

It came to Ferris D'Orr suddenly, between the first friction burn from dialing 1 and the moment the Master of Sinanju inserted his finger in the 0-for-Operator hole.

"Hello, Ma?" Ferris said, sucking on his dialing finger. He did not sound happy. Chiun stepped back, beaming. He loved reunions. They reminded him of his beautiful American dramas.

Ferris D'Orr did not talk very long on the phone, but he did listen. Finally he said, "Bye, Ma," and hung up.

"Wasn't that nice?" asked Chiun.

"Yes, very," Remo agreed.

"I want you both to know two things," Ferris said, glowering at them. "One, I am not a momma's boy. Two, I am not—repeat not—Jewish."

"Who said you were?" Remo asked.

"My mother. But she's crazy."

Remo and Chiun looked at one another. They shrugged.

"Now, if you'll excuse me," Ferris said. "I have work to do."

Remo and Chiun left the room.

"You came all the way back to America for this?" Remo asked Chiun when they were out of earshot.

"Ferris is a genius," said Chiun. "An important genius. Guarding him is a sacred trust."

"All he does is fiddle with that machine of his and melt blocks of metal."

"Titanium," corrected Chiun.

"Does it matter?"

Chiun led Remo into the living room, where the big projection TV stood. Chiun settled onto the couch.

Remo sat on the floor.

"You don't wish to sit with me?" Chiun asked.

"Couches are bad for the posture."

"Who says?" asked Chiun.

"You. Constantly."

"This one is different. It is exceptionally comfortable."

"I'll stick with the floor, thank you."

"You have that right," said Chiun in a vague voice.

"How long is this going to go on?" Remo asked after a pause.

"How long is what going to go on?"

"This guarding Ferris."

"Until Emperor Smith informs us otherwise."

"Informs you otherwise. I'm just a bored groupie. I told Mah-Li I'd be back in a week. It's almost that now."

The Master of Sinanju shrugged as if Mah-Li were of no consequence. "Then go. I am not keeping you."

"I told you I'm not going back without you."

"Then I would advise you to find work. I, who have work, will be employed for the next year. At least."

"I think we should talk to Smith about this," Remo said. "Together."

"There is nothing to talk about. I am under contract."

"I'm still trying to figure that one out. And why did you leave Sinanju at night? Without saying good-bye. Answer me that, Little Father."

"I was in a rush."

"What rush?"

"To make my flight."

"What flight? You practically hijacked your way across the Pacific."

"I did not wish to deprive Emperor Smith of one hour's worth of the allotted service due him. What if, in the absence of the Master of Sinanju, he were to be assassinated? Then I would have to break in a new emperor." Chiun shook his aged head. "No, I am too old to break in a new emperor. Old, and unwanted."

"What do you mean, unwanted?"

"I am unwanted by my villagers, and by you."

Remo came to his feet.

"That's a low blow, Chiun. Would I be here right now if I didn't want you back?"

"Guilt makes men do strange things. You do not want me. You want Mah-Li."

"I'm going to marry Mah-Li with your blessing, remember? You always wanted me to marry a Korean girl. It's been your obsession."

"Mah-Li does not want you," Chiun said.

Remo's brows ran together.

"What makes you say that?" he asked. "How could you say that?"

"Has she written?"

"It's only been a few days, and she doesn't know where I am exactly. How could she write?"

"A worthy bride would write letters day and night, sending them hither and yon until they found you. Mah-Li is probably spending your gold even as we speak."

"Fine. Let's go back and stop her."

"You go. I must guard Ferris."

"We got the guys who were after him. What are we guarding him against—unwanted calls from his mother, for crying out loud?"

"Do not shout, Remo. It is unseemly. We never used to argue like this in the happier days."

"In the happier days we would argue all the time."

"Not like this," said Chiun, secretly pleased that Remo, in his anger, had admitted those days were indeed happier.

"No, you're right, not like this. In the old days, you would carp about me refusing to go back to Sinanju with you and I would hold my ground to stay in America. Now you've managed to get it all twisted up. Only you, Chiun, only you."

"You are beginning to sound like Ferris," Chiun sniffed.

"Is that good or bad? You seem to like Ferris, for a white."

"Whites are not that bad. I am beginning to like whites, some of them. Whites appreciate talent. I feel appreciated in America."

"You are appreciated in Sinanju too, Little Father. I appreciate you. Mah-Li does too. She worships you."

"Then why did you both let me leave in the middle of the night with only three kimonos and one pair of sandals?"

"Because we didn't know you were going to pull a disappearing act!"

"You should have known. You should have seen the signs. They were everywhere."

"There are signs everywhere around here, anyway," Remo said, looking out the penthouse window in disgust. Below, the city of Baltimore lay, a mixture of old buildings and new skyscrapers. Nothing matched or harmonized. In the streets, automobiles sent exhaust fumes into the air. Remo could smell them even through the double-sealed windows.

Once America had been his home. Now he felt like a stranger here. He hadn't lived in Sinanju long enough to love it, but the only two people in the world he did love were of Sinanju. That was enough for a start. At least in Sinanju the rain was clean, and the only dirt was on the ground, where dirt belonged. With some improvements, Remo knew he could make Sinanju a paradise for Mah-Li, himself, and Chiun. If only he could convince the Master of Sinanju.

"A penny for your thoughts?" asked Chiun.

Remo was silent for several ticks of the clock before he turned to the Master of Sinanju. His voice was clear and steady, his dark eyes determined.

"I'm not an American anymore," he said.

"So?"

"It's not fair that you do this to me. I did everything you wanted. I trained, I learned, and finally I gave you the last thing you wanted: settled in Sinanju. Now you do this to me."

"Do what?" Chiun said innocently.

"Pull the rug out from under me."

"You are standing on linoleum," observed Chiun.

"You know what I mean, dammit!" Remo was shouting. There were tears in his eyes now, tears of frustration. "I'm more Korean than white now."

"You are more Sinanju than white, never Korean."

"You forget. Mah-Li told me the story about Kojing and Kojong, the twin Masters of Sinanju. Their mother raised one of them secretly so their father wouldn't know he had twins and drown one of them in the bay. Both learned Sinanju, and Kojong went out into the outer world and was never seen again. You've always said I was part Korean, and I've always denied it. Now I don't. Kojong was my great-great-grandfather or something. This is why I learned Sinanju despite my whiteness."

"Anyone would have learned as you did—with me as his teacher," said Chiun.

"Cut it out! You know that isn't true. We're part of the same bloodline. You found me, and you brought me back into the fold. It was a long hard struggle and I fought you every step of the freaking way, but now I'm where I belong."

"In America."

"No, dammit. In Sinanju. Part of Sinanju. One with Sinanju. Why do you have to screw it up now? Why do you have to screw me up now?"

"Mah-Li told the story wrong," Chiun said huffily. "You are not the offspring of Kojong. The offspring of Kojong would not speak to me this way."

"Are you coming back to Sinanju or not? Last chance. Right now."

"No," said Chiun. "I am bound to Smith by my inviolate word."

"See you later, then," said Remo, leaving the room.

The Master of Sinanju sank back into the sofa after Remo Williams stomped out. It had been the most difficult conversation he had ever had with his pupil. Chiun had had to deny Remo. But the alternative was worse. If they returned to Sinanju, he would lose him entirely, and with him lose his mastery over his village. When that happened, Chiun knew he would lose all desire for living.

In America, they could be happy. Not in Sinanju. Never in Sinanju. Remo had been correct, in all ways. Despite his carping, the Master of Sinanju was not ready to allow Remo to become a Korean. Not yet. One day, perhaps, but not yet.

Chiun brushed a tear from the corner of his eye and turned on the TV. But even the Three Stooges did not bring laughter to his hazel eyes on this bitterest of afternoons.

20

For a week, the world wondered what had become of Ferris D'Orr. The network reporters worked overtime to locate him, but without success. The FBI refused to comment. The CIA refused to comment. The Defense Department refused to comment. The President's press secretary, at a prime-time news conference called to settle the raging question of his whereabouts, assured the networks that Ferris D'Orr remained in safe hands.

Even after a well-known White House correspondent, citing his brother-in-law as an "anonymous source," claimed to know for a fact that Ferris D'Orr was a prisoner of an Iranian-backed Lebanese splinter group and failed to get the White House to produce Ferris on camera, no one had a clue.

"I know where he is," Herr Führer Konrad Blutsturz said firmly, watching the news conference from his command-center bedroom at Fortress Purity.

"You do? Where?" asked Ilsa. She was stripping him of his silk dressing gown. His bionic left arm lay on a nearby table, where Ilsa had placed it.

"At the penthouse in Baltimore."

"They moved him. Everybody knows that," said Ilsa, pouring epsom salt into a pan of warm water. She dipped a facecloth into it and wrung the cloth until it was moist but not wet.

"They did not move him, Ilsa. Ah, that feels good. If they had moved him the networks would have found him. They found him once. The networks have no restrictions on them. They are free to ask questions, poke their noses into files, and do investigatory work that would cause the ACLU to shut down any other investigative body, government or private. By now, they would have found a leak. Everything leaks. But they have found no leak. They have found no clue precisely because there is no new location. No one would believe they did not move Ferris D'Orr after his location was revealed on the seven o'clock news, but that is what they did."

"You sure? Lift, I want to get under your arm."

"If they had moved D'Orr," said Konrad Blutsturz, "they would have moved him immediately. Had they done so, Boyce Barlow would still be alive. Consider, the news of D'Orr's location broke on a Thursday night. The following morning, I sent Boyce to the safe house. It would have taken him most of the morning—probably longer, the way he gets lost—to find the safe house. By the time he got there, D'Orr would have been moved—if the FBI intended to move him. We never heard from Barlow, therefore he and his cousins are dead. Had he died storming an empty safe house, the incident would have made every news show. No doubt he was killed by the defenders of Ferris D'Orr, and the incident has been hushed up to conceal D'Orr's actual location—the one place no one would think of looking."

"That makes sense. Lower?"

"Always lower. You know what I like, Ilsa."

"So what do we do?"

"We go to Baltimore and get Ferris D'Orr and his nebulizer."

"Just the two of us?"

"We are Aryans. Together, we are equal to any challenge."

"I love it when you talk like that," Ilsa said meltingly.

The flight reservations desk was apologetic.

"I'm sorry, sir. We have no flights leaving Baltimore-Washington Airport tonight. If you'd like to come back in the morning, I believe we'll be able to accommodate you. Or you could try one of the other carriers."

"I did try the other carriers," Remo Williams snarled. "You're my last hope. Why aren't there any flights available?"

"It's complicated."

"I've got all night," Remo said, drumming his fingers on the desk. The flight reservations clerk noticed that the data on his reservations terminal was jumping in time to the skinny man's finger drumming. He tapped the side of the computer to settle it down. It did not settle down. In fact, it got worse because the man in the black T-shirt drummed his fingers faster.

The clerk, who knew his terminal was jar-proof, couldn't imagine how the man's drumming fingers could cause that kind of on-screen disruption. It was an electrical phenomenon. How could the man's fingers be interrupting the electron flow to the screen?

He decided to answer the man's question despite strict company policy against doing so.

"It's the weather, sir."

"The sun is shining," Remo pointed out. Beyond the big windows, jetliners sat bathing in the dull winter sunshine.

"In Kansas City, I mean."

"I'm flying to New York City."

"I know, sir, but Kansas City is our airline's hub. All flights either originate, or terminate, or pass through Kansas City, and they're having a blizzard out there."

"Let me get this straight," Remo said slowly. "You don't have any flights because they're all in Kansas City?"

"I didn't say that, sir. I said our hub is snowbound at present. It should be dug out by morning."

"Isn't that one of your jets out by the gate?" Remo asked calmly.

"That's right, sir."

"Why not use it, then?"

"Can't. It's our Kansas City flight."

"We both know it's not going anywhere, so why not reroute it to New York?"

"Sorry, it's against company policy. All flights have to go through Kansas City."

The clerk noticed his on-screen data had all run together to form a luminous green blob that floated in the center of the black screen. Now, that was impossible.

"Baltimore and New York City are both on the east coast," Remo informed the clerk. "Do you mean that to fly from one to the other, I have to go through Kansas City, about a thousand miles out of the way?"

"It's the way we here at Winglight Airlines operate. It's actually more efficient that way."

"How is that possible?" Remo wanted to know.

"To save transportation costs and excise taxes, not to mention local fuel surcharge taxes, all our Jet-A fuel is stored in Kansas City. The extra fuel mileage is more than made up for by refueling in Kansas City exclusively."

"That explains your problem. What about the other carriers?"

"I think they just normally screwed up, sir. Deregulation, you know."

Remo looked at the man and stopped drumming his fingers. The on-screen data blob suddenly exploded like a fireworks display. When the little green sparks settled down, the clerk noticed that they had reformed into letters and numbers. He expended a sigh of relief. Then he looked closer. The letters and numbers were inexplicably backward.

By that time, the unhappy would-be passenger was gone.

Remo Williams had to wait an hour to use a pay phone. The pay phones at Baltimore-Washington Airport had lines in front of them that were longer than the ones at the reservation desks. But at least the phones worked when you got to them.

Remo called Dr. Harold W. Smith. He called collect.

"Remo? What have you to report?"

"Nothing," said Remo. "I don't work for you, remember?"

"Yes, of course. But from what Chiun has been saying, I thought you were more or less unofficially back on the team."

"Forget what Chiun said. You should see him now. He's tricked out like some freaking Pee Wee Herman clone. Look, Smitty, I'm trying to get back to Sinanju, but I'm stuck in Baltimore. No flights are going out until morning, if ever. Can you swing something? Say, a helicopter?"

"No helicopter would carry you across the Pacific."

"I know that, Smitty. I just want to get out of Baltimore, okay?"

"Not okay. As you know, I'm responsible for allocating millions in taxpayers' dollars. I would be remiss in my responsibility if I used even a cent of it for nonoperational expenses. You are no longer a member of the organization. You admitted it. I'm sorry, I can't justify the cost of returning you to Korea."

"That's your answer?"

"Well, you could reconsider your decision to go. I have that matter we discussed. Someone is trying to kill me."

"I know how he feels," Remo said through clenched teeth.

"I'm sorry, Remo," Smith said formally. "I just can't see it your way."

"Thanks a lot," Remo said, hanging up. Behind him, a long snaky line of waiting customers groaned with one voice.

"What's eating you?" Remo asked them.

"You broke the phone," said a bony woman.

Remo looked back. The receiver was a mush of plastic attached to the dial pad. "Oh, sorry," he said sheepishly.

"That's easy for you to say. You already made your call."

"I said I was sorry."

At the other side of the terminal, Remo tried to rent a car. He was told in no uncertain terms that he could not have one.

"Give me two reasons," Remo said.

"One, they've all been rented. Two, we don't accept payment in alleged gold ingots. Please take this thing off my counter."

Remo pocketed the bar of metal.

"Do you have a credit card and identification?" the clerk asked.

"No. What if I did? You already told me you don't have any cars."

"True, but if you had a credit card we could fit you in in the morning."

"I can get a flight in the morning," Remo said. "I won't need a car then."

"The customer is always right," the clerk told Remo.

Remo decided to sit out the night in the airport cafeteria. It was mobbed. The fast-food restaurants were jammed too. Not that Remo would have eaten in one. His highly attuned nervous system would have short-circuited with the ingestion of the smallest particle of hamburger or french fry.

"Ah, the hell with it," Remo muttered to himself, looking for a cab to take him back into Baltimore. "Even dealing with Chiun is better than this crap."

But there were no cabs to be had, either, and Remo had to walk all the way back to the city.

The Master of Sinanju did not sleep that night.

He could not, try as he might. The pain was too great. Even now, his pupil was many thousands of miles away, flying back to Korea. In his heart of hearts, Chiun wished he, too, could fly back to Korea, back to the land of his childhood. True, there were many painful memories back in Sinanju, of his stern father, who trained him in the art of Sinanju, of his cruel wife and her unworthy relatives, and of the shame of having been left, at an old age, without a proper pupil to carry on the Sinanju traditions.

Remo had wiped away that shame. Remo had become the son Chiun had been cheated of having. In the early days Chiun had not expended any great effort on making Remo a fit assassin for CURE. Remo was white, and therefore inept. His unworthiness would cause him to reject the better portions of Sinanju training. And even when Chiun grew to respect Remo, he avoided getting to know the man. He was white and therefore doomed to eventual failure. There was no sense in getting friendly. Remo would only die.

And it had happened. Remo had died during a mission. But Chiun, sensing a change in Remo, revived him. Remo had come back from the dead less white than he had been when he had lived. He had come back Sinanju.

It was then that Chiun knew destiny had delivered into his aged hands a greater future for the House of Sinanju than he had ever dreamed there would be. Delivered to Chiun the Disgraced, the old Master who should have retired but was stuck in a barbarian land so backward even the Great Wang had never known of it. Chiun understood he had the greatest Master, the avatar of Shiva, in his care.

Chiun had poured his heart and his love into the training of Remo Williams after that, and Remo had grown through the stages of Sinanju. Now he was a Master himself, tied to the village by bonds of tradition and honor.

Chiun would never have believed that when Remo finally agreed to settle in Sinanju, it would be the beginning of the greatest pain he would ever know: ignored by his ungrateful villagers, cast aside by Remo for a mere girl. All that he had worked for had turned to smoke.

And so, because he dared not admit his unhappiness, he had fled to America and tricked Harold Smith into another year's service, confident that Remo would follow him. And he had.

Yet now Remo was leaving again. He was actually returning to Sinanju, alone. Chiun would not see him again for a year, or longer.

The Master of Sinanju walked to a window. A clear full moon hung in the sky. Chiun wondered if that same moon shone down on the aircraft now carrying Remo back to Sinanju. Just the thought made him feel somehow closer to his pupil.

Chiun had gambled that Remo's love for him would be stronger than his love for Mah-Li. He had been wrong, and now he was prepared to pay the price—a year of separation.

Out in the hallway, the elevator door opened. Chiun cocked his head in the direction of the door.

A soft padding sounded on the carpet. It was not the heavy tread of American-shod feet, or the crush of bare feet. It was an effortless gliding that only one pair of feet other than Chiun's could make.

The Master of Sinanju burst into the hallway in his sleeping kimono.

"Remo, my son! I knew you would return. You cannot live without me."

"My flight was canceled," Remo said sourly.

The Master of Sinanju looked stricken. Then he slammed the door in Remo's face like an offended spinster.

"I didn't mean it like that," Remo said exasperatedly.

There was no answer from the other side.

"Look, I'll make you a deal," Remo called through the panel. "I'll stick around until this Ferris thing is over, then we'll talk to Smith and get this straightened out. Okay?"

The door opened slowly. Chiun stood framed in it, moonlight silvering his aged head. His face was impassive, and his hands folded into the sleeves of his sleeping kimono.

"Deal," he said, his face lighting up.

21

Ilsa Gans sent the specially equipped van circling the block for the last time.

"It looks clear," she called back over her shoulder.

Peering through the privacy glass, seeing but unseen, Konrad Blutsturz searched with avid eyes. There were no signs of guards in the lobby of the Lafayette Building, no obvious FBI agents posted on foot or in cars. No danger.

It was night, the perfect time. Konrad Blutsturz decided everything was perfect.

"On the next pass," he told Ilsa, reaching down to unbolt his wheelchair restraints, "park."

Coming around the block, Ilsa looked for the open space she had picked out in the parallel-parking zone, the one with the spray-painted stick-figure-seated-on-a-half-circle-wheelchair-symbol—the universal sign of handicapped-only parking.

A blue Mercedes suddenly pulled ahead and cut her off.

"He took it!" Ilsa said suddenly.

"Who took what?"

"The space," Ilsa answered. "The handicapped space. That guy in the Mercedes just scooted right in. He knew I was going for that space."

"Is there another?" demanded Konrad Blutsturz anxiously.

"No," Ilsa said miserably. "That's the only one."

Konrad Blutsturz banged his hand on the armrest. "There is always only one," he yelled. "What is wrong with this country? Do they think we handicapped travel only one at a time?"

"What do I do?" Ilsa moaned.

"We must park here. Is there another space of any kind?"

"No, and even if there was, it wouldn't be wide enough to offload in."

"Ram the car, then."

"Okay," said Ilsa, turning the van around until its rear wheels rode up on the opposite sidewalk. She pointed the van at the rear of the Mercedes in the handicapped space. The driver was just stepping out.

Ilsa sent the van shooting forward.

The van hit the back of the car like a tank, which, being built of bulletproof materials, was what it really was. The van pushed into the parking slot.

The Mercedes lurched forward, throwing the driver off his feet. He picked himself off the ground, swearing.

"Hey! What do you think you're doing?" he demanded.

"This is a handicapped space!" Ilsa yelled indignantly. "Are you handicapped?"

"It's the middle of the night, lady."

"They don't regrow their legs after dark, you know," said Ilsa, stepping out.

"I'm a lawyer, and I'm going to sue you for this!"

"He's making too much noise," Konrad Blutsturz said. "Kill him."

Ilsa reached for her Luger.

"No," hissed Konrad Blutsturz. "Quietly."

"Right," Ilsa said, extracting her swastika-shaped letter opener from the glove compartment. Its edges gleamed in the moonlight.

"Catch," said Ilsa.

The man caught it. In the throat. He went down clutching himself, his fingers splitting open where they touched the multiple blades. He writhed and gurgled in the gutter.

"That'll teach him," Ilsa said, opening the side of the van. "The inconsiderate bastard."

Konrad Blutsturz sent his motorized wheelchair onto the van's hydraulic lift. Ilsa grabbed the control levers and jerked it first one way, then the other. The steel platform, carrying Konrad Blutsturz, lifted out through the side door and settled to the street with a low hissing release of sound.

He sent the wheelchair scooting to the building entrance.

"Let's go," he called.

"What about this guy?" asked Ilsa.

"He looks Aryan. Put him out of his misery."

Ilsa placed the Luger against the man's forehead to smother the sound, said, "Nighty-night" sweetly, and fired once.

"Yuck! He splattered a little," Ilsa complained, looking at her formerly white blouse.

"You should never stand that close to your kills if you insist on being fussy. Come."

Ferris D'Orr lay dreaming. He dreamed that he was a gingerbread man. He had had that dream often as a child. He was a gingerbread man, and evil men who talked in funny voices were trying to cook him in a great big oven.

Ferris kept telling the men that they had the wrong person each time they pulled him from the oven and poked their fingers into his browning stomach that was decorated with huge M&M's.

"Put him in again. He's not done," they would say. And Ferris would shout the words that they refused to believe over and over again.

Ferris D'Orr woke up crying the words: "I'm not Jewish! I'm not Jewish!"

And for the first time, a voice answered his plea. It was a hoarse voice, an old voice, and through the hoarseness, Ferris recognized the guttural accents of his nightmares.

"Of course you are not," the voice said. "You are Ferris D'Orr, the brilliant metallurgist, and I am Konrad Blutsturz, here to enlist you in a great cause."

Light suddenly flared in the room and Ferris D'Orr saw the man who spoke. He was a hideous old man with a metal arm that clenched and unclenched nervously. It whirred like a dentist's drill as it worked. The man was in a wheelchair, his face leaning close to Ferris' own. Too close.

Ferris sat up suddenly, because as ugly as the man was, the red blanket that draped the stumps where the old man's legs stopped was uglier. In its center was the twisted cross of the Nazis.

The blond girl standing beside the old man also wore a swastika. It was on an armband circling her right arm, and the arm pointed a long-snouted pistol at his face.

"You must have great night vision," she said sweetly, "to be able to see our colors in the dark."

Ferris D'Orr had only one thing to say, one word.

The word was: "Momma!"

"Thank you for treating me, Little Father," Remo Williams said.

Chiun waved dismissively as he handed his American Express card to the restaurant cashier. Tonight his suit was maroon and gold. The tie was pink.

"You said you had not eaten," he said. "Now you have eaten."

The cashier took the credit card and filled out the charge slip. Then she placed both in the charge machine and ran the embossing handle back and forth with a loud chunking noise.

"Sign here, please," she told Chiun.

The Master of Sinanju took the proffered pen and signed with a flourish. He waited patiently. When the card was returned to him with the slip, he placed the card in his wallet and threw the slip into the nearest litter basket.

"Did you see that, Remo?" he asked once they were on the street. It was nearly four A.M. and there was not much traffic.

"Yes, I did, Little Father."

"I have been thinking," said Chiun. "I do not believe that even American merchants could be so foolish as to not realize I have not had to pay for their wares."

"Oh?"

"I think the card itself is not the wondrous thing after all."

"No, then what is?"

"Why, my name, of course."

"Your name?"

"Yes, Chiun. See? Here is my name printed on this

gold card. It says Chiun, my name. This is the magic thing, not the card. Obviously it is like the old seals of the Egyptians, intended to identify royal personages to commoners. When I show this card, they look for my name and see that they are dealing with the Master of Sinanju. Then they ask me to sign, using my signature for verification the way the Egyptian seals were once used. Thus, they do not ask for gold."

"It makes sense when you say it," said Remo good-naturedly.

"This means that America has finally learned to appreciate me. Smith must have told them. Yes, that is it. In the weeks when we were gone from his service, seeing that he no longer needed to keep our past employment with him secret, he has spread word of the good service that he formerly enjoyed from the Master of Sinanju. And subordinate Master, of course."

"Of course," said Remo, hiding a grin. "By the way, what did Smith say about the bodies?"

"What bodies?"

"The three guys you eliminated, the kidnappers. Was Smith able to identify them?"

"He said something vague about their unimportance. I do not remember what."

"That's strange," said Remo. "Usually Smith's computers can identify anyone from fingerprints or dental records."

"I think these must have been special nonentities," said Chiun, hoping that Smith never found out about the bodies in the dumpster. "What difference would it make?"

"Knowing who they were might mean knowing if they were operating on their own or working for someone."

"Why do you bring this up?" asked Chiun.

"I wonder if it was a good idea to leave Ferris alone."

"What harm is in it? Ferris is asleep, and Smith had obviously spread the word that he is protected by the Master of Sinanju. Our reputation does most of our work for us, you know."

Remo started to argue, but as he turned the corner he suddenly saw Ferris D'Orr.

Ferris was still asleep. But he was asleep in the arms of an old man in a wheelchair. The old man was being hoisted, wheelchair and all, into a waiting van. A blond girl in some kind of military uniform was working the lift. Remo recognized the titanium nebulizer rocking beside the wheelchair on the rising platform.

The blond slammed the side door closed and jumped for the driver's seat.

"They've got Ferris!" Remo said.

The van backed out of the space and barreled down the street.

Remo started after it and then noticed a man lying in the street beside a crumpled Mercedes that had been thrown up on the sidewalk.

"He's dead, Little Father," said Remo. Remo didn't notice that Chiun did not answer because Remo suddenly saw the shiny object embedded in the man's throat. He removed it, and found himself holding a steel-bladed swastika.

A car screeched to a stop beside Remo's crouching form.

"Hurry," a voice called from the car.

Remo got to his feet. There was no one behind the wheel. Remo lifted on tiptoe. His head barely topping the dashboard, the Master of Sinanju gestured frantically.

The passenger door popped open.

"Quickly," Chiun said anxiously. "They are getting away."

Remo jumped in, and the car took off down the street, careening like a drunken tiger.

"Where did you learn to drive?" Remo asked.

"Back there," Chiun said.

"Back where?" asked Remo.

"Back where I picked you up."

Remo suddenly noticed the ignition had been popped. "Wait a minute. You mean you don't know how to drive!"

"What is to learn?" asked Chiun, lifting himself up out of the seat to better see over the steering wheel. "You point the car and it goes."

"Right," said Remo, grabbing the wheel with one hand. "I'll help you point."

"You might also help me with the brake," said Chiun as they took a corner on two wheels.

"What's wrong with it?"

"Nothing. But I cannot reach the pedal with my feet."

Remo shot out a foot and the car slowed and stopped, knocking over a mailbox.

Remo got out and jumped over the hood to the driver's side. "Scoot over," he said.

The Master of Sinanju folded his arms defiantly.

"If you will not let me drive, neither of us will drive."

"Fine," said Remo. "Then you can be the one to tell Smith that you let Ferris get away."

Chiun slid over and Remo got behind the wheel. The car leapt forward.

"This would never have happened if you hadn't gotten hungry," scolded Chiun.

"Save it," said Remo, pushing the speedometer to sixty. He spotted the van pulling onto a major highway. Unfortunately, it was in the opposite lane. Remo sent the car over the lane divider and did a U-turn.

"I think that is against the rules," Chiun pointed out.

Remo ignored him. He piloted the car onto the ramp and sent it hurtling after the van.

When the van came in sight a half-mile away, Remo accelerated. Streetlights flashed past. He overhauled the van with surprising ease. Even as the blond girl stuck her tongue out at them in defiance, she did not push the van past sixty-five.

Remo found out why when he tried to force the van off the road.

His left-front fender crumpled against the side of the lumbering vehicle. The van didn't even wobble. It was too heavy. Too heavy to speed and too heavy to stop.

"This is not how it goes on TV," Chiun pointed out.

Remo tried again, but this time the van came at him.

Remo felt the steering wheel wrench under his fingers. He compensated against the twisting of the front wheels as they careened out of control. The steering wheel broke off in his hands.

Remo hit the brakes, and the car spun around like a big metal top, as the van continued on into the night.

When the car stopped scraping sparks off the guardrail, Remo and Chiun got out of the wreck.

"You okay?" Remo asked Chiun.

Chiun straightened his pink tie. "Of course. How could you let them get away like that? I will be shamed before Emperor Smith."

"That thing was a tank," Remo said. "Let's find a pay phone."

"I am not reporting failure to Emperor Smith," said Chiun.

"You don't have to. I will."

"Done. Just be certain you place the blame where it belongs, on your shoulders. I told you I should have driven."

Ferris D'Orr woke up. He found himself lying on a fold-down cot inside a plush-lined van. He rubbed his stinging shoulder. The last thing he remembered was being in his bed in the penthouse and having a blond girl shoot something into his veins.

"Ughhh," Ferris said.

A mechanical whirring attracted his attention. Ferris saw the old man, the one from his nightmare.

"Ah, Mr. D'Orr. I am glad you are awake."

"Where am I?"

"That does not matter. It should concern you only that we are nearly home."

"My home?"

"No, mine," said the old man. "We will be under way shortly, I assure you. My Ilsa is running an errand."

A few minutes later, the blond girl jumped back behind the driver's seat.

"This is all I could find," she said breathlessly, waving a sheaf of papers. "Most of the pay phones were vandalized. Honestly, don't people respect property anymore?"

Konrad Blutsturz took the papers in his steel fist and riffled through them.

He shook his head. "There are so many of them," he said in disgust, and threw the papers to the floor.

One of them landed on Ferris' covers. He picked it up. It was a page of telephone listings. Ferris noticed the van's interior was littered with similar pages.

Oddly, there was one name on every page—Smith.

As the van got under way, Ferris D'Orr pulled the blanket over his head and shut his eyes until they hurt. He hoped that he would wake up back in his penthouse bedroom. But he didn't think that he would.

22

Dr. Harold W. Smith awoke on the first ring.

He awoke the way he always did, like a light bulb switching on. He lay there for the briefest of instants. Recognizing that he was in his office at Folcroft Sanitarium, he got off the office couch. His wristwatch, which he wore even to bed, read 4:48 A.M. as he picked up the desk phone.

"Yes?" he said, his voice as astringent as lemons.

"Smitty? Remo."

"Yes, Remo," Smith said uninterestedly.

"We lost Ferris," Remo said abruptly.

Smith's hand tightened on the receiver.

"What?"

Chiun's voice came on the line as Remo started to reply.

"Do not fear, Emperor. Ferris is not truly lost."

"Where is he?"

"We do not know."

"Then he is lost."

"No, merely misplaced. Here, Remo will explain his failure to you. Please do not punish him too severely."

"Thanks a lot, Chiun," Remo said away from the phone. Over the line, Smith heard them lapse into a tense exchange in Korean. He waited for the bickering to subside because he knew neither man would listen to him as long as they were arguing.

Finally Remo's voice came back on the phone.

"He was kidnapped, Smitty. We saw it happen, but the kidnappers got away. They were driving a van that must have been built of steel."

"Titanium," Chiun said in the background. "Mere steel would not have stopped us."

Remo went on after a tired sigh. "It was a girl, young, blond, with an older guy. Really old."

"But younger than me," Chiun chimed in.

"Will you let me finish?" Remo said.

Smith rolled his eyes heavenward. Even at this moment of failure, his immediate reaction was that it felt as if Remo and Chiun had never left CURE. His second was that he felt the walls were closing in.

"Anyway," Remo went on, "the old guy was in a wheelchair."

"We must have a bad connection," Smith said. "I thought you said one of the kidnappers was in a wheelchair. Repeat please."

"He was in a wheelchair. I know it sounds crazy, but there you go. Ferris has been kidnapped by a disabled person. They even rammed a car out of a handicapped parking space and killed the driver just to get the space. At least, that's how I read the scene."

"This doesn't make sense," Smith said.

"It gets worse. The guy who took the parking space had a shuriken lodged in his throat."

"A which?"

"A shuriken," Remo repeated. "It's a sharpened throwing star. Ninjas use them for killing."

"Ferris D'Orr was kidnapped by ninjas?"

"I don't think so," Remo said. "This wasn't the usual throwing star. It was shaped like a swastika, with the edges sharpened."

"Nazi ninjas kidnapped Ferris D'Orr? Is that what you're saying?" He reached for a bottle of extra-strength aspirin.

"No, I'm telling you what I saw and what I found. It's up to you to figure it out."

"Is there anything more?"

"We followed them. They ran us off the road and got away."

"Remo wouldn't let me drive," the voice of the Master of Sinanju came faintly through the receiver.

Dr. Harold W. Smith sat down in his leather chair wondering how he would explain this to the President.

"I don't suppose you managed to get the van's license plate in all the excitement?" Smith asked acidly.

"No, I didn't get the van's license plate," Remo repeated. "I don't work for you, remember?"

"But I do and did," another voice said.

Smith bolted up in his chair. "What was that? What did Chiun say?"

"Here, you talk to him," Remo said.

"Master of Sinanju?" Smith said, hope rising in his heart.

"Never fear, Emperor, I have the numbers at my command. Truly, I have learned how important numbers are in American society. You have numbers for everything, for telephones, for houses, and for American Express. I saw the numbers of the offending vehicle."

"Read them to me, please," Dr. Smith said, booting up his CURE computers. In a walled-off section of Folcroft's basement, the powerful bank of computers kicked into silent life.

"DOC-183," said Chiun.

"What state?" said Smith, in putting the numbers into the search file.

"Moving fast," said Chiun.

"I meant what state was listed at the bottom of the license plate. There is always a state name."

"I did not notice," said Chiun unhappily. "Are states also important? I thought only numbers were. Should I remember the state the next time, or the numbers?"

"Both," said Smith wearily.

"Both. It will be extra work, but I will do this in your honor, O generous dispenser of American Express."

"This is important, Master of Sinanju. Do you, maybe, remember the first letter of the state name?"

"I think it began with A."

"Alabama, Alaska, Arizona, or Arkansas?" asked Smith, his fingers poised to key in the answer.

"Yes, one of those," Chiun said confidently.

Smith's fingers went limp. "Do you remember the color?"

"White, with red letters."

"Alabama," said Smith, inputting the name.

The computer searched its memory banks and generated an on-screen readout.

"The van is licensed to the White Aryan League of

America and Alabama," Smith said. Then he thought about what he had said. "Put Remo on, please," Smith told Chiun.

"Smitty?" Remo said.

"That swastika means something. The van is registered to a neo-Nazi group."

"What would neo-Nazis want with Ferris D'Orr?"

"I can't imagine, but it's going to be up to you and Chiun to find out and get D'Orr back before anything happens to him."

"Talk to Chiun. I'm just along for the ride until this is over. Then I'm going back to Korea."

"Would you tell him, Remo?" Smith pleaded. "I always get a headache explaining even simple things to him."

Remo stopped the rented car in front of the big gates with the hand-carved pinewood sign, "FORTRESS PURITY," over them. He stuck his head out the window and called to the guard, who wore a brown uniform and a Sam Browne belt.

"Excuse me," Remo called. "Would you mind opening up?"

The guard sauntered over to the car. Out of the corner of his mouth, Remo whispered to Chiun, "Remember, keep your sunglasses on."

The Master of Sinanju adjusted his wraparound sunglasses over his almond eyes and pulled his white bowler down over his forehead. It matched his suit. His tie and breast-pocket handkerchief were a matching gold.

"Don't worry, I am cool," he said, using a word he had picked up from television. Americans used it a lot. Therefore so would he.

"What do you want?" the guard asked suspiciously.

"We want to sign up. Where's your recruiting offices?"

"We only let in the racially pure," the guard said, looking at Remo's brown eyes and dark complexion. "What's your name?"

"Remo."

"Doesn't sound very Aryan to me," the guard said slowly.

"Remo White. And this is my father."

"Chiun, Chiun Whiter," said the Master of Sinanju.

"Whiter? Whiter than what?" Remo whispered in Korean.

"Whiter than thou," answered Chiun, adjusting his tie.

"What lingo was that you're speaking?" demanded the guard in a suspicious voice.

"Aryan," said Remo. "We're the official Aryan tutors. By this time next month, you'll all be speaking it."

The guard looked at them a long time and finally made up his mind.

"Okay, you can go in. It's the big building with the flag."

"They all have flags," said Chiun as they passed through the grounds. Around them, men in brown uniforms marched in formation. "Nice ones. It is good to see the Zingh again."

"The what?"

"The Zingh," said Chiun, pointing. "It is a lucky symbol."

"Little Father," said Remo as they got out of the car and walked up the long ramp in front of the main building, "that's the swastika. It's the Nazi symbol. It's evil."

Chiun spat. "Do the Japanese own the sun because they put it on their flags?" he asked. "Or the Americans the stars? The Zingh is older than Germany. In ancient days it was a proud sign. Remind me to tell you about it someday."

"Later. Right now, I want you to let me do all the talking. These people are Nazis. They may be dangerous."

"Nazis are not dangerous," said Chiun. "They are idiots."

"Dangerous idiots, then. Just let me do the talking. We've got to pass ourselves off as good clean Aryans."

"That will be impossible. Aryans never bathed and were blood-drinking barbarians."

The man at the registration desk did not ask them if they were Aryans. He did not even ask their names. He asked only how much they made per year.

Remo said, "I'm unemployed."

Chiun said, "More than you can imagine."

"Will you pay your friend's dues?" the man asked Chiun.

"Surely," said Chiun.

"That'll be twenty-five thousand dollars for the year. Prorated."

"Do you take American Express?" Chiun asked casually.

"Everyone takes American Express," said the man, running Chiun's card through a credit-card machine.

"I'll get you your uniforms," said the man. A moment later he was back with two cardboard boxes. He handed them to Remo.

"These should fit you both. You bunk in the Siegfried Barracks."

On the way out the door, Chiun opened his box. When he saw the contents, he made a disgusted face and threw the box into a trash barrel.

"We'll need that to blend in," Remo said.

"When you wear a uniform," Chiun pointed out, "you surrender your very soul to the rules of others. Surrender nothing to these people, Remo, or they will own you."

"How else are we going to blend in with these people?" asked Remo.

"Sinanju does not blend in with others," said Chiun. "Others blend in with Sinanju."

"Uh-oh, trouble," Ilsa Gans said, looking out the window of Konrad Blutsturz' office.

"What is it, Ilsa?" Konrad Blutsturz said absently. He pored over the blueprints that lay in profusion on his desk. With one eye, he watched Ilsa's rear end as she bent over to look more closely at whatever interested her. It was a nice rear end, very round.

"Remember those two men? The ones who chased us in Baltimore?"

"Government agents. Bunglers, no doubt."

"Well, they're here."

Konrad Blutsturz looked up. He hit the operating switch and his chair spun out from behind the desk and joined Ilsa at the window.

Below, a tall man in chinos and a T-shirt walked to

one of the barracks, carrying a White Aryan League regulation uniform across one arm. A smaller man in white walked beside him, looking around curiously.

"Have them killed. I am busy. The doctor will be here shortly, and I must attend to many details."

"Oh, goody."

"Remember to use our expendable people."

"They're not as good as your lieutenants. They always screw up."

"Then use more of them. Soon we will have no need for any of them anymore. For soon I will walk like other men. And do the other things erect men do."

"I like the way you said that—erect."

Remo had given up trying to fit into his brown uniform when someone knocked at the door of the barracks room he and Chiun had been assigned.

"What?" asked Remo, realizing for the first time that Chiun had thrown out the uniform meant for him and that he had wasted twenty minutes trying to fit into a child's size.

"First duty," a voice said. "Report to the shooting range."

"I am not touching a firearm," Chiun said firmly. "Nor will you."

"Maybe we can fake it," said Remo.

They found the front door of the firing range locked and deserted.

"Maybe there's a side door," said Remo.

There was, a small one. The words "Firing Range" were scrawled on a sheet of blue-lined paper torn from a loose-leaf notebook and taped to the door.

"I guess this is it," Remo said.

The door clicked shut behind them and there was no light.

"This doesn't smell right," Remo said.

"Gunpowder," said Chiun, wrinkling his nose. "It never does."

"I mean this setup. I think it's exactly that."

They felt their way along a wall in the darkness. Remo sensed a great open space to his right, and beyond that there was some movement and the faint smell of human beings, but it was muted, as if intercepted by a barrier.

When the lights suddenly snapped on in the building, Remo saw the black silhouette targets of the firing range. They were not in front of them. They were on the wall directly behind them.

At the far end of the building, men in brown uniforms stood behind the glass ports of firing stations. They hefted rifles to their shoulders and pointed them.

"Is this a form of initiation?" asked Chiun.

"No, it's a form of slaughter. And we're the objects."

The rifles started cracking, sharp spiteful cracks. Behind Remo and Chiun white holes were punched into the black targets, and the air around them vibrated with the sounds of high-velocity slugs.

"Weaver Pattern, Little Father," Remo said.

"Agreed," said Chiun.

Remo moved toward the soldiers of the White Aryan League in a straight line. The Master of Sinanju took a parallel course. Abruptly Chiun cut across the path of Remo's trajectory, and Remo slipped behind him in a similar, but opposite, diagonal movement.

To the soldiers working their rifles, it looked as if Remo and Chiun were panicking in all directions. That was the idea of the Sinanju Weaver Pattern. Each man ran a broken line, but it was an intersecting broken line, weaving across one another's paths. It had been originally devised as a form of attack against archers at the time of Darius of Persia.

As Chiun had explained it to Remo years ago, a man running toward an assailant presented a static target that grew larger the closer he came to the attacker. A man running side to side presented a confusing target. But two men running a Weaver Pattern were confusion upon confusion, because an archer always picked the largest target. He would always fire when the two running men crossed paths to form a converging double mark. But by the time he loosed his arrow, the two men were running in diverging paths.

It had worked against arrows. It worked against bullets, which were faster than arrows, but also smaller, and easier to avoid because they required more precise aiming.

There were five riflemen. By the time they realized they could not pick their targets individually, Remo and Chiun had cleared half the space toward them.

The marksmen switched tactics and started a murderous crossfire. But Remo and Chiun were already too close to them for that and they had to revert to individual targeting.

It was too late for individual action as well.

One rifleman sighted on Remo, waiting until his chest filled his field of vision. He squeezed the trigger slowly, because that gave the cleanest shot.

He felt his weapon kick against his shoulder. He didn't feel it discharge. Nor did he feel the butt of the rifle, pushed by Remo's open palm, tear his shoulder muscles loose. The nerves had been severed and no pain signals were transmitted. The rifle clattered to the floor, and the gunman clutched his limp arm stupidly.

Remo took him out with a short chop to the neck and turned on another soldier, who was swinging his rifle around.

Remo stopped, folded his arms across his chest, and said, "Tell you what, pal. I'll give you one freebie shot."

The soldier fired. The bullet went where it was supposed to go, but strangely, his target did not fall or even grab at his solar plexus. The soldier brought his weapon up to his shoulder again, but by then it was too late.

Remo scolded, "I said one shot. You're out." He jellied the man's face.

Remo stepped over the falling body to reach Chiun, but the Master of Sinanju needed no help. He stood over the twisting form of a soldier whose legs no longer worked. Two others had Chiun between them. They kept trying to bring their rifle muzzles to bear on the Master of Sinanju, but each time they lifted their weapons, Chiun swatted them down like a child fighting off broom handles.

"I'd give it up if I were you," Remo told them. "You're only going to prolong the agony."

"Silence, Remo," said the Master of Sinanju, suddenly making the barrels fly up instead of down. "Wheee!"

The two soldiers refused to give up. One shot was all they needed, but they couldn't keep their rifles trained on where a bullet would do the most good long enough to pull the trigger. One started to blubber uncontrollably.

When the Master of Sinanju grew tired of his sport, he grasped the rifle muzzles. The action was brief, but firm, and the soldiers never knew that Chiun had squeezed the muzzles shut.

"I am tired of this," announced Chiun, and he walked away with taunting unconcern.

The soldiers couldn't believe their good fortune. Sighting down their weapons, they fired in unison. The blowback shattered the receiving mechanisms and sent metal and wood shrapnel into the faces of the guards. They dropped, still clutching their useless weapons, like toy soldiers. Which is what they really were.

"That was excellent shooting practice," said Chiun. "How many did you get?"

"Two," Remo said.

"Three," said Chiun. "I win."

"No, I think we both lose. They're onto us."

"So much for blending in."

23

They had taken Ferris D'Orr from the van still huddled in the cot. Soldiers did that. Soldiers in brown uniforms with the red Nazi armbands.

Ferris had peeked as they carried him into the big main building. It was dark. He was in some kind of compound, surrounded by guards and a high fence. There were many soldiers, and many buildings. Nazi flags flew from every roof. It looked like the photos of those places his mother used to harp about—places like Treblinka and Bergen-Belsen—places he knew couldn't possibly exist on American soil.

"Oh, my God," Ferris said under his breath. "I'm in an extermination camp."

They took him into a homey dining room, and the blond, Ilsa, stripped the blanket back and offered her hand.

"We're here," she called.

Ferris refused to get up. He wouldn't let go of the blanket either. He clutched one corner of it in his hand.

"Come on," Ilsa said sweetly. "Get up."

"Perhaps Mr. D'Orr would like to freshen up," said the guttural voice of Ferris' nightmares. "A shower, perhaps?"

"No way!" screamed Ferris D'Orr. "I know what you people mean by showers."

"He is frightened after his long journey," said Konrad Blutsturz. "Let me speak with him. You start the oven."

"I'm not Jewish!" Ferris said, jumping to his feet.

The old man laughed. "You already told us that. Ilsa is merely going to start dinner. Do you have a preference?"

"Anything," said Ferris D'Orr, "as long as it's ham, pork roast, or pork chops."

"Any of those, Ilsa," the old man called as the girl left the room. "Come, sit by my side. You are a most peculiar young man, but then, you are a genius. All geniuses are peculiar."

"I want to go home," Ferris said, sitting in the chair with the same gingerly resignation of a death-row inmate settling into the electric chair. He suddenly, desperately, yearned for a lemon Coke, but they hadn't made them in years.

"Do not be frightened. You will be here only a short time. I need your expertise. And your nebulizer."

"It's yours. Just put me on a bus."

"Soon, within the week. Allow me to show you my plans."

Ferris watched as the old man unrolled a set of blueprints.

"Some of the parts are very delicate, as you can see, but we have the molds. Can your nebulizer cast such tiny parts?"

Ferris gave the blueprints a quick glance.

"Easily. Can I go now?"

"After these parts are made and assembled."

"What are they going to be assembled into?"

"Me," said Konrad Blutsturz. "They are going to be assembled into me."

"But there are enough parts here to build a baby tank."

"Exactly."

All during that feverish night they brought in the molds and the chunks and billets of titanium. It was good-quality titanium. Ferris recognized the Titanic Titanium Technologies stamp on a few of the sections. They made Ferris melt the pieces into molds. When they were done, they had him weld the parts into mechanisms. The brown-suited soldiers took the finished components into the next room. Once, when the door opened wide enough, Ferris saw that it was an operating amphitheater.

He remembered his mother's stories of the grisly Nazi surgeries performed on conscious patients. Once he had seen in a book a photograph of two Nazi doctors. They stood with stupid pride over a sheet-covered body.

The body's legs stuck out from below the sheets and there wasn't enough flesh on the bones to satisfy a rat.

Ferris D'Orr shuddered. He didn't know what he had become enmeshed in, but he knew that it was evil. And he understood for the first time why his mother was so determined to remember the holocaust.

It was happening again. Here, in America. And Ferris was a part of it.

"What's this all about?" Ferris asked Ilsa after he had finished casting the largest pieces of the mounting for a sicklelike blade of steel.

"It's about cleansing America," she said matter-of-factly.

"Of what?"

"Jews, blacks, Asians, and icky people like that. Smiths, too."

"Smiths?" asked Ferris, remembering the telephone-directory pages.

"Yes, they're worse than Jews or the others, much worse. A Smith put Herr Führer Blutsturz into a wheelchair. But you will lift him out."

Ferris understood another thing. Hatred did not discriminate. All his life he had hidden his heritage from the world, half out of false shame and half out of fear. The evil that haunted his dreams had found him anyway. There was no escape from hatred.

"No one is safe," Ferris said.

"What, sweet thing?"

Ferris D'Orr stood up and shut off the nebulizer. A billet, beginning to liquefy, suddenly froze in its mold, only half-formed.

"That one's not done," Ilsa said.

"It is done," Ferris said firmly. "It's all done." He kicked over the nebulizer. It hit the floor with a mushy crack, and the projector tube bent. A panel popped off one side.

"Hey! Why'd you do that?"

"Because," said Ferris D'Orr proudly, "it's my historic duty. I am a Jew."

Ilsa made a face. "Oooh, too bad. We were going to let you live."

Konrad Blutsturz was beside himself. He raged. He

flopped on the operating table. The doctors, frightened, tried to hold him down. It was a critical moment.

"Herr Führer, restrain yourself," the head surgeon pleaded. "If this is true, there is nothing we can do."

"He went bananas," Ilsa moaned, tears streaming down her cheeks. "I didn't know he was going to do anything crazy. How was I to know?"

"I must walk. I must."

"We may be able to proceed," the head surgeon said. Behind him, on a series of cork panels, the blueprints for the new Konrad Blutsturz were pinned up with thumbtacks. "We cannot stop. We have gone too far. We must proceed."

"And I must walk," said Konrad Blutsturz.

"We are taking stock of the unfinished components, Herr Führer," the head surgeon said. "If necessary, we will build the incomplete portions of the mechanisms from aluminum or steel. Most of the critical titanium parts have been formed."

"The legs?" demanded Konrad Blutsturz.

"They are being assembled now."

"Are they complete?"

"Nearly. Let me finish attaching the arm."

"Finish it, and bring that man to me."

"What man?"

"The traitor, D'Orr."

"Gotcha," said Ilsa.

The doctors had opened up the stump that was Konrad Blutsturz' left arm and inserted a titanium coupling into the bone marrow, as they had done with both leg stumps. The old steel hand lay in a corner. In its place they were attaching the bluish jointed arm that ended in a fully articulated hand. It possessed four fingers and that ultimate symbol of humanity, an opposable thumb.

"No pain?" asked the doctor.

"This is a moment of rebirth," said Konrad Blutsturz. "The pain of birth is the pain of life. It is to be savored, not endured."

"I could put you under, if the local anesthetic is not enough."

"Only to stand erect will ease the pain. Only to take

the throat of the man who put me in this position will be enough."

Ilsa brought in Ferris D'Orr at gunpoint.

Konrad Blutsturz had only one question: "Why?"

"I am the son of a Jew."

"And for that you would cheat me of my dream? Fool. I meant you no harm."

"Your kind has seared the conscience of the world."

"Fool! We Nazis did not hate the Jews, or anyone else. It was a political hatred. It was not real, not true. The Jews were just a focusing point, a scapegoat to rouse Germany out of the hell of inflation and defeat after the First World War. Had the Reich triumphed, we would have abolished the death camps. There would have been no need for them. We would have pardoned the Jews."

"And who would have pardoned you?" asked Ferris D'Orr.

"So you have placed yourself in this jeopardy because you wish to avoid a repetition of your holocaust. Correct?"

"Yes."

"Ilsa, make him kneel. On my left side, please."

Ilsa forced Ferris D'Orr to his knees and pulled back his hair until his eyes were stretched open.

Ferris D'Orr stared at the blue metal arm lying next to him. Parts of it he recognized; he had molded them.

"The first years were the worst," intoned Konrad Blutsturz, his words as distantly angry as far thunder. "I could not move. I was in an iron coffin staring at the ceiling. I wanted to die, but they would not let me die. Later, I would not let myself die. I would not die because I wanted to kill."

The titanium hand clicked into a fist. Then it opened. It moved soundlessly, with a near-human animation that was as repulsively fascinating as watching a spider eat.

"I dreamed of this moment, Harold Smith." Konrad Blutsturz spoke to the ceiling. The operating lights blazed down upon his unformed body.

"Ilsa, place Smith's neck in my new hand. I wish to feel its strength."

"Smith?" Ilsa asked blankly.

"Our prisoner."

"Oh." Ilsa obediently pushed Ferris D'Orr's head down onto the operating table.

The blue robot hand clenched Ferris' neck, digging in. Ferris D'Orr clutched at the edge of the steel operating table. He pushed against it. But his body would not move. The hand held his neck, his spine, his life. There was no escape. His breath caught and came hard.

"Did you think you could escape me, Harold Smith? No? Yes, you thought I was dead."

Ferris D'Orr choked, his face purpling.

"I was not dead. I was in hell, but I was not dead. I lived only to hold your neck in my one strong hand, Harold Smith," said Konrad Blutsturz, not looking at the struggling man in his hand, but at the ceiling, as he did in the early days when he could not move, lying in the iron lung.

Ferris D'Orr clawed at the unyielding stainless-steel table, and when that did no good, he clawed at the arm that acted with smooth, unfeeling life—the arm of titanium that he had helped to make. He clawed the way they had clawed the walls in the death camps, after the doors were shut and the gas was pumped in through the shower nozzles.

The others looked away. Except Ilsa. She bent down to get a better look at Ferris' blood-gorged face.

"Do their tongues always stick out like this?" she asked.

"Do you feel fear, Harold Smith?" Konrad Blutsturz' voice ground lower. "Anger? Remorse?"

But Ferris D'Orr did not feel anything. There was a sudden taste in his throat that he thought must be blood, but oddly, it tasted like lemon Coke. Then he was dead.

"I think you can let go now," Ilsa said.

The body of Ferris D'Orr slipped to the antiseptic floor in a heap of inert flesh.

"He is dead?" Konrad Blutsturz asked, his eyes clearing.

"Yep," said Ilsa. "I'll have someone get rid of the body. Imagine that, a Jew named Smith."

"Smith," said Konrad Blutsturz, and the rage came into his eyes again.

Ilsa sponged the blood off his titanium hand and went out to see if the two new recruits were dead yet.

The new recruits were not dead. There was no sign of them on the firing range. Instead, five White Aryan League soldiers lay in contorted positions.

One of them, his legs shattered, still lived.

"What happened?" Ilsa asked, kneeling at his side.

"They were superhuman. Bullets could not touch them. We tried. We truly did." His voice congealed on itself.

"How could you fail? You are an Aryan. They are mongrels."

The soldier uttered a final gurgle and his head lolled to one side. Ilsa stood up numbly.

Ilsa Gans had always believed in Aryan supremacy. She had first learned it from her parents, who had come from Germany after the war because living in America was better than suffering in a broken and divided land.

She had met Konrad Blutsturz in Argentina, on a family vacation. Her parents always vacationed in Argentina, where they felt free to speak of the old Germany and of the Reich that was now ashes. They and their friends told bitter stories of failure and shattered hopes. It seemed so boring. But Konrad Blutsturz had actually met Hitler. Konrad Blutsturz made it come alive for her.

Even in a wheelchair, he was a giant. Ilsa had thought so at age eight, and the next year, and every vacation after that.

One year, Konrad Blutsturz had asked her to stay on. Her parents were at first apprehensive, even horrified. There was a scene. In the name of the Reich, Konrad Blutsturz had commanded them to release their daughter to him. And they had refused.

Konrad Blutsturz had come into her bedroom the night before she was to leave Argentina, and sadly, with grandfatherly patience, explained to Ilsa, then sixteen, that her parents were dead.

Ilsa had no words. The shock was too great, and to fill

the silence Konrad Blutsturz had explained that the Jews had killed her parents, Jews who chose to persecute the vanquished soldiers of Germany.

"We'll get them," Konrad Blutsturz had promised. "And their leader, the evil one incarnate."

"Who?"

"His name is Smith, Harold Smith."

"Is he a Jew?"

"He is worse than a Jew. He is a Smith."

Ilsa became his nurse, his confidante, and the only one he would allow to tend him. She learned to hate the Jews, the blacks, and the other inferior races. When Konrad decided to return to America to seek out Smith, Ilsa had gone along willingly. By that time, he had taught her to kill.

Just as he had taught them all to kill. He had instilled in the White Aryan League the confidence of racial superiority. Even the ones who weren't exactly Aryan. And he had passed out enough rifles to equalize their racial shortcomings.

Yet five crack White Aryan League soldiers armed with rifles had been killed by only two non-Aryans.

There were security cameras built into the ceilings of every Fortress Purity building. Ilsa got a stepladder and used it to collect the videotapes of the day.

As she walked across the darkened compound, her brow puckered as she recollected of Konrad Blutsturz' words in the operating room. He had said that the Jews were really not inferior. Perhaps it was stress that made him say those things. After all, he had called the metallurgist Ferris D'Orr by the name of Harold Smith. Sometimes Ilsa worried about her mentor. The strain was becoming great. They had to get to Smith soon, while Herr Führer's mind was whole.

Ilsa had no time to wonder further because across the compound she saw the two new recruits, Remo and Chiun, prowling through the Fortress Purity parking lot.

They were looking for something.

"This is it, Little Father," the taller one said. "Same van, same color and license plate."

"Next time I will remember the state too," the shorter one said. Ilsa thought his accent was peculiar.

She started to draw the Luger that was always holstered at the small of her back, but then she remembered the five high-powered rifles that lay uselessly beside the bodies of the trained soldiers.

Ilsa Gans hurried on. Whoever these two were, the videotapes would show how dangerous they really were.

24

"No one has attempted to kill us in several hours," the Master of Sinanju said.

"The van is empty," said Remo.

"Of course. It is for transportation, not storage."

Remo closed the van door. He hadn't expected to find anything inside, but discovering the van was a final confirmation that they were in the right place.

"Ferris has to be around here," Remo said.

"In the big building," said Chiun. "Where something important transpires."

"What makes you say that?" said Remo.

"Important personages are always to be found in the largest buildings. That is why they are large. Do emperors live in huts or hovels? Even Smith, who claims not to be an emperor, although he is, lives in a fortress."

"Smith lives near a golf course," Remo said. "He only works at Folcroft."

"An emperor lives within himself. Wherever he is, he is home."

"And what makes you think something is going on in the main building? This place is like a ghost town."

"Exactly," Chiun said. "No one has tried to kill us in several hours. Obviously, they are preoccupied."

"Maybe they're afraid of us?"

"We only killed five. Whoever commands here would not quake when but five soldiers fall. Commanders do not feel fear until their elite guard has fallen. It is the way of such men."

"I didn't notice this before," said Remo slowly.

"Notice what?"

"The design on the side of the van, the repeating one. It's a series of swastikas hooked together like a chain."

"The Zingh," Chiun corrected. "I must tell you about that."

"On the way," said Remo. "Let's try the big building."

"An excellent choice," said Chiun. He had taken off his sunglasses now that the sun had fallen behind the hills. "The Zingh is older than Germany, older than the Greeks. The Indians knew of it."

"American Indians?"

"They, too. But I refer to the Indians of the East, the true Indians, the Hindus. Their Lord Buddha wore this symbol tattooed to his body as a sign of his goodness."

"Really?"

"Yes, the Zingh was a lucky sign in olden days. Although not so lucky for some."

"I detect a legend coming on," Remo said.

"Once, a Master of Sinanju was in service to a caliph of India," Chiun recited. "This particular caliph was having problems with the priests of his province. They objected to his taxes or something. I do not remember because their offense is not the point of this story. And so the caliph sent the Master, whose name was Kik, to slay the priests."

"For not paying their taxes. Just like that?"

"Merely because priests wrap themselves in holy words, that does not make them holy. Or even less mortal. The priests, hearing of the Master of Sinanju coming to their temple, were beside themselves with trepidation. They knew they were powerless against the Master of Sinanju. They could not fight him. They could not defend their soft bodies from his blows. They could not reason with him, for they spoke not his language. In their fear, they sought a charm to ward off the Master's attack."

"The Zingh?" asked Remo.

"The very same. They knew that their Lord Buddha anointed his largeness with this very symbol, and so with pigments they anointed their bodies with this emblem of luck and goodness, trusting that the Master Kik would perceive their good intentions and spare them."

"You make the Zingh sound like the old peace symbol hippies used to wear."

"No, that is the Urg. Another thing altogether.

The Zingh is more like that funny yellow circle people wear with the dots for eyes and the insipid smirk."

Remo looked puzzled. "A smile button? The swastika was the Hindu version of a smile button?"

"The Zingh. Exactly," said Chiun. "And so when the Master of Sinanju stood outside the gate of this temple, he called the priests out to face his wrath. And the priests came, stripped to their loincloths, their bodies anointed with the Zingh, and their fat bellies quaking in fear, and the Master of Sinanju flew upon them, chop, chop, chop, and in a twinkling they fell dead."

"The Master of Sinanju did not recognize the Zingh, huh?"

"Oh, he recognized it," Chiun replied cheerfully, "but he did not know it as the Zingh, but as the Korean Buk, the symbol of storm and lightning and combat. You see, to a Hindu it meant 'Have a nice day,' but to a Korean it meant 'I challenge you to fight to the death.' And so the fat-bellied priests died."

"And the lesson?"

"There is none."

"Really," said Remo, "no lesson? I don't think I've ever heard a Sinanju legend that didn't come with a lesson attached to it."

"That is because this is not a lesson legend, but a humorous legend. Masters of equal ranks use them to pass the hours. Now that you are a full Master, I may tell you other such legends. But remember, these are not stories to tell the villagers or others. These are between Masters, to be appreciated by Masters only. To tell such lessons to villagers is to diminish the solemnity and dignity of the Sinanju histories."

"That last part sounds like a lesson to me."

"That is because you are new to full Masterhood," said Chiun, chuckling.

When Remo did not chuckle back, Chiun asked what was wrong. They were approaching the long ramp that led to the main building's entrance.

"This place is wrong, Little Father."

"It is ugly, yes, I will agree to that."

"It shouldn't exist. Not here in America, not ever."

"Soldiers are as numerous as ants. You step on one

anthill, and they build another elsewhere. What can you do?"

"These people aren't soldiers," said Remo. "They're racists."

"No!" said Chiun, shocked. He had heard the word spoken in very disapproving tones by white newscasters many times on television. "Racist?"

Remo nodded grimly. "This place is a racist paradise."

"Racism is despicable. It is a plague among the inferior races, especially sub-Koreans. Why do Americans not stamp out these foul racists?"

"Because these people are Americans too. They claim the same rights as other Americans, and they use those rights to preach hatred against other Americans."

"If they are Americans as you say, then why do they fly the Zingh flag of Germany?" asked Chiun. They had come to the door of the main building.

"They think Nazi Germany had the right idea about some things. Or maybe they just like the losing side. Most of these people also think the fall of the Confederacy was the end of civilization. I don't know, Little Father. None of it makes any sense to me either."

Remo found the double doors locked. Because he wanted to continue his discussion with Chiun, he knocked instead of breaking the lock with his hands.

Chiun asked, "Then why do they not live in Germany?"

"It's hard to explain," said Remo, waiting patiently. "They think they are the only true Americans, and that everyone else is inferior."

"Everyone else?"

"Mostly blacks and Jews and members of other religions they don't like."

"Koreans too? That is hard to believe. I have lately found Americans to be very enlightened people."

"You could ask him," said Remo as the door opened and a square-faced man with a beet-red complexion and brushcut hair glared at them.

"You are both out of uniform," he said. And then, noticing Chiun, he asked Remo, "What's he doing here?"

"We're taking a poll," said Remo. "It's a word-association poll. We'll say a word and you say the first thing that comes into your pointy head. Ready? Start. Chinese."

"Scum."

"See," said Remo. "You try, Little Father."

"Japanese," said Chiun.

"Sneaky."

"Vietnamese."

"Sneakier."

"Actually," said Chiun, "they are more dirty than sneaky, but you are close." Turning to Remo, the Master of Sinanju demanded, "How can you call this intelligent and true American a racist? He got two out of three correct."

"Ask him about Koreans," Remo said.

Chiun addressed the man. "Koreans."

"Worse than Japs. Stupider, too."

Chiun puffed out his cheeks in indignation.

"Racist," he said loudly. "Foul despicable round-eye racist. You are like all stupid whites. Ignorant."

The man suddenly pointed a handgun at the Master of Sinanju's angry face.

"I don't like being called names."

Chiun said to Remo, "He is truly ignorant, isn't he?"

"I don't think he knows who you are. Why don't you tell him?"

"I am the Master of Sinanju," Chiun said proudly. "Currently I am in disguise."

"What's that mean?"

"It means I am a Korean, possibly the most awesome and merciful creature you could ever imagine."

"You make yourself sound perfect." The man sneered, cocking his revolver. "Well, this gun makes me perfect."

"By what reasoning do you claim that?" asked Chiun.

"Because I can shoot off your gook head for what you called me."

"No, all that proves is that a gun, correctly aimed, can kill. Everyone knows that. It has nothing to do with your alleged perfection. It proves nothing."

"Good-bye, gook," said the man, pulling the trigger.

"Good-bye, racist," said Chiun, his open palm batting upward. It struck the muzzle of the pistol a precise quarter-second before the hammer fell, and because exactly a quarter-second after Chiun struck it the pistol was pointed up into the soft underside of the man's jaw, the bullet mushroomed against the man's tongue and the top of his head geysered a spray of blood and confused thoughts.

Remo and Chiun stepped past him.

"Let us find Ferris quickly so that we may be gone from this nest of inferior racists," said Chiun. He was unhappy because Remo had proven that there were Americans who were not as enlightened as Chiun had claimed.

Ilsa Gans ran the videotapes simultaneously on three monitors. The videos covered three angles, one head-high and the others from the ceiling. Each one told the same story, and the story was that the two spies who called themselves Remo and Chiun were invincible.

Ilsa watched them intently. The overhead films showed clearly why the five soldiers had been confused. First, the two men ran faster than the camera could record. Ilsa set the VCR for slow motion, but even then they were just slow-moving blurs. The blurs looked like they were running through a crossfire of water pistols. The bullets were real, though. Ilsa saw the walls behind them collect dusty bullet pocks.

The men were superhuman, both of them. They were more superhuman than Konrad Blutsturz, who Ilsa thought possessed superhuman will and drive. But the Führer's superiority was that of a man painstakingly overcoming great odds. These men seemed to be routinely superhuman, as if it were as normal as walking or breathing.

Ilsa watched the tapes over and over with glowing eyes. The taller one's movements were strangely exciting, like a tiger slinking through the jungle, only this man slinked at high speed. The play of his lean muscles and the flash of his limbs, even from the overhead views, held Ilsa spellbound.

A quick glimpse of his face, handsome, even cruel in a slight way, made her heart skip a beat. It was as if the eyes could see her, even though his eyes were only a videotape image. Those eyes made Ilsa feel like she was prey. She shivered deliciously.

Ilsa forced herself to stop watching. She pulled the tapes and went running to the Fortress Purity auditorium, now being used as the operating amphitheater.

Ilsa burst in breathlessly.

They were wheeling Konrad Blutsturz out on a hospital gurney.

"Oh no," she moaned.

"Ilsa, it is finished," Konrad Blutsturz said, his face a ghastly gray hue.

"But you're not walking. You're not walking. It didn't work?"

The head surgeon interjected himself.

"We won't know for several days. We were able to repair the nebulizer. All the parts are in place, but the surgical openings we made in Herr Führer's stumps must heal first."

"We've got to get out of here before then," Ilsa pleaded.

"Out? Why, Ilsa?" asked the pitiful face of Konrad Blutsturz.

"Those new recruits. They didn't die at the rifle range. They killed our brave Aryan soldiers like they were children. They aren't human. Look at these tapes."

"Bring the tapes to my bedroom."

"Herr Führer," the doctor began, "you must not exert yourself."

"Hush! Ilsa knows danger. Come, Ilsa."

In the bedroom, Konrad Blutsturz was laid on a specially reinforced iron bed. Six hulking soldiers handled him. He was covered by sheets. The sheets draped a complete human form.

It excited Ilsa to think that he was whole at last, but she quickly loaded the first tape and, after Konrad Blutsturz had dismissed the others, they watched it together.

After they had seen all three tapes, Konrad Blutsturz spoke.

"You are right, my Ilsa. They are a great danger. And I am too weak to face them just yet."

"I'll bring the van around."

"No. There still may be a way. Remember my plan to invite the Harold Smiths of America to Fortress Purity? I have just now thought of a way to test the feasibility of that plan and to rid ourselves of all of the people who stand in our way."

"Just tell me what you want me to do."

"Call a meeting in the auditorium immediately. Everyone must attend. Tell them I will make a great announcement. The doctors, too. We do not need them anymore."

"Okay. Are you sure you're up to it? You're supposed to rest."

"My fury will give me strength. Do this, Ilsa."

"Look at this, Little Father," said Remo. He pointed to a painting on the wall. They were in an office they had found. Two guards had attempted to stop them in the corridor but Chiun had taken their guns and, after learning that they knew nothing of Ferris D'Orr, spoke to them very quietly on the evils of racism. He held their hands to keep their attention. Sometimes he squeezed to emphasize key points.

By the time the Master of Sinanju was finished lecturing them, the two guards were on their knees nodding in furious agreement.

Chiun had locked them in the next room, where they were collaborating on a paper extolling the superiority of the Korean people—especially those hailing from the fishing village of Sinanju. Chiun had told them he would collect it on the way out.

On the wall where Remo pointed was a portrait of the old man in the wheelchair they had seen kidnapping Ferris D'Orr in Baltimore.

"Another clue," said Chiun. "Does this mean we are closer to Ferris?"

"Probably," said Remo. Hearing footsteps coming down the hall, he glided to the door. "Someone coming," he said.

"Probably another racist," spat Chiun.

Remo caught the person as he entered. The he was a she.

"Oh!" said Ilsa Gans, struggling in Remo's arms.

When her struggles only caused the arms to tighten around her, she looked into the face of her captor. "Oh!" she said again. There was fear in her voice, but an undertone of pleasure too.

"It's the blond girl from Baltimore," Remo told Chiun. "Where's Ferris?" he asked her.

"Somewhere," Ilsa said. His eyes, close up, were brown and very large. They looked as warm as polished wood. For some reason, that made her tingle.

"I want an answer," Remo warned.

"I'll give you everything you want. Just squeeze me harder."

"Damn," said Remo, suddenly thinking of Mah-Li waiting for him back in Sinanju. "Here, you take her, Little Father," and he sent Ilsa spinning across the room.

Chiun plucked her wrist, bringing her to a skidding stop.

"Oohh, you're some kind of icky Oriental," Ilsa cried, looking at the Master of Sinanju.

Chiun released her wrist disdainfully.

"And you are some kind of icky racist," he said. "I am losing my faith in American enlightenment, Remo."

Remo pushed Ilsa into a leather chair and towered over her.

"Answers," he said, pointing to the wall portrait. "Who's he?"

"Herr Führer Blutsturz. He is a great man."

"That's open to discussion. He's in charge here?"

"Until you got here," Ilsa said meltingly. She was staring at Remo's belt buckle hungrily. "There's something I must tell you. It's very important."

"Shoot," Remo said.

"I'm a virgin. I've been saving myself for someone else, but you can have me if you want."

Remo groaned inwardly. Women always reacted like this. It was some kind of animal magnetism generated by Sinanju rhythms. It had been a long time since he had enjoyed the effect he had on women. Usually it was a bother turning on the airline stewardesses or secretaries he happened to encounter. Sometimes Remo could use it to his advantage. A little Sinanju sexual stimulation could be a quick interrogation technique. But that was in the past, before Mah-Li.

"I want some answers," Remo said.

"Not until I get what I want."

Remo grabbed Ilsa by an earlobe. He squeezed. Ilsa screeched. Her eyes watered.

"Get your mind onto business. Why did you and this Führer what's-his-name—Bloodsucker—kidnap Ferris D'Orr?"

"Blutsturz," Ilsa moaned. "We needed his nebulizer."

"For what?"

"To make Herr Führer walk. He has been in a wheelchair since the war. The creepy Jews did it."

"He's lucky they didn't do worse," said Remo, noticing Ilsa's Nazi armband.

"We needed the nebulizer to rebuild him in titanium. It was important. We tried to kill the Smiths one by one, but there were too many."

"What Smiths? You were talking about the Jews."

"Harold Smith is the leader of the global Jewish conspiracy."

"Harold Smith?" asked Remo.

"He was the evil one who destroyed Herr Führer's magnificent Aryan physique. During the war. We've been trying to locate him for years."

Chiun sidled up to Remo and whispered, "Would that Smith be our Smith?"

Remo shook his head doubtfully. "There are zillions of Smiths."

"That is too many," said Chiun.

"Where's Ferris?" Remo asked Ilsa.

"I don't know." Ilsa pouted. "Dead somewhere."

"Aeeiie!" wailed the Master of Sinanju. "Did you hear that, Remo? Ferris is dead. O woe! O misery! We are lost."

"I didn't know you liked the guy that much," Remo said.

"Like," spat Chiun. "I despise that wretch. First for allowing himself to be captured and second for not defending his life with his last breath. Did he not know that by dying he would disgrace me in the eyes of my emperor? Had he no consideration? How will I break this to Smith? O calamity!"

"Smith?" said Ilsa.

"A different Smith," said Remo. "Our Smith doesn't head any conspiracies, Jewish or otherwise. Next question. The nebulizer?"

Ilsa Gans hesitated before answering. It was growing clear that the sexual creature who called himself Remo was not going to take her. Not now, not ever. She took a deep breath and gained control of her passion. She would save it for the man she had always been saving it for—Konrad Blutsturz.

"All your questions will be answered at the meeting," she said.

"What meeting?"

"The great meeting. Herr Führer is going to make an announcement of his future plans. I came here to tell everyone," she added, indicating with her head a public-address microphone sitting on the desk.

Remo hesitated.

"Everyone will be there," said Ilsa. "You can ask us all your questions then."

Remo turned to Chiun. "What do you think, Little Father?"

"If we get all the racists together in one place," Chiun said bitterly, "maybe the room will catch fire and there will be fewer racists in the world. Do not ask me, I am inconsolable over the loss of the metallurgist."

"Okay," Remo told Ilsa. "Make your announcement, but no tricks."

"No tricks," said Ilsa, picking up the heavy microphone and flicking the switch that would send her voice out through the broadcast speakers installed in every building in Fortress Purity. "I could not possibly trick superior beings like yourselves."

"This one at least is educable," Chiun sniffed.

25

Konrad Blutsturz lay staring at the ceiling. He imagined himself back in Argentina, in the green room, in the 1950's. Only by reliving the horror of those days could he steel himself for what he was about to do, the great test of his will.

The doctors had told him he must have a week's rest. The new limbs were attached through surgical implants and were detachable, replaceable, but the incisions made for the implants that were fitted into the shattered bones of his stumps required time to heal. Unnecessary movement was restricted, even forbidden.

And so Konrad Blutsturz lay on his bed, as helpless as in the days when he was a one-limbed abortion, flopping and twisting in his nightmares.

Except now he was not limited by the lack of limbs, but by the weight of his new limbs. His shining blue titanium limbs.

It was dangerous, but again, Konrad Blutsturz had no choice.

And so he willed his left arm to move.

It lifted, heavily. Good. He pushed himself to a sitting position using both arms, the strong good one and the stronger blue one. The bed creaked in agony.

He whipped the sheet off his body. The legs twitched like an insect's mandibles. They gleamed like locust armor.

With an effort that sent pain searing along his nerves, Konrad Blutsturz stood up. It felt strange, giddy, to stand so tall after so long. For nearly forty years he had looked at the world from the eye level of a small child. Now he stood as tall as any man. Any erect man.

In the corner stood the motorized wheelchair which had meant freedom and mobility to him. But it belonged to the past. He would crush it, but he needed its use one final time.

Konrad Blutsturz walked to the wheelchair. His legs, powered by battery packs implanted in the limbs themselves, moved with the soundless animation of a marionette.

The first step was easy. The second easier. The motion was smooth. Mere will made each step happen, like real legs. Microcomputers controlled the striding gait. His unfeeling legs carried him with a rolling motion, as if he were on a ship.

With his strong titanium left arm, Konrad Blutsturz lifted the heavy wheelchair.

He walked out of the room, straightening his torso to control the imbalance. But even the weight of the wheelchair did not deter him. He noticed his walk was becoming smoother as the titanium parts grew used to their task. He grinned.

Passing a hall mirror, he saw himself completely for the first time. But instead of pride, he felt anger. He saw a gleaming monster. He cursed the name of Harold Smith under his breath and strode on.

The Fortress Purity auditorium was deserted. The rows of collapsible chairs had been cleared for the operation, but now even the operating table was gone. There was just the platform stage and a dark stain where Ferris D'Orr had had the life squeezed out of his neck.

Konrad Blutsturz did not think of Ferris D'Orr. Ferris D'Orr belonged to the past. Konrad Blutsturz belonged to the future.

The wooden access ramp cracked under his massive weight as he mounted the stage and set the wheelchair facing where the audience would stand. He was nude, but not as nude as he had been. Something pink and rubbery dangled from the hairlessness of his crotch. But he did not think of that now either as he ripped the great red Nazi banner from the back wall. He thought only of the menace of the two men who had followed him to Fortress Purity.

Konrad Blutsturz wrapped himself up in the flag he no longer believed in and settled into the wheelchair. It squealed under his weight, the spoked wheels bending into useless ovals. He arranged the red flag until his entire body was shrouded like a mummy on an ancient throne.

He waited. Soon Ilsa's announcement would come. Soon the White Aryan League of America and Alabama would be assembled before him. And soon they would all fall like grass before a mower.

They filed into the auditorium slowly at first, then in a hurried rush. He regarded them with black eyes that were so glazed with pain they barely saw. But soon the pain would be a thing of the past. Soon he would have his two greatest desires, Ilsa's supple body and Harold Smith's limp corpse.

The assembled Aryan League stood before him, muttering under their breath. They had heard that their Führer was to undergo a miraculous operation. But there he was, gray-faced and sickly, wrapped in a red blanket, in his wheelchair. What had happened?

Konrad Blutsturz' eyes came to life when Ilsa stepped into the standing-room-only crowd. With her were the two dangers to his life, the man called Remo and the other one, the Oriental. They saw him, and started through the crowd toward him. But the crowd was thick.

He saw Ilsa lock the great double doors behind them. Good. She understood. He had already locked the side door. Now there was no exit from the windowless room. No exit for any of them.

This is how it was to be with the Harold Smiths, thought Konrad Blutsturz. He would invite them all to this room with some ruse. A giveaway or sweepstakes lure. Every Harold Smith who could be the Harold Smith. And after the doors were locked . . .

The two men were halfway through the crowd already. They seemed to find the paths of least resistance in the mass which pressed closer to the stage in anticipation.

Konrad Blutsturz raised his voice.

"I have summoned you, men and women of the White Aryan League of America and Alabama, because a grave danger threatens our purity. Infiltrators, enemies of the White Aryan League."

The crowd tensed. They looked at one another fearfully. They remembered what had happened the last time their Führer had said such words. One of them had died.

"These enemies are among us now," said Konrad Blutsturz. "They are in this room. One of them is white, the other is not."

"I think he means us, Remo," said Chiun, in the crowd.

All heads turned toward the squeaky sound of Chiun's voice.

"Now you did it, Little Father," said Remo.

"You see them," called Konrad Blutsturz. "Now deal with them!"

The crowd exploded. Remo and Chiun were inside a boiling tangle of humanity that was clawing, squeezing, groping for them.

Chiun whirled in place like a miniature dervish, and the people in his immediate vicinity flew away from him like gravel off a flywheel.

Remo took the opposite tactic. He grabbed the reaching hands and pulled them toward him. Bodies followed Remo's yanking motions, colliding into other bodies.

Konrad Blutsturz watched in amazement touched with admiration. Two men against hundreds. Two unarmed men against a disciplined mob. And not only did they remain untouched, but they continued to advance on the stage, effortlessly, inexorably.

It was at that moment, unnoticed by the furious mob, that Konrad Blutsturz rose from the crushed wheelchair to his full height.

Towering on the stage, he sucked in a triumphant breath. He could smell the sweat of humans in conflict, see their frenzy, almost taste their bodies. Even in this elemental state, they were but masses of organs and tissue and bone. He was all that and more. He was titanium and servo motors and over six feet tall. And as he willed it, his artificial knee joints whirred, and like a telescope stretching out, he rose from six feet to six and a half and then to a figure of flesh and blue metal that stood over eight feet tall.

He held out his hard left arm, and at a thought, there was a loud snick and a shining blade of metal clicked out from his forearm and into place.

At a signal, Ilsa switched off the lights.

In that first hush of darkness, Konrad Blutsturz stepped off the stage like a silent juggernaut.

The darkness meant little to Remo and Chiun. Actually, it helped. Their eyes, trained in Sinanju, knew how to turn the dimness into clarity. But the eyes of their opponents saw only blackness. People milled about them in confusion.

That made it easier to pick them off. A chop here, a pressure on the neck nerves there. Every hand that reached for them was turned into a handle to use against the attacker.

Grunts and groans and panicky screams started to fill the room.

Remo's ears picked out a different kind of sound in the noisy confusion, a heavy tread, not human, not flesh. Remo looked toward the stage. He saw the dim outlines of a wheelchair, but it was empty.

Then there was a loud, thunking sound, simple, harsh, final, like an ax digging into a tree trunk. Into a spongy tree trunk.

Someone screamed shrilly. "My arm! My arm!"

The tart scent of blood floated to Remo's nostrils.

"Chiun! There's something loose in this room," Remo warned.

"Yes," said Chiun, kicking the legs out from under two assailants. "I am!"

"No, something different."

The hazy shadows of milling bodies blocked Remo's vision. He had a brief glimpse of an arm rising and falling, and at the end of that arm there was a swordlike blade.

Every time the arm fell, someone screamed and another body thudded to the floor.

The screaming turned into wholesale panic.

Remo moved, sighting on the flashing blade.

"Chiun, get these people out of here! They're being massacred."

"I am massacring them," said Chiun, knocking two heads together.

"Chiun! Do it!" yelled Remo. He moved toward the electrical field he sensed just ahead.

The thing towered over Remo, its movements strange. He circled behind the man or thing or whatever it was.

Remo had learned one thing years ago, a great truth that Chiun had impressed upon him. When facing an unknown threat, never attack first. Observe. Understand. Only when an enemy revealed his weakness to you was it safe to go on the offensive.

Remo did not know what he faced in the blackness of the auditorium. His feet grazed fallen bodies, dismembered limbs. The floor was slick with blood, and the scent of it stung his nostrils with the sickness of wasted life. The thing was too tall for a man, yet it had a manlike heartbeat. Lungs, tired, laboring, respirated with difficulty.

At the same time, the thing carried an electrical field, low but powerful. Remo poised for a first feint.

Suddenly light spilled through the opened double doors. Chiun had broken them down.

Remo saw the thing clearly then. It was Konrad Blutsturz, no longer a withered old husk in a wheelchair, but a thing half-man and half-machine, his face terrible with rage and wrinkles.

"Ilsa," Konrad Blutsturz shouted. "Do not let them escape! Any of them."

"Nobody's escaping," said Remo. "Especially you."

Konrad Blutsturz turned at the sound of Remo's voice, his face contorting wordlessly.

He raised his titanium arm. It descended toward Remo, the curved blade snapping out from the forearm.

Remo dodged the blade easily. It retracted, ready to slice again.

Remo slipped behind him. The blade mechanism appeared to be a spring-loaded sickle that retracted into the artificial forearm like a gigantic switchblade.

Remo poked with a steel-hard finger and broke the

spring. The blade dropped, swinging uselessly on its hinge.

"I'd take that back," Remo said lightly. "It's defective."

"I will not be stopped now. Not by you."

"How about by me?" Chiun said.

"By neither of you," said Konrad Blutsturz, his face wild and twisted.

"Be careful, Little Father," warned Remo.

"What is it?" asked Chiun in Korean as they circled Blutsturz warily.

"Bloodsucker. They've turned him into some kind of robot," said Remo.

"I can see that," snapped Chiun. "What I wish to know is what are its capabilities."

"Let's find out," said Remo.

"Let's wait," said Chiun.

"He killed Ferris. We owe him for that." Remo moved in.

Blutsturz' titanium hand clicked into a fist. He sent it sweeping before him, back and forth, back and forth, like a mace.

Remo ducked under his weaving arm and let go with an exploring kick.

Blutsturz' leg gave with the blow. The eight-foot figure wobbled on one leg until the off-balance limb found its footing.

"It is strong," said Chiun. "And nimble for a machine."

"It's only metal."

"Titanium," said Chiun worriedly. He slashed at the metal hand with his fingernails, which scored the metal, but the arm did not paralyze with pain, the way flesh would.

"It does not feel pain," said Chiun.

Konrad Blutsturz lunged for the Master of Sinanju. Chiun spun in a double-reverse movement that took him clear of the lumbering man-machine. He swept out an arm and took Remo by one wrist.

"Hey!" said Remo.

"Come," said Chiun. "We will fight this one another time. His techniques are unfamiliar."

"Nothing doing," said Remo, slipping loose.

Konrad Blutsturz bore down on him. Remo met him

halfway. This time Remo went for the flesh-and-blood arm. He sent a two-fingered nerve thrust to the elbow joint.

"Arrh!" howled Konrad Blutsturz. He felt the shuddering bone-shock of Remo's blow. He clutched his elbow with his other hand, not thinking. His titanium fingers grabbed too hard and he screamed again at the pain he inflicted on himself.

"Ilsa!" he called in his anguish.

Remo got behind the shuddering form. He kicked at the back of the knee joint or where the knee joint should be. Konrad Blutsturz went down on one metal knee. But almost as rapidly, he rose to his full height again.

"Come, Remo," said Chiun nervously.

And when Remo did not come, the Master of Sinanju intervened.

Chiun came up behind his pupil, while Remo's full concentration was on the awkward man-machine. While Remo was distracted, while Remo could not defend himself.

Chiun, his face warped with the pain of what he was about to do, struck Remo at the back of the neck—a short, clean chopping blow.

Remo tottered, and Chiun snapped him up, taking him under one leg and by the neck. Carrying his fallen pupil across his shoulders, the Master of Sinanju bounded for the doors.

On the threshold, he stopped and called a challenge to the weaving thing that was Konrad Blutsturz.

"You win for now, inhuman creature," he said, "but we will meet again. The Master of Sinanju promises it."

Konrad Blutsturz barely heard the taunting challenge. The pain in his stumps was now too great to endure. His legs refused to move. His good arm hung limp at his side. The other one raised and lowered uncontrollably, like a child having a tantrum.

"Ilsa!" he called.

Ilsa Gans sent the van careening through the night, away from the hell that had been Fortress Purity. Fear rode her soft features. She bit her lower lip. It bled.

In the van's dark interior, lying on the floor, was the thing that was Konrad Blutsturz. He slept now. But it had taken all her strength to get him into the van when the carnage was over.

She had been forced out of the auditorium when the doors burst open. The crowd had nearly trampled her. She had stumped to the ordnance room and had gotten a machine pistol.

She shot her way back into the auditorium, shot without discrimination, without mercy. All that mattered was reaching the side of Konrad Blutsturz.

When she found him, he was sinking to the floor. There was no sign of the two enemies, Remo and Chiun. They weren't among the butchered bodies that lay everywhere in macabre profusion. But they no longer mattered. Getting her Führer to safety did.

She talked Konrad Blutsturz to his feet, because he was too heavy to lug. But he could not stand. He was barely conscious. There had been only one thing to do. She dismantled the limbs of which he had been so proud. She had uncoupled them from the titanium knobs implanted in each stump.

And carrying him in her arms, Ilsa had deposited him in the back of the van, on the floor, because there was no time to make him comfortable.

She would never have gone back for the blue arm and the insectlike legs, but in his delirium, Konrad Blutsturz had insisted. Just as he had insisted she bring the nebulizer.

Now she was speeding into the night. She did not know where she was going. She did not care where. All she wanted was to escape.

26

Dr. Harold W. Smith was thinking of going home. He believed the immediate danger to himself was past, perhaps even averted. For over a week now no one named Harold Smith had been murdered or reported missing anywhere in the continental United States.

Smith sat at his administrator's desk at Folcroft Sanitarium. The killer should have found him by now, but he had not. There'd been no disturbances at Folcroft since Remo's sudden appearance. Smith had explained away Remo's attack to his guard staff as a former patient who had tried to readmit himself the hard way. The guards—none of whom was seriously injured—had accepted Smith's explanation that the patient had been turned over to the local police, and the matter was resolved.

Smith knew that if he were to be attacked, it would happen at his listed address—Folcroft. But to ensure his wife's safety, he was having his house watched. Two FBI agents were staked out at Smith's house to watch for what Smith's anonymous directive called "suspected terrorist activities." If anything happened there, his wife would be protected.

Smith wondered if it was now safe to call off those agents and return to a normal life. He wasn't sure. The killer had struck in a logical state-by-state itinerary. Folcroft should have been next. Perhaps it still was, Smith thought. Perhaps the killer didn't dare try to penetrate the security of Folcroft. Perhaps he was waiting for Smith to leave the grounds before striking. Could he have been arrested or intercepted?

Finally Smith decided he would stay put, at least for another day.

The secure phone rang. The CURE phone that Remo reported through.

Smith picked it up.

"Yes?"

"Smitty?" It was Remo's voice. He sounded upset. "Bad news."

"What?"

"Ferris is dead. We were too late."

"The nebulizer?"

"Gone."

"Find it." Smith's voice was harsh. He didn't want to report failure to the President.

"Hey, I'm just making a courtesy call here," Remo said. "I don't work for you."

"I'm sorry," said Smith, thinking that if he upset Remo he would have to deal directly with Chiun. Smith preferred to deal with Remo. "Please tell me what happened down there."

"That's better," Remo said, mollified. He liked Smith better when he was polite. "We're at Fortress Purity. This place is a cesspool. Run by this old Nazi, Konrad something. I can't pronounce it. It's German."

"Go on," Smith said. Remo never could handle details.

"This old fart is some kind of cripple. One arm, no legs. But he's the guy who kidnapped Ferris. You'll never guess why."

"You're right," said Smith, who was picked to head CURE because he had no imagination. "I won't. Tell me, please."

"He needed the nebulizer to rebuild himself. You heard me right. When we caught up with him, he had artificial legs and an arm rigged with a meat cleaver. He's some kind of bionic half-man, half-machine."

"Cyborg."

"Huh?"

"The technical term for what you just described is a cyborg, a human being reconstituted with artificial parts."

"If you say so," Remo said. "He was supposed to be the leader of this freaking place, but when we caught up to him, he was slaughtering every one of these neo-Nazis. I can't figure why."

"I ran a background check on the White Aryan

League," said Smith. "It was founded by a Boyce Barlow. A few days ago his body, and the bodies of his two cousins, were discovered in a Maryland dump. Obviously this Konrad person got them out of the way."

"But why? To take over? He ended up killing almost everyone."

"I can't explain that part. Where is this person now?"

"Got away."

"How?"

"I was zeroing in on him when Chiun jumped me. He was afraid I'd get hurt. You know how he is when he has to deal with something outside of his experience. If it's not in the Sinanju histories, you don't mess with it. Run now, fight later."

"Where is Chiun now?"

"Teaching what's left of the survivors why Koreans are the true master race. Look out, Smitty. When he's done, the first Korean-supremacy group in world history will set up in Alabama."

"Remo, it's very important that we recover the nebulizer."

"To you and me both. I could have strangled Chiun when I woke up from that nerve chop. The sooner I end this thing, the sooner Chiun and I can have it out about going back to Sinanju."

"Have you any leads?"

"When Chiun is finished, I'm going to work these people over myself. I'll come up with something."

"Keep me informed."

"Say the magic word," Remo said airily.

"Please."

"Thank you." And Remo hung up.

Smith's thoughts were more troubled than ever. The death of Ferris D'Orr would not be easy to explain to the President, but if the nebulizer were recovered, it would salvage the situation.

Unfortunately, Smith could not report the nebulizer's recovery just yet. Another man in his position might have been tempted to wait a day or two to report in the hopes of giving his superior more positive news. Not Smith. Even if it meant his removal from CURE—a possibility, given the failure to protect Ferris D'Orr—Smith would not shirk his immediate duty.

Without hesitation, he picked up the red phone.

Almost as rapidly, he replaced it.

The CURE computer terminal had beeped twice, a signal of urgent incoming data.

Smith turned to the console, all thought of the President evaporating from his mind.

The computer told of a murder in the sleepy town of Mount Olive in North Carolina. A man named Harold Q. Smith, age sixty-two, had been murdered. He was found on the stoop of his home, his head lopped off as if by a guillotine. Police were investigating. The man had no known enemies, and there were no obvious suspects.

Smith punched up his tactical map of the United States and added the name of Harold Q. Smith to the list of Smith victims, now numbering fourteen. He added the place of death, and the number fourteen appeared within the borders of North Carolina, corresponding to the locale of Mount Olive.

Smith hit a key and a green line zipped between the locale of the last Harold Smith killing, Oakham, Massachusetts, and Mount Olive. The line was long, straight, and paralleled the east coast. It went through lower New England and New York State, right past Long Island and Rye, New York.

The killer had bypassed him. Completely.

Smith wondered if he had made a mistake in calculating the killer's methods. Perhaps he was not traveling by road, as Smith had surmised. Possibly he was not selecting his targets by telephone listings either.

It should have been a relief. It was not.

It injected a maddening note of randomness to what Harold Smith had, with his rational mind, perceived as a logical system. If the killer was deviating into another pattern, Smith, in the long run, remained the probable target.

The agony of waiting could be prolonged indefinitely.

Smith groaned inwardly, and settling himself, prepared to attack this new factor with all his rational skill.

Harold Q. Smith had heard a knock at his front door.

He was watching a football game, in which his team was leading by three points in the fourth quarter. He was not happy at being interrupted, and so went to the door grumbling.

The girl standing on the porch was young and very pretty. Smith had never seen her before, and because Mount Olive was a college town, he automatically assumed she was a student. Maybe she was here to sell him a magazine. Sometimes the students did that for spending money.

The girl smiled sweetly, and Smith's bad mood went away. She had that kind of smile.

"Hi! Are you Harold Q. Smith?"

"That's right, young lady."

"I have a friend of yours in my van."

"Friend?"

"Yes, he'd like to speak with you."

"Well," said Harold Q. Smith slowly, thinking of his football game, "tell him to come in."

"Oh, he can't," Ilsa said sadly. "He can't walk, poor thing."

"Oh," said Harold Q. Smith. "I suppose I have to go to him."

"Would you?"

Smith would, and did.

The blond girl hauled open the side door. Harold Q. Smith stuck his head in before stepping up into the van and saw the most hideous face he had ever seen. Ever.

The face belonged to a body covered to the neck in blankets. An old man. Very old, with tiny ears and bright black eyes. His body didn't seem to make a normal outline under the rough cloth.

"Smith!" the man hissed.

"Do I know you?"

Then Smith felt the gun in his back. He did not have to turn around to know it was a gun. In fact, he didn't think it would be a good idea to turn around at all.

"Inside," the blond girl said, her voice no longer sounding of honey and sunshine.

Smith stepped up. He had to bend over to stand in the cramped interior. It was okay, though, because it made the fall when the girl clubbed him over the head that much shorter.

"I have waited for this moment, Harold Q. Smith," Konrad Blutsturz intoned. "Forty years, I have waited."

"I think he's out."

"Eh?"

"He can't hear you," said Ilsa. "I guess I knocked him out. Sorry."

"Bah!" spat Konrad Blutsturz. "It does not matter. He is not the right Smith and I am too weary to kill him. Drag him back to his porch and shoot him there."

"Can I cut his head off instead?" Ilsa asked, eyeing the curved blade from Blutsturz' blue left arm.

"They gush when their heads are cut off," Blutsturz warned.

"I'll stand clear," Ilsa promised.

"Please yourself," he said, closing his eyes. "Just as long as he is dead."

"Oh, goody," said Ilsa, grabbing Harold Q. Smith by the heels.

Ilsa Gans replaced the pay phone in the gas station that, even in winter, smelled of a mix of sweet magnolia blossoms and gas fumes.

She scooped up the pile of dimes she had used to make her calls. She had started out with forty dollars in change. Now there was only sixty cents. But she had found what she wanted. She couldn't wait to tell her Führer.

She trotted back to the waiting van and climbed behind the wheel.

"I found the perfect place," she called back.

In the dim rear of the van, lying on a fold-down cot, lay Konrad Blutsturz.

"Where?" he croaked.

"Folcroft Sanitarium. It's in New York. It took me a zillion calls to find a place, but this one is perfect. The admitting person assured me it's one of the best in the country. They'll accept you right away, and best of all, they'll let me stay with you as your personal nurse. Some of the others would have taken you, but not me. I knew you didn't want us separated."

"Good, Ilsa," groaned Konrad Blutsturz. His stumps ached, they ached to the bone. With his real hand he pulled the blankets tighter. They were coarse. Army blankets. They itched, and somehow the itch was more maddening than the pain.

"And you'll never guess what," Ilsa went on in the cheery voice she used when his spirits were low. "The man in charge of Folcroft, his name is Smith. Harold Smith. Isn't that wild?"

"Smith," said Konrad Blutsturz. And his eyes blazed.

27

Remo Williams left the headquarters office of the White Aryan League of America and Alabama and rejoined Chiun in the adjoining conference room.

"What did Emperor Smith say?" the Master of Sinanju asked. Chiun stood before the assembled survivors of the White Aryan League, who squatted on the floor, their hands clasped behind their heads like POW's in a war movie.

"He's not happy, but if we bring back the nebulizer right away, I don't think he'll fire you."

Chiun's facial hair trembled.

"Fire?" he quavered. "Smith said I might be fired? No Master of Sinanju has ever been fired. Never."

"He didn't say fire, exactly," Remo admitted, "but he's very upset."

"Then we will recover this device," said Chiun firmly.

"How?"

Chiun yanked one of the seated men to his feet. The man came up like a springing jack-in-the-box.

"This one will tell us," Chiun said.

Remo looked at the man. He was frightened, but there was a streak of surly arrogance in his meaty, middle-aged face. His thick eyebrows and brush mustache were the same whisk-broom color.

"What's your name, buddy?" Remo demanded.

The man squared his shoulders. "Dr. Manfred Beflecken."

"You say that like it means something."

"It does. I am one of the finest surgeons in the world."

"He is the one who created that vile thing," said Chiun.

"Did you?"

"I had that privilege. Bionics are my specialty."

"You created a monster," Remo said.

"No," said Dr. Manfred Beflecken. "Konrad Blutsturz was already a monster. The war made him so. I made him a better monster."

"Insane," said Chiun. "This physician is insane. And he is a racist, possibly the worst one of all. I tried your word game on him, Remo. He hates everyone. Even these other racists. He thinks Germans are the master race. Germans! The only thing Germans were ever good for was soldiering—and when was the last time they won a war?"

"These others are nothing," said Dr. Beflecken. "Mere tools to achieve Herr Führer's ends."

"The only end I care about is ending that thing's life," Remo said grimly. "Where can I find him?"

The doctor shrugged. "Who can say?"

"You can, and you will," said Remo, grabbing the man by the shoulder. Remo dug his thumb into Dr. Beflecken's beefy shoulder muscles until he felt the hard ball of the man's shoulder joint. Dr. Beflecken's face flushed. He struggled, but Remo's hand squeezed the fight out of him.

"What you did to Blutsturz I can undo. To him. To you. To anyone," Remo warned. "Last chance."

"I am a loyal German of the Reich," said Dr. Beflecken.

Remo pressed. The man's shoulder separated with an audible pop.

Tears squeezed from Dr. Beflecken's eyes. His right arm dropped lower than his left by a noticeable inch.

Remo switched shoulders.

"There is a cabin," Dr. Beflecken gasped as he felt Remo's thumb seek his other shoulder joint. His knees felt like tires leaking air. "In the Florida Everglades. Near a place called Flamingo. Herr Führer lived there before coming to Fortress Purity. He may go there."

"Hear that, Little Father?"

"No," said the Master of Sinanju. "I hear only the voice of my ancestors, accusing me of becoming the first Master of Sinanju to be laid off like a common ditchdigger."

"This wouldn't have happened if you hadn't stopped me. I could have taken Bloodsucker or whatever his name is."

"And you wouldn't have been foolish enough to believe you could take him if your lust to return to Sinanju had not clouded your thinking. How many times have I told you, never assume that just because familiar things fall before your skill, that it will be so with unfamiliar things. Your arrogance could have gotten you killed. And then where would my village be?"

"In Korea, where it's always been," said Remo. "And where I wish I was right now."

"You would abandon me in America, Remo? Alone, the only perfect person in a land of fat racists."

"No, Little Father, I would take you back to Sinanju. With me. Where we both belong."

Chiun's parchment visage softened. He turned away so that his pupil could not see his face.

"We will discuss it later," he said. "After we recover the nebulizer and ensure my continued employment."

"Fine. Let's go."

"What about these vermin?" said Chiun, waving a hand at the cowering members of the White Aryan League of America and Alabama. "Should we not dispose of them? Perhaps Emperor Smith would appreciate a few heads to set upon the gates of Fortress Folcroft. Heads are wonderful for warding off enemies. I see some good ones here."

"We don't have time."

The Master of Sinanju shrugged, and followed Remo out the door.

"What about me?" asked Dr. Beflecken, clutching his useless dangling arm.

"Oh, right," said Remo, stepping back into the room. "You rebuilt Bloodsucker, didn't you?"

"Blutsturz. Yes."

"And you could do it again? With someone else?"

"I am very skilled."

"Good-bye," said Remo, driving two fingers into the man's eyes. Dr. Manfred Beflecken collapsed into a pile of dead flesh.

"You were right, Little Father," said Remo. "It's a handy stroke."

"Remind me to kill you later," Chiun said to the surviving members of the White Aryan League in parting. Moe Stooge had used it often in similar circumstances, and the Master of Sinanju was certain that the great entertainer would not mind his using it.

Dr. Harold Smith removed the special briefcase from his office locker. He opened it and checked the mini-computer and telephone hookup that would link him to the CURE computers during his planned trip to North Carolina.

Before he closed the briefcase, he slipped his old automatic into a special recess that would enable him to get it past airport security.

On his way out of the office, he spoke to his secretary.

"I will be away for at least a day, Mrs. Mikulka," Smith told her. "I'm sure you'll be able to handle matters until my return."

"Of course, Dr. Smith," said Eileen Mikulka, who prided herself on the fact that she could easily run Folcroft's day-to-day operations while her boss was out of town.

"I will be in touch."

"Oh, Dr. Smith?"

Smith turned. "Yes?"

"They're admitting that new patient now. The one who survived a botched surgical procedure. I thought you might like to welcome him, as usual."

"Thank you for telling me," said Dr. Smith. "What is his name?"

Mrs. Mikulka consulted a desk log. "A Mr. Conrad."

"Fine, I will do that."

Smith took the elevator to the main lobby, where he saw the new patient being wheeled through the big glass doors by two burly attendants. A young blond girl in a white nurse's uniform hovered over the man on the gurney, concern pricking her soft features.

Smith strode toward them.

"Hi! I'm Ilsa," the blond nurse said. She had the

chipper personality of a health-care worker fresh to the field.

"Welcome to Folcroft Sanitarium," Smith said, briefly shaking her hand. "I'm chief administrator of this facility."

"Oh! Dr. Smith."

"That's right."

"I've heard of you," Ilsa said brightly. "Allow me to present Mr. Conrad."

The man on the gurney stared up with glazed black eyes, his face as dry and bloodless as if it were carved from shell. The dry lips were drawn back over brownish gums in a deathlike rictus.

Smith offered a tentative hand, but quickly shoved it into a pocket when he realized the man had no legs. The covering sheet lay flat where the man's legs should have been. Smith couldn't be certain the man wasn't also missing his arms. Better not to find out the uncomfortable way.

Ilsa bent over the patient. "This is Dr. Smith. I told you about him. Dr. Harold Smith."

Suddenly the black eyes brightened with life.

"Smith," he hissed.

Dr. Smith recoiled at the violence with which the dry husk of a man spoke his name. The old head trembled, lifting off the pillow. One arm, strong, muscular, but horribly scarred, flailed out from under the sheet. The patient's gnarled hand clawed the air. It seemed to claw at him.

"Calm down," soothed Ilsa. "It's all right. I'm here."

"Smith," the man hissed again. "Smith!"

"He sometimes gets this way," Ilsa told Smith as she gently forced Konrad Blutsturz' agitated head back onto the fluffy pillow.

"Er, yes," said Dr. Smith. "Let me assure you he'll get the best of care at Folcroft."

Dr. Harold Smith hurriedly escaped out the door, even as the poor patient kept repeating his name over and over again. Smith shuddered, even though he had seen worse cases come through the Folcroft gates. Patients like Mr. Conrad were often bitterly mad at the world. Even so, the utter venom that seemed to coat the way he spoke Smith's name was disturbing. It was almost as if the man knew him. And hated him.

But that, of course, was impossible, thought Harold W. Smith. He had never seen Mr. Conrad before.

Smith drove off the Folcroft grounds wondering what terrible tragedy had reduced the man to his present pitiful state.

Mrs. Harold W. Smith stood before the floor-length mirror in the bedroom of her modest Tudor-style home, examining herself critically.

"Frumpy," she decided aloud.

The other two dresses made her look the same. She had just purchased them, and while they had seemed to flatter her full figure in the store dressing-room mirrors with the perky salesgirl insisting they all made her look "fashionable," in the privacy of her home she saw herself as she had always been—a frump.

There was no help for it. Even as a teenager, she had possessed only a certain dowdy charm. Harold had married her anyway. And as the years passed by, blurring the modeling of her face, etching motherly wrinkles about her eyes, and filling out a body that, even at twenty-five, belonged to a middle-aged woman, Harold Smith had continued to love her.

True, Harold had peculiar attitudes about matrimonial love. He had never surprised her with perfume or flowers or new clothes, even in the early years of their life together—because he considered any purchase that didn't come with a five-year, fully refundable guarantee frivolous. The most romantic gift Harold Smith had ever given her was in 1974, when he had purchased a riding lawn mower for her use. The neighborhood boy had raised his rates ten cents an hour and, because Harold's hours were impossible and there was no other boy to do the work, Harold Smith had splurged on the tractor mower because he didn't want her to tire herself with the chore.

Mrs. Smith had accepted it all, down through the years. She told herself that when the time came for Harold to retire, she would finally have him all to herself. But age sixty-five came and went for Harold W. Smith, and there was no talk of retiring from Folcroft.

"I'm too important," he had said the one time she had broached the subject. The years had worn down his slight frame, and she had been worried about him. "Folcroft couldn't get along without me."

It was after that brief conversation that Mrs. Smith had begun to suspect that her husband did not run a health sanitarium. Not really. Certainly he ran it, but even more certainly his job at Folcroft was a blind for something less mundane. Harold's intelligence background suggested it. That and the fact that he seemed to age faster after his early retirement from the CIA than before it.

Mrs. Smith clicked into the next bedroom, unsteady on her new high heels. She was not used to high heels, had never worn them. But they were back in style and maybe they would make her seem taller, her legs slimmer, and her carriage appear less . . . frumpy.

Vickie's bedroom was the same as when she had left it to go off on her own. It was hard to believe that her only daughter was now a grown woman. Where had the years gone?

On the vanity Vickie's cosmetics sat where they always sat, waiting for the holiday visits, as she always explained it to Harold whenever he suggested converting the bedroom into a den. In truth, she had kept the room as a shrine to the young girl she thought had grown up much too fast.

Sitting at the vanity, Mrs. Smith went through the trays of cosmetics. She never used makeup. Harold had always disapproved of it. She sometimes wondered if he really objected to makeup or to the high prices for the stuff. Thinking back to the lawn mower, she decided it was the cost.

She gave up on using the makeup and applied just a touch of perfume behind each ear. That would get his attention.

Satisfied, Mrs. Smith called a taxi.

During the ride, she worried about what Harold would say to her when she showed up at the gate of Folcroft Sanitarium. Would he be annoyed that she had come unannounced? In the more than twenty years Harold had worked at Folcroft, Mrs. Smith had never visited. And so it had come as a pleasant surprise when he had suddenly invited her to see his office and meet his secretary.

That had been a week ago. In that week, she had not seen her husband. In that week, he had regressed from the new, attentive Harold Smith to the withdrawn machinelike Harold Smith of too many years of dull marriage. Each day, his voice seemed edgier, more harried. Each day, she could feel him slipping away from her.

Today she was going to stop that erosion—even if she had to pull him away from his office by force.

But maybe Harold would be upset. He might even send her home, never noticing her new dress and the coy hint of Chanel No. 5 behind each ear.

When the cab pulled up to the Folcroft gate and Mrs. Smith handed over $28.44 and tip for the fare, she stopped worrying about what Harold would say to her about dropping in unexpectedly.

He was going to kill her for not bargaining the cabdriver down to a lower flat rate. She just knew it.

28

"Are you sure this time?" asked Ilsa Gans. "I mean, really sure?"

"It is Smith," said Konrad Blutsturz. He lay on an adjustable hospital bed. "I recognize his eyes, his face, his manner. He has not changed. Not much. Not since Tokyo. How can he have changed so little after I have been changed so much?"

"Do you want me to kill him for you?"

"No! I must do it myself. It is him, Ilsa. It really is this time."

"Wild," said Ilsa. "I was thinking, before we kill him, if I should do something about his skin. His skin looked kinda dry. Maybe I could send him some baby oil or something. I don't think I'd want to bind my diary in skin that yucky."

"It really is him," whispered Konrad Blutsturz. "Ilsa, I want you to find out everything you can about him. Talk to him. Talk to his employees. I must know what he has been doing all the time I suffered."

"Okay. Then can we go after the Jews?"

"The Jews?"

"Yeah, after we kill Smith, then we can go after the Jews. They killed my parents, remember?"

Konrad Blutsturz pushed himself up in bed painfully. He balanced on his right arm. The bluish connecting knob gleamed amid the rawness of his left arm stump.

"Ilsa, there is a book among my things. In the van. Get it, please."

Ilsa returned moments later.

"Read it," said Konrad Blutsturz.

Ilsa looked at the title, *The Diary of Anne Frank*. "Oh, yuck! I don't want to read this."

"Read it. Now. When you are done, come back to me."

"If you say so, but I think I'm going to throw up."

Two hours later Ilsa Gans returned to his bedside. She was in tears.

"You cannot kill the Jews," said Konrad Blutsturz. "Hitler tried, and although six million died, the Jews emerged stronger than ever, with a nation of their own. Do you think a culture that produced such a person as that brave young girl can be extinguished by you or by anyone?"

"No," said Ilsa sobbingly.

"Good. The Jews did not kill your parents, Ilsa. Someday I will tell you that story. And when I do, you must take care to understand that anything I did in the past, I did for us. The Jews do not matter. No one matters. Only Smith and I matter. Do you still want to kill the Jews, my Ilsa?"

"No," Ilsa said definitely. "I want to kill the blacks. No black could write a book like this."

Konrad Blutsturz sighed. "I have taught you too well. Enough, we will discuss this another time. Find out what you can about Harold W. Smith, my mortal enemy."

Mrs. Smith was surprised.

She had expected her husband's secretary to be younger, more attractive. Instead, Mrs. Mikulka was not much younger than she was, although possibly less frumpy. More matronly than frumpy. She wondered if Harold was sometimes attracted to the matronly type.

"I'm sorry, Mrs. Smith. Dr. Smith left several hours ago," Mrs. Mikulka informed her pleasantly.

"Oh. Did he say where he was going?"

"No, he didn't," said Eileen Mikulka, wondering if she should mention the fact that Dr. Smith had gone out of town. It was odd that Dr. Smith should go out of town without telling his wife, who seemed pleasant enough, if a tad frumpy.

Mrs. Smith frowned. "Oh dear. I'm so worried about Harold. He hasn't been home in over a week. But he's called every day," she added hastily.

That decided Mrs. Mikulka. "I believe he mentioned something about a short trip," she said hopefully. Perhaps Dr. Smith had tried to call his wife, but missed the connection.

"Oh dear." Mrs. Smith twisted her purse about with both hands. "I guess I should have called."

"I'm sorry."

"Do you suppose . . ." started Mrs. Smith. "I mean, it may be an imposition, but I've never been to Folcroft."

"Yes?"

"Might I see Harold's office?"

Eileen Mikulka smiled reassuringly. "Of course, I'd be glad to let you in."

"You're very kind."

"Not at all. I was about to run down to the cafeteria for a bit of lunch. Could I get you something?"

"Orange juice. And a Danish."

"I'll be right back," said Mrs. Mikulka.

And the two women smiled at one another in that tentative way two women who had a single man in common often did.

Ilsa Gans asked directions to the office of Dr. Smith. Along the way, she flashed her smile at every male who looked like he worked at Folcroft and asked, "What's Dr. Smith like?"

The answers fit into two uniform categories.

The polite people said he was dull, but nice.

The more honest people called him a miserly Scrooge.

No one seemed to like him much.

There was no one seated at the big reception desk outside Dr. Smith's office.

"Darn," said Ilsa Gans. "I'll bet his secretary would have spilled plenty."

Ilsa put her ear to the door to Smith's office, and hearing nothing, tried the door. It gave. She entered carefully.

"Oops!" said Ilsa when she bumped into a frumpy woman in a blue print dress.

"Excuse me," said Mrs. Harold Smith politely.

"I'm looking for Dr. Smith," Ilsa said uncertainly.

"So am I. I'm his wife. I came to have lunch with Harold, but I guess I should have called first because

Harold has left for the day and no one seems to know where he is." Mrs. Smith giggled nervously.

"His wife?" asked Ilsa. "Maybe you'd like to meet Mr. Conrad."

"Mr. Conrad?" Mrs. Smith said blankly.

"A very good friend of your husband."

"Oh, really. I don't think I've ever heard the name before."

"Oh, they go back years. To the war. Here, I'll take you to him. Just let me drop this off on Dr. Smith's desk."

"A bottle of baby oil?" asked Mrs. Smith.

"For his skin."

"Oh," said Mrs. Smith, who thought it very odd that this young girl would leave such a thing on her husband's desk. But she was such a cheerful little thing that Mrs. Smith was more than happy to accompany her.

Dr. Smith returned to his office, his face even more bitter than usual.

"Good morning, Dr. Smith," said Mrs. Mikulka. "How was your trip?"

"Unsatisfactory," said Smith, tight-lipped. He had taken a chance, flying to Mount Olive, the scene of the last Harold Smith killing. Using forged identification that credited him as an FBI agent, Smith had made the rounds of the Mount Olive police and the friends, relatives, and neighbors of the late Harold Q. Smith.

He had turned up exactly nothing, no clues to the person or persons who had decapitated Smith's fellow name carrier.

"I'm sorry to hear that," said Mrs. Mikulka, as Dr. Smith stamped into his office. "Did Mrs. Smith reach you?"

Smith paused. "Reach me?"

"Yes, she was here yesterday. I'm afraid I couldn't tell her where to reach you. She was very worried. Funny thing, I left her in the office while I grabbed lunch and when I came back she was gone."

"Gone." The word croaked from Smith's throat. Suddenly he remembered calling home from the airport and receiving no answer. It didn't mean anything at the time, but now . . .

"Please get my wife on the phone," Smith said.

At his own desk, Dr. Smith pressed the button that raised the concealed CURE computer terminal. He keyed in a report request on the FBI agent he had secretly detailed to watch over his house.

The report came back. Subject reported taking a taxi at 11:22 the previous day. No record of return. No other unusual activity.

Smith tripped the intercom.

"No answer, Dr. Smith," said Mrs. Mikulka. "Shall I keep trying?"

"No," said Dr. Smith. "Please have the head of security sweep the grounds for any sign of my wife."

"Sir?"

"Do it!"

The head of security reported directly to Dr. Smith an hour later. A search of the grounds had been instituted. The only untoward item was the sudden disappearance of a patient, a Mr. Conrad.

"Conrad," said Smith, dismissing the man. That was the multiple amputee patient. There was no connection there.

The CURE line rang. It was Remo.

"Smitty," Remo said. "I think we have a lead on the nebulizer. We're going to follow it up."

When there was no answer, Remo said, "Smitty?"

"My wife has been kidnapped," Smith blurted out.

"Sit tight. Chiun and I are on our way."

"No," said Smith. "You stay on the nebulizer. That's your first priority."

"Don't go cold-blooded on me, Smitty. We can help. This is your wife we're talking about. The Smith killer?"

"I think so. It's hard to tell. I don't know."

"You sound pretty rattled. Are you sure you don't want our help? Chiun and I may be going on a wild-goose chase anyway."

"This may be a personal matter," said Harold Smith, regaining control of his voice. "And I will handle it. Personally."

"Suit yourself," said Remo, hanging up.

Smith stared out the picture window, unseeing. If anything had happened to his wife . . .

Mrs. Mikulka buzzed. "Call on line one, Dr. Smith."

Dr. Smith picked it up without thinking, toying with a bottle of baby oil on his desk. What was baby oil doing here? Had his wife left it?

"Dr. Smith?" a voice asked. A very old voice. "I have your wife."

Smith knocked over the bottle. "Who is this?"

"I have been searching for you a long time, Harold W. Smith. Since June 7, 1949. Do you remember June 7, 1949?"

"I do not," said Smith. "Where is my wife?"

"Where you will not find her. Without my help."

Smith said nothing.

"It was in Tokyo," said the cracking voice. "Do you remember Tokyo?"

Smith's brow furrowed. "No, I don't think—"

"No!" the voice hissed. "No! I have lived in hell since that terrible day and you do not remember!" In a calmer voice he went on, "Do you remember yesterday? In the lobby of your place of work? Do you remember a man so crippled you dared not shake his hand?"

"Conrad," said Smith. Suddenly it made sense. The Smith killer had been smuggled in as a patient.

"No. Konrad Blutsturz."

"Blut—!" It all came rushing back to Harold Smith. The mission to Tokyo, the chase through the Dai-Ichi Building, and in a kaleidoscope of boiling fire, that last image of Konrad Blutsturz' blackening form slipping to the ground covered in flames.

"Ahhh," said Konrad Blutsturz. "You remember now. Good. Now listen carefully. I want you to go to the town of Flamingo in Florida. There you will rent one of those flatboats they use in the Everglades. You know the kind of which I speak, with the big fan in back? In the Everglades nearby you will find a nice cozy cabin. I will be waiting there for you. Come alone. Perhaps I will let you say good-bye to your wife before I wrench the life from you."

The line clicked dead.

On the flight to Miami, Harold W. Smith allowed

himself to doze off. He knew he would need all his strength for the confrontation that lay before him.

As he dozed, he dreamed.

He dreamed he was back in occupied Japan, a young agent in the waning days of the OSS, standing in the just rebuilt Tokyo Station. The train, when it wheezed into the station, was a wreck of broken windows and rust scabs. Smith got on the one new car which bore a sign reading "Reserved for Occupation Forces" in English and Japanese.

The train rattled past firebombed pockets of ruin that had been the prosperous Asakusa district. An American MP sat across from him, reading a copy of *Stars and Stripes*. Smith kept to himself.

Smith got off at Ueno Park, walked past what had been called Imperial Tokyo University, and found the little rice-paper-and-wood home his briefing had described right down to the reedy gate and untended shrubbery.

Smith did not loiter, because loitering would attract attention to himself. He walked right to the sliding front door, shoved it open, and tossed in a tear-gas grenade.

He waited for the gas to clear and then barged in, his automatic held steadily before him.

The house was empty. At first Smith thought he might have made a mistake. Then he noticed there was no family scroll in the traditional parlor alcove. No Japanese lived in this house.

There was a small explosives factory in the bedroom. Smith recognized the materials because during the war he had worked with the Norwegian underground. Explosives were his specialty.

Smith found a street map of downtown Tokyo, with several different routes marked on it in red ink. The routes led to a building that Smith, with a shock, recognized as the Dai-Ichi Building—the headquarters of General Douglas MacArthur and the occupation government.

Smith hurried out to the street and flagged down a *basha*, one of the taxis that, during the hard war years, had been converted to burn wood instead of gasoline.

As he hectored the driver into going faster, he wondered if even Konrad Blutsturz was stubborn enough to attempt to blow up the American occupation headquarters four years after the war had been lost.

Smith knew little about Blutsturz. His superiors had told him he was the head of a secret Nazi cell placed in the U.S. before the war. The cell had been intended as a reserve force that would take control over the United States government if Germany conquered Europe and headed for American shores.

Blutsturz had fled the U.S. and kept one step ahead of the FBI. His trail had been lost until informants had tipped the occupation that a German had made contact with Japanese militant holdouts in Tokyo itself and was planning to foment public sentiment against what so far had been a peaceful occupation.

Smith's job was to locate Blutsturz and capture him or eliminate him. As the *basha* deposited him in front of the imposing Dai-Ichi Building, Smith prayed he would not be too late.

Smith identified himself at the greeting desk.

"Smith, Harold," he said, showing his identification. "I've been cleared by SCAP."

And just as he turned, he saw Konrad Blutsturz walking in.

Blutsturz did not know Smith, but he knew the expression on Smith's face when he saw it.

Smith drew his weapon and identified himself again.

Konrad Blutsturz did not run out the front door, although it would have been the sane thing to do. He plunged into the elevator.

Smith's first shot missed. The second dented the closing elevator door. Seeing that the elevator cage was sinking toward the basement level, he took the stairs.

In the basement, Harold Smith decided not to take Konrad Blutsturz alive. The man had been carrying a briefcase. Smith was certain it contained an explosive or incendiary device.

It was dark. There were no windows. Smith paused, holding his breath, listening.

The sound was the faintest of clinks. A toe striking a piece of coal or broken glass.

Smith fired at the sound.

A roaring fire lit the basement, and in the fire a man danced, screaming. Screaming in a lung-ripping way that Smith, hardened by wartime conflict, had never heard before.

Smith's first thought was to put a bullet through the man to end his death agonies, but the fire—it was only that and not an explosion—was creeping along the floor carried by a volatile liquid propellant.

Smith ran to get help, the sound of those screams forcing him to cover his ears. . . .

Smith awoke as the captain announced the descent into Miami International Airport. He barely heard the captain's tinny voice. He could still hear the screams of Konrad Blutsturz echoing down forty years of memory.

The fire in the Dai-Ichi Building had been extinguished and then hushed up. Konrad Blutsturz had been pulled from the basement, clinging to life, his skin sliding off in charred patches where the rescue team had to touch it.

Smith was on an Air Force transport within a day of the incident, his work done. Digging back through the layers of memory, he could not recall if he had ever heard that Blutsturz had lived. He had always assumed not. Obviously, Blutsturz had. Somehow, sympathizers must have spirited him out of the military hospital in Tokyo. An embarrassing security lapse that was no doubt also hushed up, Smith thought bitterly.

As the plane touched down, Smith thought how none of those other deaths—those of the fourteen Harold Smiths who had died in his stead—would have happened had he not identified himself to Konrad Blutsturz instead of just gunning him down in the Dai-Ichi foyer. And he vowed to complete the job he had left unfinished in Tokyo nearly four decades ago.

"Enjoy your stay in Miami," the stewardess told Smith as he deplaned.

"Yes," Harold W. Smith said grimly. "I shall."

29

Ilsa Gans struggled with the arm. It was heavy. She dragged it across the floor to where Konrad Blutsturz lay, because the bed would not support his weight. Not with two legs of bright titanium, each leg weighing over three hundred pounds.

"This may hurt," she warned him.

"Pain does not matter now," said Konrad Blutsturz, and his face squeezed up tightly as Ilsa forced the jutting implant into the socket receiver. She threw the tiny switch that powered the arm.

The legs already hummed with that quiet power that caused the short hairs along her arms to rise.

"You're all hooked up," Ilsa said, stepping back. "Are you sure you want to go through with this?"

"Smith will not waste time," said Konrad Blutsturz, hoisting his upper body to a sitting position. His shoulder ached where the implant stressed the bone. "He could be here at any hour. I must be ready for him."

With another effort, he curled the legs, stiff like the forelimbs of a praying mantis, and climbed upright. On his feet, he swayed drunkenly.

"You don't look too steady," Ilsa said doubtfully.

"The stabilizers will steady me. Quickly, the blade."

"Here," said Ilsa, carefully carrying the curved sickle with the edge pointed away from her. Konrad Blutsturz held his arm out while she hooked it up.

"I hope it holds," she said.

With his good hand, Konrad Blutsturz forced the blade into the recess of his titanium forearm. It clicked into place. And held.

"Good," he said.

Ilsa looked doubtful. "I still think we could have killed him at Folcroft."

"No. This is better. There is his fear for the safety of his wife. This will be more satisfying. Besides, at Folcroft he had many guards at his command. Here he will have no one."

"Don't you think you should put something on? I mean, your, um, thing is hanging out and everything."

"I am proud of my new body, Ilsa."

"Is it real? I mean, can it—"

"Can it do everything a real one can?" said Konrad Blutsturz. "It is a rubber prosthesis. I can relieve myself standing up now, not sitting like a woman. It is also inflatable."

"Will it, like, feel like a real one?" Ilsa asked. She couldn't take her eyes off it.

"What difference does it make, my Ilsa?" he asked, advancing on her. "You have never felt a real one inside you."

Ilsa shrank back to the wall of the cabin. The raucous cries of Everglades birds echoed eerily in the swamp outside. The muggy heat filtered in through the windows, which had been sealed for many months.

"Shouldn't we wait?" asked Ilsa in a scared voice. "I mean, I want to and all. You know I do. But right now? You're still weak."

"I have ached for you, Ilsa," said Konrad Blutsturz, crowding her against the wall. "Ever since you were a child, I have ached for you, your smooth skin, your youthful flesh."

"My parents didn't like you."

"They were in my way. Now they are in the past."

"In your way! What do you mean?"

"Foolish girl. They were not murdered by others. I eliminated them. Because I wanted you, because I needed you."

"You!" Ilsa cried, shocked. And even before the tears began, she started to scream and pound her small fists against the bare, scarred chest of the man she had believed in for so many years. "You lied to me! You killed them. Not the Jews, not Smith, you!"

Ilsa stopped screaming when the blue hand took her by the throat and began to squeeze.

When she slipped to the floor, Konrad Blutsturz

looked at her still form for a long moment of regret. "Ilsa," he whispered. "I did not mean to hurt you."

When she did not answer, he began to inflate himself. Death would not rob him of his prize.

Dr. Harold W. Smith cut power to the airboat. There was an islet ahead, tangled with mangrove growth. The water split in two directions around it. He did not know which way to go.

Smith had rented the boat in Flamingo and sent it across a flat expanse of swamp grass until he had reached the mangrove swamp. The air was heavy, and alligators sunned themselves in the black mire at the edge of the increasing number of islands covered with mangrove and moss-draped trees. Despite the climate, Smith still wore his gray suit, his Dartmouth tie knotted tight at the throat. A briefcase lay at his feet.

Smith chose right and kicked on the great propelling fan which whirred inside a protective cage directly behind the pilot's seat.

A hundred yards ahead, Smith saw the cabin. It looked deserted. Smith cut power and let the flat-bottomed boat glide to the hump of an island. An egret flashed by through the close dark trees.

From out of the silent swamp came a voice. A now-familiar voice. Smith tensed.

"There have been four great moments in my life, Dr. Smith," the voice called out.

Smith did not reach for the automatic in his shoulder holster. He did not want to betray the fact that he was armed. Not yet.

"The first great moment was in Berlin, when Hitler himself selected me for the work in America," the voice called.

Smith looked about carefully. The growth was thick. The voice didn't seem to be coming from the cabin.

"The second great moment was when I first sat in a wheelchair. You might think, Harold W. Smith, that sitting in a wheelchair is not a moment of celebration, but compared with what I had been through, a wheelchair was glory."

"I prefer to see who I'm speaking to," said Harold Smith.

"The third great moment was achieved when I stood erect for the first time in forty years," the voice of Konrad Blutsturz went on. "But you will see what you have wrought soon enough, Smith."

"Where is my wife?" Smith demanded. He kept his voice under control. But he did not feel under control. He felt rage. "You offered me the chance to say good-bye to her. I claim that right."

"And the fourth great moment lies just before me. It is the instant when I take your throat in my hard left hand and squeeze the life from it. I hope it is a long moment for I have waited very long for it."

A figure emerged from the growth. Smith saw Konrad Blutsturz. His left arm gleamed unnaturally, and as Smith watched, a curved blade of metal snapped out; its glittering blade ran along the back of the blue-colored hand, protruding in a wicked point past the pointed metal fingertips.

Cyborg, thought Smith. Was it possible?

Konrad Blutsturz crushed his way to the mossy bank, and Smith watched the shiny artificial legs sink into the spongy earth almost up to the ankles. And he knew. Somehow, it all linked together, Blutsturz, the nebulizer and Remo and Chiun.

But there was no time for Smith's logical mind to connect all the pieces together, because suddenly Konrad Blutsturz was growing.

Tiny whirrings came from the man-machine's bionic knees. They spun, cranking out unfolding panels of titanium and pushing the leg sections upward.

When Konrad Blutsturz had gained two feet of height, he stepped into the still waters and advanced on Smith's boat like a metallic travesty of a stork.

"My wife," Smith said.

"You will never see her again," said Konrad Blutsturz. And he bared his teeth. It was not a grin. It was something that mixed pleasure and pain.

Smith switched the big fan to life and sent the boat surging at the ungainly wading thing.

"Idiot!" Blutsturz yelled, throwing his arms before his face.

Smith jumped from the boat before it struck.

Konrad Blutsturz wobbled slightly—only slightly—and sickled off a corner of the boat's flat snout. The craft took on water and began to sink.

Smith, scrambling up the mushy bank, plunged toward the cabin.

"Where are you?" he called.

Behind him, the croaking voice of Konrad Blutsturz laughed mockingly.

The body was nude below the waist. Someone had shoved the pants down about the ankles.

Smith saw that it was Ilsa, the blond nurse he had met at Folcroft. She was dead. His heart in his mouth, he ran from room to room. He found nothing, no one. The cabin was empty.

"Where is she?" he said to himself. "My God, where is she?"

Remo came to the fork in the swamp creek and asked Chiun, "Right or left?"

"Left," said Chiun firmly.

Remo sent the airboat skimming down the left-hand channel. The Master of Sinanju stood at the head of the craft like a bizarre figurehead. He wore a Hawaiian shirt over duck pants, because everyone in the Everglades settlements wore them.

"I still think we should be helping Smith instead of running around like this," Remo complained.

"Smith told you he did not wish our help," said Chiun. "He is the emperor. His word is law."

"If this place is empty, I vote we turn back for Folcroft."

"You turn back," said Chiun. "I will remain to await the coming of the man-machine, Bloodsucker, should he return."

The left channel ended in an empty cul-de-sac.

"You were wrong," Remo pointed out.

"I was not wrong," said Chiun huffily. "I simply was not absolutely right."

"Same difference," said Remo, turning the boat around.

"Listen!" Chiun said suddenly. "I hear something."

Remo shut off the motor and heard a voice filter through the sun-dappled trees.

"Smith! Harold W. Smith!" the voice screeched.

"It is him," said Chiun. "Bloodsucker."

"Through those trees," said Remo, sending the craft piling onto a bank. They jumped out and flashed through the undergrowth as if they had machetes attached to their bodies.

On the other side of the bank, they found the right hand channel. Standing in it, the deep water not even reaching his hips, was Konrad Blutsturz.

"Smith," Blutsturz called.

"Hold, abomination!" cried the Master of Sinanju. Konrad Blutsturz heard the voice and half-turned. One leg lifted and moved, storklike, and he pivoted to face the new threat.

"So," he said. "You have found me."

Remo started into the water. Chiun pulled him back. "Wait. Let him come to us."

"Okay, Little Father. You call it," said Remo. He shifted off to one side so that he and Chiun presented separate targets.

"Smith," cried Konrad Blutsturz as he advanced. "Harold Smith. Come out and see the vengeance I mete out to my enemies."

"Is he referring to our Smith?" asked Chiun.

"I don't think so," said Remo, who changed his mind when a familiar figure in gray stuck his head out of the nearby cabin.

"Smitty," Remo called. "What are you doing here?"

"That thing kidnapped my wife."

"You know each other?" said Konrad Blutsturz, surprise filling his bloodless face.

"Don't you know?" said Remo coolly. "We work for him. We've been onto you from the start."

"For Smith? All along?" Blutsturz turned to face Smith. "I have been stalking you and you sent these two after me? Amazing. You are more resourceful than I expected, Harold Smith."

"Forget Smith," said Remo. "You have to deal with us first."

Chiun called to Smith, "Look in the cabin, Emperor Smith. The device we seek may be in there."

Smith disappeared inside.

"He is out of the way, good," said Chiun. "Let us show this nearly dead thing how Sinanju deals with its enemies."

"I'll see what I can do, Little Father," Remo said as Konrad Blutsturz reached their moss bank. Blutsturz lifted a leg. It broke through a chunk of earth and slipped back into the tea-colored water.

"What?" wondered Konrad Blutsturz, dumbfounded.

"He cannot leave the water," Chiun told Remo. "Too heavy."

"Now," said Remo.

Remo took the left, coming in on an inside line—the traditional Sinanju path for close-quarters fighting—and the flashing blade rose to meet him. Chiun cut in on the right, taking the outside-line approach.

"I will kill you," howled Konrad Blutsturz, and chopped down with the wicked blade.

Remo twisted out from under it and jabbed a stiff-fingered blow at, not the metal arm, but the flesh of the stump above it.

Konrad Blutsturz let out a scream of deep agony. He duck-walked back from the bank as if his legs were being pulled by invisible strings.

Chiun kicked out a sandaled toe and caught one metal leg as Blutsturz hopped back. The leg buckled, then recovered mechanically. Blutsturz' torso twisted like a scoop of ice cream on top of a tipping sugar cone.

"The leg machines move on their own," Chiun called to Remo in Korean.

"Gotcha," said Remo. He plunged into the water.

Chiun followed him in.

Konrad Blutsturz, holding his bleeding stump of a shoulder, stepped back, circling on one leg like a giant compass drawing a circle. He peered into the brown water. He saw nothing. He looked for air bubbles, but oddly, there were none. Did these two not breathe air?

Then one of his legs quivered from a blow—the

right. Yelling, Konrad Blutsturz lashed out, kicking. Water splashed furiously. He was like a wader who suddenly discovers a poisonous jellyfish between his knees. He kicked. He howled. But his titanium legs connected with nothing.

"Peekaboo," said a squeaky voice behind him.

He turned. It was the Oriental.

"Come and get me," taunted Chiun.

Konrad Blutsturz did not come and get Chiun. He stepped back. And felt both legs lock. He strained, but something kept his legs from moving. Something in the water. Of course, the young one. Remo.

"I can have him tip you into the water," said Chiun. "He has you by both legs. If you fall, as heavy as you are, you will drown."

"No!" screamed Konrad Blutsturz. "I will not be cheated. Not after forty years. Smith! Smith! Call them off, Smith. Face me like a man. I dare you to face me, Smith!"

Harold Smith emerged from the cabin. He was struggling with the nebulizer. Its wheels kept sinking into the muddy ground.

"Don't kill him," Smith called. "He's the only one who knows where my wife is."

The sound of Smith's voice carried underwater, where Remo held Konrad Blutsturz' stiff legs in place. He climbed to the surface like a man climbing two poles, without releasing either titanium leg.

When he cleared the water, Remo asked, "What do I do, Little Father?"

"Do not listen to Smith," said Chiun in Korean. "We have Bloodsucker where we want him now."

Blutsturz swung at Remo, but his arm was too short. He raged inarticulately. Remo shook the legs violently in annoyance. Blutsturz groaned.

"But you heard Smith," Remo said. "This guy knows where Mrs. Smith is."

"Emperors' wives can be replaced," retorted Chiun. "This thing must be extinguished now before he causes more harm."

"I thought you always taught me to obey an emperor," Remo reminded him.

"You obey your emperor," said Chiun, "after you obey your Master."

"Maybe I can do both," Remo said, yanking hard.

Konrad Blutsturz felt himself twisting, tipping. He fell hard, his upper body crashing into the mangrove growth. He clawed at the solid ground, retracting his legs behind him.

Remo and Chiun climbed up after him, but Blutsturz was already on his feet when they reached him.

"It will be harder now," Chiun snapped at Remo.

"Smith wants him alive," Remo said. "He gets him alive."

Konrad Blutsturz flailed wildly at both men with his titanium blade. They ducked his blows, twin blurs of unstoppable motion. Each time he swung, the swing passed right through them. Or seemed to. He knew they were not human. But then, neither was he anymore.

And each time he missed, they would send a tormenting blow to his naked torso, where he was vulnerable.

"He is weakening," said Chiun in Korean.

"I have an idea," said Remo. "Try kicking a leg out from under him."

"It will do no good," said Chiun, aiming for the right leg. The leg gave before his lightning blow. For a half-second Konrad Blutsturz was poised on one long leg; then the other found its footing, controlled by computerized internal stabilizers.

"See?" said Chiun.

"Try again," said Remo, circling behind the towering, sweating figure.

Chiun struck again. This time Remo also kicked. Both kicks moved with the striking power of a piston. Both aimed at the precise same point—the leg section below the collapsible knee joint.

The leg, touched by the kick of the Master of Sinanju, retreated with microprocessor speed.

And collided into Remo's striking toe.

Titanium parts collapsed, spitting off in all directions.

Konrad Blutsturz staggered, his maimed leg waving crazily, seeking footing and stability.

Like a fantastic living tree, Konrad Blutsturz fell, raving, to the ground.

"Smith!" he yelled. "I will not be cheated! We are not done yet!"

And he wasn't. Konrad Blutsturz threshed like the machine he was, chewing up plants and sending clods of swamp muck into the air.

"Stay back, Little Father. He's still dangerous."

"I know," said the Master of Sinanju.

"Remo! Chiun! Stand clear," Harold Smith called from the cabin door.

"What?" shouted Remo.

"I said stand clear." When they moved out of the way, Smith triggered the nebulizer.

On the ground, the churning mechanical limbs of Konrad Blutsturz began to waver and blur. What had been hard metallic joints threw off globs of cold slag, melted, and ran.

In a matter of an instant, the dried husk that was the human part of Konrad Blutsturz flopped in a liquid puddle that was dribbling down the bank and into the water.

With a savage cry, Blutsturz pushed free of the pool of titanium and scrambled at Harold Smith. He hopped on the stumps of his legs in a horrible mockery of human locomotion, keeping his body upright with his one arm.

Harold Smith saw the thing bearing down on him, and it was like being attacked in a nightmare. What was now Konrad Blutsturz was less than three feet tall, but over and over again he cried one word in a voice that sent the alligators plunging into the safety of the water for miles around.

"Smith! Smith! Smith!"

And Harold W. Smith, shaken by the hatred that animated the thing creeping toward him, was forced to shoot.

He pumped two bullets into Blutsturz' hobbling form, but even that did not stop him.

The third bullet did. It slammed Blutsturz into a low somersault.

Smith drew close to the bleeding body that was a head and a torso and not much more, his automatic shaking in his fist—the same automatic he had carried in Tokyo.

"My wife," Smith demanded. "Where is she?"

"Dead," croaked Konrad Blutsturz. "Dead. I am revenged in that at least. Revenged."

And Smith, horror riding his features, fired a last bullet into Blutsturz' head.

"I'm sorry, Smitty," Remo told him.

Smith stood with a stupid expression on his face.

"Dead," he said weakly. "She's dead."

"We will scour these Everglades," cried Chiun. "We will recover the body of the emperor's wife so that she may be buried with honor." And he kicked the corpse in spite.

"No," said Harold Smith. "No. Just . . . just take me back to Folcroft. Please."

30

Dr. Harold W. Smith walked stiffly into his office. It was late at night, and outside the picture window a heavy snow was falling.

"Are you sure you want to stay here?" Remo asked gently. "Wouldn't you rather be home?"

"There is nothing there for me anymore," Smith said dully, dropping into his age-cracked leather chair. "Folcroft is my home now."

Smith got out the red phone and waited while the line automatically rang an identical phone in the bedroom of the President of the United States.

After a moment, Smith spoke.

"My report, Mr. President. I regret to inform you that Ferris D'Orr is dead. Murdered by kidnappers. . . . Yes, it is regrettable. My person did all he could. However, the nebulizer is secure and we have eliminated the persons responsible. There will be no more difficulty from that quarter."

Smith paused, listening. Finally he said, "Thank you for understanding, Mr. President," and hung up.

"I don't get you, Smitty," said Remo. He had been wanting to ask him a question, but during the flight back, Smith had insisted, for security reasons, on not sitting with them on the plane. "That was your wife we left back there. Why wouldn't you let us hunt for the body?"

"And how would I have reported her death?" asked Smith bitterly. "Any police inquiry would automatically include questioning me. They would ask for my whereabouts on the day of the murder. They would place me in Florida and then what would I tell them? CURE's security would have been jeopardized."

"Is the organization so important that you couldn't take the risk?" Remo asked.

"CURE is all I have now," Smith said tonelessly.

"How will you explain away her disappearance?" wondered Remo.

"I'll think of something."

"Where's Chiun?" asked Remo suddenly. "I thought he was right behind me."

"I saw him talking to a guard on the way in. Why don't you go to him, Remo? I would prefer to be alone just now."

"Yeah, I know how it is."

"No, you do not," Smith said flatly.

Before Remo could leave, the Master of Sinanju breezed into the room. He was not alone.

Smith looked up, shock melting the haggardness of his features into surprised joy.

"You're alive!"

"Oh, Harold," said Mrs. Smith, running into his arms. "It was awful. I met one of your nurses. She took me to the most horrible man. He said he knew you. They tied me up and I thought they were going to kidnap me or something like that. The last thing I recall was asking for some water and then I woke up in a dark room filled with garden tools. I thought I was going to starve to death until this kind gentleman found me."

"Where? How?" asked Remo in Korean.

The Master of Sinanju beamed. "Emperor Smith gave up too easily. On the way in, I spoke to a guard. Smith's security is too tight. All leaving vehicles are searched. No one could have spirited out a kidnapped woman beyond these walls. So I looked around Fortress Folcroft until I found a woman who looked like she would be married to Smith."

Remo nodded in understanding. "Where was she?"

"In the basement."

"Good going, Little Father," said Remo.

Harold Smith released his wife from the grip that threatened to crush her.

"Please wait outside, dear," he said quietly. "I must speak to these men in private. I'll be with you directly."

"Hurry, Harold," said Mrs. Smith. She smiled at the

Master of Sinanju, her rescuer, in gratitude and slipped out of the room.

Smith cleared his throat noisily. "Master of Sinanju, I can't thank you enough. Ask anything."

Chiun bowed. "I ask only that I be allowed to continue in your generous employ for the duration of our contract."

"Done," said Smith.

"Hey!" cried Remo. "I thought we were going to discuss this."

"We just have," said Chiun placidly.

"I didn't get a word in edgewise."

"Can I help it if you are slow on the uptake? Perhaps the leisurely pace of life in Sinanju has dulled your formerly quick reflexes."

"You old pirate," said Remo. "What am I going to do now?"

"You can return to Sinanju and await my possible return," said Chiun. "Or you can demonstrate your strength of character and delay your return until I am free to accompany you."

"I am prepared to let you rejoin the organization, Remo," Smith interjected. "I'm very grateful to you both."

Remo paced the floor. "Nothing doing! Christ, Chiun, you always have to do this to me!"

"I do not know what he is talking about, Emperor," Chiun confided to Smith. "He has not been himself since the engagement. I think it is the premarriage jitters. Perhaps Remo is not yet ready to settle down."

"I'm ready to settle down," Remo said. "You're just not ready to let me settle down. All right, all right, I'll make you both a deal."

Chiun cocked his aged head to one side. "Yes?" he asked.

"You're stuck working for Smith for the next year. Right?"

"Not stuck," said Chiun. "Privileged."

"I'll stick around. But just for one year. And I'm not working for Smith. I'm strictly along for the ride. Only to see that you don't get into trouble. Understand?"

"Yes," said Smith.

"Perfectly," said Chiun happily. He clapped his hands together in undisguised glee. "Oh, it will be just like old times."

"Now that that is straightened out," said Dr. Harold W. Smith, "will you both please leave? Security, you know. And I want to take my wife home."

Remo stared up at the ceiling.

"It's going to be a long year," he sighed.

"Let us hope," added Chiun.